The Wishing Well

The Wishing Well

a novel by

Joyce Veranda Gray

Q-Boro Books
WWW.QBOROBOOKS.COM

An Urban Entertainment Company

Published by Q-Boro Books

Copyright © 2008 by Joyce Veranda Gray

ISBN-13: 978-1-933967-48-6
ISBN-10: 1-933967-48-X
LCCN: 2007933675

First Printing July 2008
Printed in the United States of America

10 9 8 7 6 5 4 3 2 1

Q-BORO BOOKS
Jamaica, Queens NY 11434
WWW.QBOROBOOKS.COM

Acknowledgments

the Creator,

the Ancestors

and

Isaac Gray, Mary Gray, Andrew Gray, Iris Robertson, Kenneth Robertson, Debra Gray, Pamela Reynolds, Allen Reynolds

Introduction

What happens to our souls once the body is gone? What happens when we are no longer earthbound and living in linear time? When the spirit is free of earthly boundaries, what becomes of it? Many believe that the spirit will go to heaven if the grace of God so deems it. The spirit will dwell amongst others that have passed into the heavenly realm. Some believe that you will leave the body only to reincarnate again and again, taking on different identities depending upon the karma from the previous life; that you live many lives until Illumination. There are some who believe that the earthly existence is the only existence, and once expired, life ceases to exist at all. You have one chance at it, and that's all. As my friend would say, "It's not a dress rehearsal." Every believer is certain that their belief is the right one, but what seems to be misunderstood is the commonality that is held within each of them. The basic principle that lies beneath is that it is a belief. There is no evidence to the contrary, so it must be true.

The only souls that really know truth are those that

have passed on. Unfortunately they can't seem to tell us what they've learned, so we allow our beliefs to dominate our journey through life. Most of us try very hard to do what our beliefs tell us we should, in the hopes that it will take us to the place of eternal peace. But for some, regardless of how they live their lives, the direction the soul takes may not be theirs to decide. When we wish for something that is not ours to have and will not accept *no* for an answer, the impact that wish has on others can be devastating.

There are some souls that get interrupted and never make it to their final destination. They are promised salvation or reincarnation through a heavenly journey, but they are forced into an existence of neither heaven nor hell. They are swept up before the heavenly father has a chance to embrace them. When evil is at play, the souls of many can be trapped in a hellish nightmare that they cannot escape from. Many of these souls should transcend to their heavenly place where loved ones await them, and when they do not arrive at their appointed time, they become suspicious of evil offerings in moments of grief and pain. The hands of mortals are used to find them and free them. The angels must guide someone who has the heart and the courage to persevere.

All of us believe that life can be hard. Some weather the storm better than others, but everyone has their moment when acceptance of the here and now is difficult and sometimes painful. We wish that we could change things; we wish that we could change their minds; we wish that we could be stronger so that the loss won't hurt so much. What happens to our wishes? Do they come true? And if they do, does it give us the peace that we sought?

When a wish becomes a burden to bear, was the wish for you? We often believe that God answers all prayers. If you ask for it, in His name, He will give it to you in His time. We also believe that God is all knowing and already knows what's good for us and will give you what your heart desires. What if the answer is no? What if what's on your heart is not what God has destined for you and the answer is no? What do you do?

For many, accepting the eventual loss of a dream is devastating. Many of us cannot cope and will do anything to get our hope back. We live our lives through our dreams; we call it hope. We know that tomorrow may never come and yet we plan for it daily. We build our tomorrows on the relationships that we form today, not knowing that we cannot predict nor control the direction of a relationship. Trust is here today, but not tomorrow. Love is here today, but not tomorrow. Joy is here today, but not tomorrow, and thus we share our lives with people who are destined to leave us or for us to leave them and the eventual creation of a new dream is always one day away.

The loss of a dream can be more than we can bear, and when we come to a breaking point we may allow ourselves to succumb to our primal need for survival. The breaking point is the point of survival. For a moment in time we believe the truth that we can't go on without the dream. We believe that life is not worth living and the joy that gave your existence value and purpose must exist in order for you to exist. We wonder why God would do something like this to us. We try to live right, and yet we are always struggling to hold on to what we think is rightfully ours to have.

But, what if it's not rightfully yours to have? What if the answer is no? For most of us, that is unacceptable, and we know that we are supposed to be happy so, my God, we're going to be, even if it kills us. At the moment, we are willing to give all of everything to keep anyone or anything when we have already lost it. It is hard to believe that something you could want so badly may never be yours to have. I guess the question is: Why do you want it? What makes you think you have to have it? Your heart. Your heart makes you think that you can't live without it and surviving the devastation that will follow the loss becomes unbearable because we can't understand why we can't have it.

Torrin Wilhelm was a young man, new to America. He had his life and dreams all laid out in a beautiful box. He was at peace with God and himself and wanted nothing more than to raise his family on the beautiful land of his loving home. But maybe the answer was no and this was not God's plan. We all think that everyone's life should mirror everyone else's or you're considered different, an outcast. But what if it is your journey to live a different life, a life alone, a life of struggle, a life without hope ? Can one imagine that God would ordain such an existence on any man? I suppose Job could answer that question. Unlike Job, Torrin could not accept that God would strip him of his joy. He would not take no for an answer, and through a moment of weakness, he shook hands with the devil and changed the destiny of everyone he knew.

When you make a wish to have what is not yours to have, are you stealing someone's dream? If you keep the souls that are rightfully God's, have you snatched away a life that should be? We rarely accept the will of God, even though we tell ourselves we do. We want what we want, and we make the need greater than our love for God and do anything to get it. When Torrin threw the coin in the well, he changed the destiny of all those to come. He closed his mind to the terms of the pact and allowed himself to live in the moment and have what he wanted today without regard for tomorrow.

But when tomorrow comes, the devastating act plagues all those touched by the wish and robs them of their dreams, their tomorrows. We all must find the courage to face what is ours to have. It may not be the same as our hopes and dreams, but nevertheless, it is ours. So our hopes and dreams must be as fluid as our lives. They cannot be steadfast, because change is outside of our control. It is said that change is the one true constant, and if your dream is steadfast, it will break in the wind.

Torrin was not willing to reinvent himself when his storm broke his dream, and now Alec must bear the burden of Torrin's weakness and face a long-standing wrong. He and an unwilling friend must face their demons and purge themselves of earthly pain before they can reach for their elusive goal.

Alec and Tremaine are forced into a world that defies space and time, and forces them to confront the horrors that plagued their lives and pulled them farther and farther away from the love of God. We all carry our burdens day in and day out. We carry our wanting of material things, jealousy, envy, guilt, hate, and other selfish pleasures that seem to rule our lives. Before Alec and Tremaine enter the holy realm, they must free their souls of that which haunts them and come to terms with what is most important in their carnal lives. The only things that matter in this world are the things your heart can carry into the next.

PART ONE

The PACT

No matter where you go or what you do, you live
your entire life within the confines of your head.
—Terry Josephson

Chapter One

Be careful what you wish for

Her screams were deafening. The baby was breeched, and the midwife was sure she would not survive the birth of her first child.

Melanie and Torrin arrived in the New World as man and wife two years ago, and fifteen months later they were expecting their first child. Torrin Wilhelm was Scottish, and Melanie was a native of Britain. They met when Torrin was on a hunting trip in the highlands of England when he accidentally shot and killed Melanie's beloved dog. He was so distraught over her loss, he found her a new pup and they began a long courtship.

When he decided to move to America, he wanted her to join him. She said *yes*, and they were married and began a wondrous journey that led them to a small village in the wilderness of North America, the territory of Oklahoma between the Chickasaw Nation and the Cherokee Outlet. The year was 1897, and Torrin had established himself as a hard-working farmer and a loving husband. He and Melanie were delighted to learn of her pregnancy nine months earlier and had been waiting in anticipation of the blessed day. But, the day did not turn out as hoped. The child was turned around feet-first, and in 1897, without a doctor's guidance, little was known about delivering a breech baby. The midwife tried to turn the baby around, but did not have much success.

"I don't think she's going to make it," the midwife said.

The scruffy-looking woman was frail and white as a sheet. Her face was weathered and beaten from years of hard work in the fields. She inherited the job of midwife from her mother, who assisted many of the village people into the world. Her long, gray hair was pulled up into a bun, and her black and gray clothes were two sizes too big. She wore spectacles over her dark brown eyes, and a few of her teeth were missing, but all in all, she had a pleasant face and a calming demeanor, which made midwifery a perfect job for her.

Melanie screamed again. Torrin gripped his chest. He couldn't stand it. He ran into the room and looked upon her face and cried at the thought of losing his beloved Melanie. He couldn't bear the thought. He ran out of the two-room cabin and into the barn. He wandered around in there until she screamed again. He panicked and ran. He ran until he was out of breath. He wasn't sure where he was. The road he was on was now stone and gravel. Beyond him was a forest of tall trees. He looked back, and he could see his farm in the distance.

As he stood at the edge of the forest, a strange feeling came over him. Something was beckoning him to enter the forest. There was a small path that pulled at him as he looked down it, deep into the trees. The mystery of the forest was alluring to him, and he wanted to know what was on the other side of the trees. *Do they go on forever?* he thought.

A warm breeze graced his brow, and he felt at ease and

peaceful. An image came to mind of him holding the baby and smiling at Melanie as she sat at the kitchen table. He smiled at the thought and wanted so much for everything to be all right. He was afraid to go back for fear of what he might find.

He looked down the path and stepped upon the rocks and grass and walked into the trees. He walked until he entered an open field. He wandered around until he stumbled upon a well. He wondered how it got there and who used it. *There must have been people nearby at one time*, he thought. He looked around, hoping to see some sign of a lost village that perished in a fire or something, but there was nothing, only the forest that surrounded the single well.

Torrin walked toward the well and peered down inside. It was dark, and he couldn't tell if water was at the bottom or not. He picked up a rock and tossed it into the well and waited to hear the eventual splash. He heard nothing. He wondered if it was bottomless and maybe the rock could still be falling.

He thought of his loneliness and grief if Melanie should die. *It would be bottomless, like the well.* He cringed and fell to his knees. Tears rolled down his face as fear gripped his heart.

"Please, God, please don't take her. I can't live without her. She is my life, she is so pure. Take me instead. Take me. Please, please don't take my love."

"It is he that calls for her," a voice came from the well. "But I can save her."

"Who is it? Who speaks to me?" Torrin came to his feet quickly and looked all around. He tried to find the source of the voice, but could not.

Suddenly, a voice from behind him startled him. "It is I."

Torrin turned quickly to find a man standing by the well. "Who are you? Where did you come from? I should have seen you come upon me. Are you man or ghost?" he asked suspiciously.

"I am one who can answer your prayer," the tall man said. He was rather cold and lifeless with dark, stringy hair and dark eyes. His pale face seemed distant and stern. He smiled slightly and peered into Torrin's eyes as if he were looking through him. His stare was frightening, but calming.

Torrin knew innately that something was wrong, but he couldn't stop himself from listening. His assumed grief over Melanie and the baby overshadowed any fear or distrust he could have for this man.

The man's long narrow arm and thin hand reached out to touch Torrin's shoulder, but Torrin stepped back.

"I don't know you. You're not from around here, are you?" Torrin was beginning to feel a little sick in his stomach. He wanted to run, and he convinced himself that if he could only turn around, he could escape the cold stare, but he couldn't.

"No, I'm not from these parts. I've lived everywhere. I have been all over the world, whereever I am needed. You see, there's always a place for me amongst humankind. For some reason, people embrace me without realizing it."

"Why?" Torrin began to back away.

"I don't know. Maybe because I give them what they want."

"Like what?"

"Like the life of a loved one," he said as he moved closer to Torrin. "You see, I can help you."

"You can save Melanie?" Torrin asked with a hint of hope in his voice.

"Yes, and the child too."

"How? How can you do this? You don't know us. You don't know what's going on."

"Oh, but I do, Torrin. I know many things about many people." He smiled and nodded his head.

"You know my name. How?"

"As I said, I know many things. I know that you don't have much time. Melanie's life is fading, and she will lose the baby as well. I can bring her back to you if you let me. It is the least I can do for the great support mankind has given me. Please let me help."

"You are evil, I know it. But, I can't lose Melly, I can't. What do I have to do?" Torrin asked shamefully.

"I won't ask for much. All I want is the village," he said as the stepped back and opened his arms humbly.

"The village? How can I give you the village?" Torrin asked. "I don't own it."

"Oh, but you can. All you have to do is throw a coin in the well, and I will do the rest."

"Throw a coin in the well? How will that give you the village?' he asked with a quizzical look on his face. "Why do you want the village anyway?"

"I will give them what I gave you, what you want . . . life. I will give you life eternal. Accept my gift and I will give life to all."

"Only God can give life eternal life," Torrin said.

"I would not deceive you. I will give you what you want."

"I don't have a coin," said Torrin as he searched his pockets.

"That's all right. I have one."

The man reached inside his coat pocket and pulled out the most unusual coin Torrin had ever seen. The coin was imprinted with the face of an angel. It was a bright gold that shimmered in the sunlight. The opposite side of the coin was the same angel crying with a look of fear and horror upon her face. This face was frightening and caused Torrin to drop the coin and step back from it.

"Do not fear it. It only represents good and evil, which is something that all men possess within them," the man said.

"Which side is the stronger? Which side will prevail?" asked Torrin.

"The one that you feed." The man picked up the coin and placed it back in Torrin's hand. "Now, toss it into the well and go home to your wife and child."

Torrin moved closer to the well and thanked God for his blessings and tossed the coin into the well. This time he could hear the coin hit the ground and ring echoes of the angel crying back to him .

His heart sank as he realized that he'd just made a pact with the devil and there was no turning back. He did not know what the outcome would be and hoped that it would be something minor that he could live with. He didn't want to think about his act of indiscretion. He only wanted Melanie to be all right. He looked into the eyes of the man standing beside him and realized that the evil that lay beneath the surface was more hellish than anything he could imagine. He couldn't speak. He started to step away as he stared into the man's deep red eyes.

"What do you fear, Torrin?" the man asked.

"I fear that I have transgressed upon my neighbors and their souls are doomed to hell."

"It was always to be so; your wants are greater than your needs, and thus your sacrifices are selfish."

"What have I done? Oh God, what have I done?" cried Torrin.

"You gave me the village. I have their souls and the souls of all of their descendants for an eternity."

The man laughed. The evil beneath the surface showed through his face, and Torrin cried as he looked upon the face of the entity that he just paid for the life of his wife and child and the death of their souls.

"You saved their lives and forsook their souls." He

laughed again and turned away. He looked back at Torrin as he walked into the forest. He laughed an ominous laugh as he walked into the trees and out of sight.

"I can't worry about that now," he said. "I have to get back to Melly. I have to see if she's all right."

He turned and ran toward the cabin. He ran as fast as he could and hoped that what just happened was all a dream and that everything would be all right. He didn't think about it anymore. His only thought was about Melanie and the child. He knew he had made a choice not only for himself, but for the village people that they could never forgive him for, but all he could think about was the here and now—what was happening now, and saving Melanie and the child.

He reached the cabin and he heard nothing. Melanie was not screaming. *Could she be dead?* He slowly walked inside and saw the midwife holding the infant. She looked up at him and smiled. With gaps in her teeth, her joyous smile told Torrin that everything was all right.

"It's a miracle. A miracle, I say. I don't understand it. The baby just turned itself around. Just like that, just decided to turn his self around. She didn't scream no more and the baby came right out. It was the most amazing thing I ever seen. It's a miracle, that's what it is, all right."

Torrin stepped into the room where Melanie was lying. He looked into her brown eyes and kneeled down beside her. He stroked her dark brown hair and caressed her small hand. Tears flowed from his eyes as he thought about his encounter at the well and how it was all worth it to see her smile. He laid his head on her breast and held her. She stroked his hair and let him cry.

The years passed swiftly for Torrin and Melanie as they cherished the life of three-year-old Michael. He was full of life as he walked around the small cabin, ex-

ploring everything in sight. Torrin built another room on
the cabin so that Michael would have a place to sleep
when he got older. Melanie was far along in her second
pregnancy and was hoping for a girl. Torrin, of course,
wanted another boy who would eventually help him
with the farm. They planned to have many children, so
Torrin expected to get lots of sons who would tend the
farm and pass the land to his grandchildren and great-
grandchildren.

The village had grown into a town over the past three
years. Many children had been born, and many newcomers
came from everywhere with ideas for new businesses and
innovative ways to make the village grow.

Torrin walked outside to draw some water from his
well when he heard a group of boys playing near his
farm. The town known as Earlsboro, named after a beloved Black barber named James Earls, was moving
closer to his small three-acre farm. The main street was
once so short, it couldn't be seen from the farm, but now,
Torrin could see the main street that ran through the town
from his front yard. Many of the farmers nearby him sold
their land to business owners and moved their farms farther out, away from the encroaching town. Torrin was
still far enough away that he felt comfortable about staying, at least for a while. He knew that he too would eventually have to sell and move if he intended to keep a farm.

Torrin watched the boys play and run around until
they started running toward the forest. He looked at
them and waited to see what they intended to do. He remembered that fateful day in the forest at the well when
his despair forced him to make a terrible decision. So far,
nothing had happened. He had not seen any result of his
pact. He was hopeful nothing ever would come of it, but
he was very nervous about the boys going near the forest
for fear that they would meet the evil around the well.

He turned toward the house and remembered his love for Melanie and Michael. He turned and ran toward the boys. He wanted to stop them before they entered the forest, but he couldn't catch them.

As the boys reached the edge of the woods, they stopped and peered down the same path that Torrin had three years ago. Jacob, the older boy, was curious about the forest and wanted to step inside.

"Let's go in. It's just some trees," he said.

"I don't know," said Virgil. "It seems dark and gloomy in there."

"What do you mean? The sun is shining," said Jacob.

"I don't want to go," said Harry, the youngest of the three. "There are spiders in there."

"Well damn, it seems that I'm hanging with a bunch of girls. Sissy girls, afraid of spiders, are you? Well, I'm going in. There's nothing in there."

As Jacob took the first step down the path toward the center of the forest, a warm breeze startled him and caused him to stop. He thought for a moment about his choice, but knew that if he turned back he would be seen as a coward. He looked back at Virgil and Harry and smiled. He turned and kept walking.

Virgil and Harry followed him, feeling very apprehensive and nervous.

By the time Torrin reached the forest edge, the boys had disappeared inside. He stopped and took a deep breath. He did not want to go into the forest, but he knew he had to stop the boys from doing anything that may cost them their lives. He remembered what the man said about our sacrifices being selfish, and he took the step down the path. He kept walking until he could see the boys standing around the well.

"Wow, look at this. I wonder who put it here?" asked Virgil.

"I don't know. It does seem strange for a well to be out here where nobody is," said Jacob. He looked all around, wondering if anyone lived nearby used the well. "It's probably dry anyway," he said as he took a coin from his pocket and tossed it into the air.

Torrin walked up just as the coin flew into the air and descended into the well. They heard a cry. It startled them as they jumped back. It was the same cry Torrin had heard the day he threw the strange coin into the well. It was the cry of the angel. Torrin remembered the cry and cringed at the sound.

"What are you boys doing here? You shouldn't play here," said Torrin angrily. Torrin startled the boys as they began to run.

Jacob stopped when he realized who the man was. "Mr. Wilhelm, we weren't doing anything wrong. It's just a old dry well," he said.

"You shouldn't play here, find somewhere else to play," Torrin said adamantly.

Jacob looked at him, puzzled by his reaction to their playing in the forest, and then he looked at the well and wondered what the connection was. He decided not to pry and turned and ran behind Virgil and Harry.

Torrin stood by the well for a moment and looked around, wondering if he would see the dark stranger again. He calmed himself and walked back through the trees.

Just as he entered the edge of the town, he heard screams and people moving about and a great amount of chatter from the local market. He walked down the street and saw women crying and covering their faces with handkerchiefs. The men moved in and out of the store and stood around out front.

Torrin walked up to Paul Hendricks and inquired about

the commotion. "What happened here? Why are they crying?"

"Something awful happened to Old Man Hasting. He was getting Miss Simmons some salt pork when he just dried up and died," said Paul.

"Dried up and died? What do you mean?" Torrin walked toward the entrance and peered inside. He looked at the townsmen standing around a body on the floor and wondered what could have happened. He walked closer and spoke to Winston Drake. "What happened, Winston?"

"Torrin, it's the strangest thing I've ever seen. I was standing by the vegetable stand when I heard Miss Simmons scream. I looked around and Hastings was drying up, as if all his organs were melting away, and his skin turned into leather, and that's all that's left," he said as he pointed to the body on the floor. "Poor Miss Simmons. She'll be scared for life after this."

Torrin stared at the dead body that had turned into a flat shell of a man without substance or motion. He lay lifeless and stiff as if someone took a straw and sucked out every bit of fluid in his body. His curled up hands and crooked mouth, which seemed to be screaming for help, blared at Torrin with agony and pain. Hasting was alive, and his body melted away a little at a time, obviously causing excruciating pain.

What happened ten minutes ago? Torrin thought. He thought of the boys throwing the coin into the well. He tried to tie the two events together, but couldn't. He dismissed it and told himself that this was just an abnormal incident that left a man dead. He had a feeling of anxiety and apprehension. He kept thinking of the well, and worried that the death of Mr. Hasting and the coin the boys threw in were connected.

Torrin walked home and tried to relax, but deep down

he felt that the evil man caused Mr. Hasting's death. He knew he was responsible, but he didn't have proof. It could have been a single incident that may never happen again. He told Melanie about the awful event and held her, knowing that he may have to deal with the consequences of the decision he'd made three years ago.

The years rolled by without incident. Michael was ten years old and had two siblings and another on the way. Kate was seven, and John was three. Kate's auburn locks of curly hair bounced about as she ran around the yard, playing with her two brothers. John had dark hair and lots of baby fat that made walking difficult for him, but it was funny to watch. Michael grew into a handsome young man. His small frame and long brown hair were striking. He had a beautiful smile and a commanding voice that made him seem far older than he was. Torrin was proud of him and knew that he would become a find young man someday. Melanie was expecting their fourth child by winter.

Seven years had passed since the death of Old Man Hasting, and the town had tried to forget the horror of the incident. Every now and then you would hear the story of his death from one of the original village folk, but mostly they tended not to talk about it. It was never explained, and doctors came from all over to study the remains to try to determine the cause of death. There were no answers. He was eventually buried, and the reports written by the doctors became part of the medical history as an anomaly.

Torrin tried to put the day out of his head. He knew that the death was somehow linked to the wishing well, but couldn't be sure, so he decided not to address it with anyone and hoped that time would erase the entire event from history.

By the early 1900's, the town had grown close to Torrin's farm. On one side of the farm, new homes were
built to accommodate the new arrivals and young mar-
riages of the townfolk. Across the road in front of the
farm was a new store. It was huge for the early 1900's
and had everything in it that a person could want.

Torrin did not like the way the town encroached upon
his farm. He wanted to move, but he loved his land and
had spent years cultivating the soil to make it just right
for an abundance of growth. Part of him wanted to get as
far away from the well as he could, but the other part felt
that he needed to keep stewardship over it. He wanted to
make sure that no one went near it, for fear that it could
provoke another incident like Mr. Hasting's demise.

Access to the well was more exposed. There was a time
when the open field behind the forest was completely
hidden from the town, but as time went by and the town
grew, much of the forest was taken to expand the town,
and now the well was just beyond a group of trees. Torrin watched intently to see if anyone went near the trees
toward the well. As he worked the fields and fed the livestock, his eyes never strayed far away from the trees.

"What are you searching for out there, Torrin?"
Melanie asked as she scanned the area, hoping to see
what he saw.

"It's nothing, Melly, nothing." He kissed her forehead
and smiled.

Melanie could hear the children playing in the back
yard. Kate's laughter was lighthearted and warm. *A
child's play is a wonderful sound*, she thought. She and Torrin peeked around the back of the house and saw
Michael chasing Kate around the clothesline, threatening
to harm her if he caught her. Of course, he could have
caught her many times over, but he allowed her to run
and believe she was ahead of him and winning. She fell

to the ground laughing to tears as he pounced on her and rolled around in the dirt. It was joyous to watch.

John tried to join in by climbing on Michael's back and holding on. Michael stood and ran around with John on his back, giving him the ride of his young life. John laughed with such joy that it made Melanie cry.

"Summertime is a time for play and frolicking about," said Torrin.

"Yes, and another one will be rolling in the dirt next summer with them," said Melanie as she rubbed her stomach gently. She looked up at Torrin lovingly, and he kissed her sweetly.

They turned to walk back to the front of the cabin when Torrin noticed three young men lurking around the edge of the trees where the well was. He stopped and stared intently.

"What's wrong?" she asked.

"I wonder what they are doing there. What do they want over there?" he asked.

"Who?"

"Those kids. They shouldn't be over there," he said.

"Why not? What's over there that's wrong, Torrin? What is it?" she asked, fearful of what she might hear.

"I just don't like it, that's all. It's too close to the forest, and they shouldn't play over there."

"They are not little children; they will be fine. Don't worry," she said as she caught Kate running by from the corner of her eye.

Her eyes followed Kate as she ran around the cabin yelling, "You can't catch me, you can't catch me."

Michael followed shortly thereafter and stopped when he noticed his father staring at the boys at the edge of the forest. "What is it, Father?" Michael asked.

Torrin looked at him strangely, his face stressed and worried. "Do you know those young people, Michael?"

"Yes, that's Bill Lakley, Jerry Wright, and Leslie Aaron. Why? Is something wrong?" Michael asked.

Melanie stood by Michael and tried to figure out what the problem was. They could see nothing wrong. Torrin looked back and watched Melanie walk into the cabin, but when he turned back around, the young men were gone. He looked all around but did not see them.

"Where did they go?" asked Torrin.

"Into the trees. There's nothing there. It shouldn't be a problem," said Michael.

Torrin began walking toward the trees. His heart started to race as he got closer. Michael yelled at him to wait for him.

"No, you stay here. Just wait, I'll be right back," said Torrin as he walked faster and faster to get to the well before the three young men did.

Melanie heard Torrin tell Michael to wait, and she stepped back out onto the porch and watched Torrin run toward the trees. They were concerned, but decided not to follow him.

He stopped just as he approached the trees and looked inside. He could see the young men standing around the well. He waited a moment until he saw one of them take a coin from their pocket and began to make a wish. He felt sick with the same sour feeling he'd had the day he threw the coin in the well.

"I wish that Mary Alice would go to the dance with me and—"

"What are you doing here?"

Bill stopped when he heard Torrin's voice from behind him.

"We are just wandering around," said Bill. "Is this your land?"

"No, but you shouldn't be back here," said Torrin.

"Why?" asked Leslie. "We aren't doing anything wrong."

"You shouldn't play around the well," said Torrin as he moved closer.

"We aren't playing. We were just looking for something to do. What's wrong with being here? It's just an old dusty well. It's probably dry anyway," said Bill as he tossed a coin into the air to see if he would hear a splash if the coin hit water.

Torrin watched as the coin went into the air and began to plummet to the bottom. He yelled in anguish, "Nooooo, oh God, no."

The puzzled young men looked at him, completely surprised by his reaction to the coin going into the well.

"What's the big deal? It's just a dry well," said Bill.

"You're right. I guess I shouldn't be so concerned. I guess I just don't want anyone to get hurt around this old well, that's all."

Torrin started slowly backing out of the forest and onto the road. He calmed himself and kept thinking that it would be all right, nothing was going to happen. But before he could finish his thought, he saw Bob Perkins run into the road. He fell to his knees and cried in horror. Torrin knew then that tossing the coin into the well meant the death of someone in the town.

Bob's mother, Emily, was ninety-eight years old. She was the oldest surviving member of the early village folk. No one expected her to live much longer, but they didn't expect her to die like that. Emily's body was dry just like Mr. Hasting's had been seven years ago. All of her organs and body fluids were gone. She died sitting on the sofa, where her stiff, leather-like body reached out for help, but couldn't move fast enough before her life force was taken from her. She didn't have time to react to the sudden loss of her entity that left her mummified and cursed through eternity.

The townspeople gasped at the sight of her. The doctor arrived within minutes and had the body moved to his office. He pulled back the cover and gagged at the sight of the fear that taunted her. Her face seemed bewildered with what was happening to her, and the look of desperation shadowed her.

The doctor had the body taken to his office and immediately went to some of the journals that were written about Mr. Hasting. Mrs. Perkins' remains looked as described in the information about Mr. Hasting. Dr. Smith had no idea what this was. He did not think it was contagious, because it had happened before and it did not cause an epidemic then. They didn't know what caused it then, and he didn't know now either. He took a piece of her skin and studied it under his microscope. There were no signs of human tissue, no cellular structure at all. All signs that life ever existed were completely erased. It was as if her skin was like a brown leather bag that once held her organs—just a lifeless bag. It had only been moments since this happened. Something should have still been there.

Torrin walked through the crowd that gathered outside of the doctor's office. He stepped inside and demanded to see the body.

"This has nothing to do with you, Torrin. Why are you here?" asked Dr. Smith.

"I must see her, I must," Torrin said frantically. "You don't understand, I must see her!" He pushed his way to the back room and stared upon the wretched face. He yelled for mercy. "God, please, I didn't mean it. I-I can't, I can't let this happen. What can I do, please, God, tell me? What can I do?" he cried.

The people in the room stared at him, wondering what he believed he could have done to prevent this from happening. They tried to understand why Torrin believed he had something to do with this.

"Torrin, what are you yelling about? Have you gone mad?" Ronald Jamerson inquired.

"Ronnie, Ronnie . . . I-I caused this. I know I did. What can I do?" He grabbed Ronald's shirt and placed his head upon Ronald's shoulder and cried.

"Look here, man. What's gotten into you? This had nothing to do with you. You couldn't have caused this if you wanted to. No, this is the work of The Devil. It is. It's just like before. We need to cleanse the town. We need to free the town of this evil," said Ronald.

"Yes, yes," the voices came from behind in agreement to find the culprit and burn him out.

"Someone is in favor with The Devil, that's what this is," a voice from the crowed cried.

Torrin hung his head and walked out onto the road. His lifeless body drug itself back to the well, where he sat and cried.

"What can I do?" he asked. "What can I do to fix this? I didn't mean for this to happen. I wish I could take it back. I need to talk to you. Where are you?" Torrin yelled. "Where are you?" he yelled again.

"I am here," said a voice from the well.

"Let me see you. I need to talk to you," said Torrin, and suddenly, there he was, the same dark man from ten years ago, unchanged and unholy.

"I have been expecting you," he solemnly said.

"Please, please stop doing this . . . please. I'll do anything, anything," cried Torrin.

"Anything, Torrin?" the dark man asked.

"Anything."

"Even sacrifice Melanie and Michael?"

"No, no, please don't take my wife and child. Please, I beg you."

"What do you want me to do? We made a pact. I held up my side of the bargain; they are alive. Now you have to hold up your side, remember?"

"But the way they die, it's horrible. I can't keep letting this happen." Torrin fell to his knees.

"Their souls are mine, as you promised, and I take them before they die. They were going to die anyway. I just help them along a little. If I wait until they expire, He will take them swiftly, and I will gain nothing. Yes, it is horrible, but it is my way." He smiled ominously.

"There's got to be a way out of this. Nothing is forever. There's got to be a way," said Torrin.

"You are right, this isn't forever. It is only until the last descendant of the original village people is dead, and then it will stop."

"But what happens to them? Where are they?" asked Torrin.

"They are with me for an eternity."

"No, no there must be a way to redeem myself. There must be. God would not forsake me this way," Torrin said.

"He did not forsake you, you forsook Him, and now you and all that is yours is mine," he said.

"There is a way, I know it, I know it," said Torrin.

"There is," he said.

"There is?" Torrin came to his feet and hoped with all his heart that there was a way to stop this.

"Yes, of course there is. We all make mistakes. I'm not without mercy, but you made a deal, and something must be paid for my kindness and generosity," he said.

"What? What? I'll do anything, whatever it takes," said Torrin.

"Find the place where the forces of life begin and end,

and there you will find the source of power to free the people of the well. Find the holy crystal rose. It must be done by a descendant of the village. With this power, the descendant will find the coin that you threw in ten years ago and must carry it into the light of the sun, and as the angel in the coin is released, so shall be the souls in the well," he said.

"Release their souls? What do you mean? I want to erase the pact. Let's be even with what you have now," said Torrin.

"Oh no. I can never do that. But you have an opportunity to release them if you can find the rose," he said.

"A holy crystal rose? There is no such thing. What is it? Where is it?"

"It is in the world beyond. It lies beyond the highest place and into the lowest place. It is not of this world, and only those with the faith of a thousand angels can ever get close to it." He laughed.

As the little hope he had began to fade, Torrin pleaded with all his heart. "No such thing exists. This is a lie. Why do you torment me?"

"Oh, it exists, all right. It has been among the angels forever. It is what gives hope to all things, and joy to those who believe in goodness and light. It must be far away from mankind in order to sustain the light, but even at its distance, it maintains harmony between the souls and a connection with all that is good. It is the only thing that will release the souls, but mind you, once you remove it from its rightful place, the world will begin to deteriorate. The evil side of man will manifest itself, and goodness will not walk upon the earth."

"If I find it and bring it here, will mankind perish?" asked Torrin.

"If the rose is returned to its rightful place, it shall be

so that all souls shall be released to the Father that followed him and mankind shall dwell in light."

"I don't know where to start," said Torrin.

"Take this piece of information, and from there, you can begin."

"What? What is it?"

"Seek those who know the wind and let it carry you to your destination," he said as he stared into Torrin's eyes. He saw Torrin's confusion and smiled, knowing that he would never figure it out.

"Oh God, what does that mean? I have no idea what you are talking about." Torrin hung his head and covered his face in anguish and confusion. He started pacing around and ranting on about the meaning of the verse. He cried out in agony, "What do you want from me!" He turned and looked back and the man was gone. He heard a reply that echoed from the well.

"I want the village," the voice said as it faded into the darkness of the well.

Torrin was beside himself. He sat on the ground trying to figure out what the riddle meant. "Seek those who know the wind . . . What does that mean? I must find this rose, I must. But where to start? I don't know where to start."

Torrin knew that he had to leave Melanie and the children. He knew that he would never see the birth of his new baby and the life of Michael, Katy, and John. He realized that the moment he made the pact, he'd given away his future and the future of his children. He was so depressed. He loved his family and cherished Melanie. Leaving them was the hardest thing he had ever thought of doing, but the reality was, he was going to lose them anyway. He took solace in the fact that their lives were spared, but now he realized the price he must pay for that promise.

He had to find the crystal rose. He had no idea how to start or what direction to take. He knew that when he started walking that he could be walking in the wrong direction and may never find it. *What is the right direction?* he thought. The consequences for not finding it were too unbearable to think about. The souls of the entire village would be lost in a hellish nightmare for eternity. Then, if he found it and released the souls and couldn't get it back, the entire world would be doomed to destruction and despair. The worst of mankind would dominate, and the world would fall into chaos. Evil would win in either case. Somehow he had to be sure that if he couldn't reach the rose, someone else would know of the story and would try to find it. Someone else must try.

Over the next few weeks, Torrin sat in the barn and wrote the fantastic story of the past ten years. He dipped his fountain pen into the inkbottle and began to tell the story from the beginning. He told of Melanie's breech birth and her imminent death. He told of his meeting with the man at the well and the pact he made. He described the coin and drew a detailed picture of it. He remembered it like it happened yesterday. He told of the death of Mr. Hasting after the young boys tossed the coin into the well and again with Mrs. Perkins. He linked the wishing well to the deaths and told that for every coin tossed, a descendant of the original village people would die a horrible death. He said that their souls would become lost in darkness for an eternity unless the rose was found and brought back to release them. He emphasized the point that the rose must be returned to its original place or all would be lost for mankind, for it was the light of life that rested upon the earth. His tears marked the pages as he wrote the words:

The rose is in the world beyond. It lies beyond the highest place and into the lowest place. It is not of this world, and only those with the faith of a thousand angels can find it and embrace it.

You must see those who know the wind and let it carry you to your destination.

He wrote in the journal that he did not know what the riddle meant, but that he had to try and find a way to release the souls.

He wrote to Melanie how much he loved her and the children and wanted to erase what had been done. He cherished her life and the life of the children so much that deep inside he knew he would make the same choice if he had it to do over again. He also knew that he would have to pay a price someday, either with his life or his sanity.

He wrote:

I do not know where I am going. I believe that I shall go in the opposite direction of the well and hope that God guides me toward the path that I must take.

The last words he wrote were to Melanie and the children:

Melly, I love you with all my heart and that love caused me to act irrationally, and I took something that was not mine to take—the souls of our children. I hope you can find it in your heart to forgive me for my transgression and for leaving you and the children alone. Michael, you are the man of the house now. Stay vigilant over your family and see them through the hard times. Kiss your sister and brother for me, and tell them about their father so that they never forget.

Torrin closed the leather binder and tied the leather string around the metal hook to keep the binder closed. He held the binder close to his chest and cried. He knew that once he departed from it, life as he knew it would be over.

He waited until Melanie and the children were asleep and he pulled together a few items that he would need for his long journey. He had been storing things in the barn over the past few days, preparing for the trip. He woke Michael and asked him to step outside for a moment.

Michael awoke from a deep sleep and struggled to pull himself together. He eventually made it outside where Torrin was waiting.

Torrin walked Michael to the barn, where he gave Michael the journal and told him what he had to do. He wanted Michael to understand that he was not just abandoning his family and that he was truly sorry for leaving, but knew that he had no other choice.

Michael was frantic when he heard the story and didn't believe a word of it. He wanted to go to the well and see for himself, but Torrin forbade him from ever going to the well.

"Michael, you must trust me and know that what I say is truth. I would never want any harm to come to you, so I must insist that you never go to the well. It is not safe, and the evil one will not come for you yet; you are young and innocent. You can only pray that I find the crystal rose and return it before your life has passed, and therefore mine. Look after your mother and do as she says until you are of age. This family is yours now. Look upon them with great care."

Torrin kissed Michael and grabbed his gear. He walked to the barn door and looked back at him and tried with all his strength not to let him see his father cry. He turned and walked out of the barn and out of the yard. Michael stood at the door and watched him. Torrin walked to the path that led to the well and turned to face the opposite direction. He began his walk on the outskirts of town toward the horizon.

Michael watched him walk into the darkness and out of sight. He could not control his tears. He held on to the hope that his father would return someday and life would be as it once was.

Just as the farm was fading in the distance, Torrin turned for one last look. He stared for a moment and then he stepped into the night sky, never to be seen again.

Chapter Two

Tremaine

Tremaine Fleming was a troubled seventeen-year-old child who worked desperately at ruining his life and everyone's around him. He never knew his father. He lived with his mother, Alaya, in Oklahoma City. They lived in the one of the poorest parts of town, and he walked the inner city streets in areas that the police wouldn't enter. His mother did not graduate from high school, and she tried to support him on a minimum-wage job in a Laundromat. She was a tall lady with long, black hair. Her slender figure and high cheekbones made her an attractive woman who could have any man, but she didn't date anyone. She didn't want Tremaine's life filled with any more drama than he already had.

She was full-blooded Navajo. Her family moved to Oklahoma City when she was a child and tried to start a new life. Her father worked on construction sites and made a minimal salary, and what he didn't gamble away, he drank up. He was soon killed in a bar room fight when she was ten, and her mother died not long after. She was raised in foster homes and was pregnant with Tremaine at seventeen. She never finished high school;

instead, she went to work and tried to make a home for herself and her new baby. Alaya wanted more for him, but with few skills, she could never reach higher than her minimum wage job and low-income housing.

Tremaine was part White and part Navajo. He hated his mixed heritage and never truly identified with either group. He didn't seem to belong anywhere, and it seemed that no one wanted him. He created a great deal of chaos in his mother's life for many years. After she sold her car to pay the bail to keep him out of jail, she told him that was the last time. If he did anything else wrong and got caught, he was on his own. She had already sold every valuable thing she had to keep him out of jail and in school, but her efforts failed. He fought her every wish.

She understood where the anger came from. He was different, and he wanted to embrace the native heritage, but saw it as a lost way of life. When he was a boy, his mother took him to his great-grandfather's farm on Navajo land in Arizona. He felt at peace there, but different.

Even though his facial features were more like his mother than his father, the young people around him called him half-breed and he hated the name. Tremaine was tall with very dark hair that hung to his shoulders. He had dark eyebrows and deep-set eyes that accented his high cheekbones. His light brown skin made him pale to his native brothers, and he wished that he could be more like them.

As he got older, he spent hours in the sun to get rich brown tans that accented his native features. He was glad that he looked so much like his mother. It prevented a whole lot of questions about his father; people just assumed that he was Navajo too. Tremaine saw pictures of his father from his mother's photo albums. He was a handsome man. Tremaine got his broad shoulders and square chin from him.

At seventeen years old, Tremaine was the man of the house. He enjoyed the role and would flex his muscles with his mother whenever he could. She was quite wise and would let him prowl around like a caged cat until he stepped over the line, and then she'd reel him back in and remind him that he was just seventeen.

He came home looking pleased with himself one day and gave her a big kiss. She looked at him and was unsure how to react. She could never tell with him. It could be that he was genuinely happy to see her, or it could be that he had done something terrible and she would have to pay to keep him out of jail and the joyous moment was his way of easing the path to the confession. On this day, it was the latter.

"I decided to buy us a car, you know, to replace the one that you had to sell. I never wanted you to have to do that, and I thought you needed another one, so I bought one. Here are the keys, go outside and see." He handed her the keys.

"You bought a car? Tremaine, where did you get the money to buy a car?" she asked.

"That doesn't matter," he said defiantly.

"Oh yes, it does. Now tell me, where did you get the money?"

"Mother, I'm a man. I can buy a car or whatever I want if I can afford it."

"Is the car stolen?" she asked.

"No, it's my car. I bought it," he yelled.

"If you did not work for this money, we cannot keep it."

"Oh, I worked for it, all right," he said with a sly look on his face.

She was so disappointed in him. She couldn't believe that after everything they'd been through together, he would risk his life or freedom for an old broken-down car.

She looked into his eyes, and with fierce anger she

said, "I love you, but I don't like you. You came from me, so I blame myself. I should not have gotten pregnant at such a young age. I was ill-prepared for the task of raising a child on my own. I should have figured out a way to get out of this slum so you could be raised in a better environment. It's my fault, yes, it's my fault, and that's something I will live with for the rest of my life, but I will not let you destroy me as you have yourself." Tears rolled down her face.

He looked into her eyes, knowing that she was different this time. He felt fear and anxiety and almost knew what she was going to say and dreaded it.

"I will help you in every way, but I will not help you be a thief."

"I didn't steal the car," he said adamantly.

"No, but you stole the money to buy the car, and that's just as bad," she said.

"Look, we needed a car, I got us one. I did it for you, Mother."

"Oh no, don't use me for your dirty work. I will not tolerate it. If you did not legitimately work for the money for that car, it will not stay here. You can't keep it."

"How are you going to tell me what I can and cannot keep? It's my car, I bought it," he said as he moved toward her.

"Are you going to try and intimidate me?" she asked. "Is that your plan? Because if it is, I have news for you. No one can intimidate me in my home, so if you plan to do this, you must live somewhere else." Her stare was piercing.

He stepped back.

She stepped forward and got in his face. "So, now, if you live here, the car goes back and so does the money you stole to buy it. Is that clear?"

Tremaine decided that today was the day to take a

stand. He wanted to keep the car, and he knew that if he backed down this time, he would never have any freedom to do what he wanted to do.

"No, Mother. The car is mine," he said softly.

"Well, I'm happy for you. I hope you and your car are happy together, but you will be happy somewhere else."

"Are you throwing me out?" he asked with a confused look on his face. "You can't throw me out because I'm a minor and I won't leave."

"As I stated, I will not let you destroy me as you have yourself. I take full blame for you and your awful ways, and I only hope that you do not take another person's life in your quest for self-destruction. But it will always be a hope, because unless it ends up on the eleven o'clock news, I won't know about it. I did the best I could, and now I'm finished. The rent is due tomorrow, and I have decided not to pay it. I'm going home, and I'm not taking you with me. Your life is your own. You are a man, as you say, do what you want with it. I don't care, I'm tired. You will be eighteen in a few months, and maybe by the time the authorities figure it out, you'll be old enough to be legal. If they try to look for me, they won't find me and they will try to put you in foster care until you are eighteen. Hopefully you can stay clear of them for a few months. I hope so. I pity the poor family that ends up with you. It doesn't matter to me anymore. I've done all I know how to do. I guess this is what they call tough love." She turned and walked into her bedroom and closed the door.

He stood in the living room, wondering what he should do. He had no place to go, but obviously he couldn't stay here.

His pride would not let him beg her. After all that talk about being a man, he had to get the courage from somewhere to step out of that apartment and never look back.

He knew she was right, but for him this life was the only life he knew and he didn't have the courage to try and fail and try again. He didn't think he was worth much anyway, so the sooner he was caught and put away for life, the easier it would be for everyone. *I might as well start my path to prison or death right now*, he thought.

Alaya called for a cab and started packing all of her personal possessions into two suitcases. After thirty minutes, she dragged them into the living room and placed them by the door. She saw Tremaine still standing in the middle of the floor, looking quite foolish and confused. She didn't say a word to him. She walked around him as if he wasn't in the room. She went into the kitchen and began to pull food from the shelves and utensils from the drawers and cabinets. She stuffed a bag with the things she wanted to keep and discarded everything else into the trashcan.

After thirty minutes, she re-entered the living room and placed the bag at the door with the suitcases. She walked past Tremaine, who was still standing in the middle of the floor, and picked up her keys from the table. She removed the door keys and placed them on the coffee table. She picked up her Bible and a few photographs from around the room and stuffed them into the small bag. She heard the horn blow from outside, and she peered out the window to see the cab at the front entrance. She walked back to the door, threw the small bag over her shoulder, picked up the suitcases and walked out.

Tremaine was shocked. He didn't know what to do. He walked to the window and watched her get in the cab and drive off. She never looked back.

But, I'm still a minor, he thought. *She can't just leave, can she?*

He looked around and wondered what to do. "Well, I

got a place for the night. The rent isn't due until tomorrow. I'll figure something out," he said.

He took the keys from the table and put them in his pocket and went outside, determined to find the money for this month's rent. He got into his car and turned the key, but the car didn't start. He tried again, but it was dead.

"Damn, that's all I need. I just bought this thing. I'm taking it back and get my money." He laughed. "I ain't got the money to get it towed back."

He got out the car and started walking. He wandered around for a few hours. Soon it would be dark, and he needed to be ready to do whatever he was going to do by nightfall. He walked the streets, looking into the shop windows and wondering which product would get him the most money on the streets. He stopped at a jewelry store and stared inside. *This would be good,* he thought, *but I couldn't sell this stuff quickly. Hot jewelry will be easy to trace.*

He kept walking until he came to an electronics store. *Yes, this is it. These things will sell fast. iPods, videos, CDs—yeah, this is it.*

"Don't do it."

The man's voice startled him as he turned quickly and stumbled to hold his footing.

Tremaine stood in front of the store filled with electronic equipment that he was sure would sell swiftly. Just as he'd made up his mind to go for it, the stranger standing in front of him peered into his thoughts and stopped him.

"What do you know?" Tremaine said angrily. "Don't do what?"

"It looked to me that you were planning to break into that store," the man said as he pointed to the store window.

Tremaine turned and looked at the window as if he

didn't know what the man could be talking about. He shrugged his shoulders.

"No, no, I wasn't. I mean, I wasn't planning anything like that." He stared into the man's eyes and wondered how he knew.

The man was tall, medium build with short dark hair. He had a scar over his left eye as if from a hard-fought battle. There was something odd about him. Tremaine noticed that his dark skin was a stark contrast to his bright blue eyes. His eyes were deep water-blue, but he was obviously Black.

"Your eyes . . . your eyes are different, I mean for a Black person," Tremaine said

"Really? I hadn't noticed."

"You hadn't noticed? How many Black people do you know with blue eyes?"

"I don't know many Black people," he said.

"What?" said Tremaine with a very confused look on his face. "You are a Black person who doesn't know any Black people? That's strange." Tremaine started to back away. The man seemed strange, and he wanted to get far away from him. "Well, I guess I'll be moving on."

"Moving on to where?" the man asked.

"Just on," replied Tremaine as he turned and walked faster.

"I am going that way too. I will join you," the man said.

"I'm not going any particular way. You don't have to join me." Tremaine looked back at the man and wondered why he was pushing himself on him.

"Ok," he said as he continued to follow Tremaine.

Tremaine was starting to get very angry. He needed to make some money tonight, and this man was blocking. He couldn't focus on what needed to be done.

"Can you go away now?" Tremaine demanded.

"Go where?" he asked with a quizzical look on his face. Tremaine looked at him, bewildered. "What kind of question is that? Where did you come from?"

"Nowhere in particular."

"Then that's where you should go back to."

"I'm not sure how to get there," he said.

"Get where?" asked Tremaine.

"To nowhere in particular," the man said.

"Ok, this is stupid. I don't think I'll keep talking to you." Tremaine started walking, hoping to ditch the man, but every time he looked back the man was there.

"WHAT THE HELL DO YOU WANT?" yelled Tremaine.

"Nothing," he said.

"Oh, the hell with this," said Tremaine in great frustration as he began to run. He ran for about twenty minutes and knew that he had escaped the daunting stare of the man with the bright blue eyes. He stopped to catch his breath and smiled at his ability to ditch the man.

"Hello," the voice said from behind him. "Why did you run? You can run pretty fast."

Tremaine was afraid to look back. *It's not possible. There's no way he could keep up with me, no way,* he thought. For a moment he was speechless.

"Are you going to run again?" the man asked.

"Yes, I am and I will continue to run until I am free of you." Tremaine took a deep breath and started to run as fast as he could.

He ran for another twenty minutes, stopped for a moment, and ran some more. Tremaine didn't pay much attention to where he was running. It seemed that someone or something was guiding him. He knew he wasn't going toward the apartment or any store in town that could provide the goods he would need to sell. He was running away from the town. He didn't know why, he just kept running. He wanted to get as far away from the stranger as possible. He looked back every now and then and didn't see anyone.

When he found himself coming upon a small park graced by beautiful trees and flowers, he stopped and wondered where he was. In the distance was a gazebo with wooden benches where people could sit and enjoy the beauty of the trees and flowers. The place was so serene and calming. The park took his mind off everything. For a moment he seemed to transcend time and space. He felt light and free of burden and fear. He gazed at the scenic view for a moment.

Then he heard the voice of a man behind him.

"There was once a time when the trees were all the way out to there," he said as he pointed down the road. "Yep, the trees were thick. You couldn't see this open area from the town back then. You had to enter the trees, and there it was."

"Who are you?" Tremaine asked calmly. He realized that the man was not going away. He couldn't figure out how he was always there, and decided not to try to escape him anymore. It was obvious the man wanted something from him.

"I'm nobody really, just a lost soul just like you," he said.

"Is that what I am, a lost soul?" He looked into the man's eyes. "Yes, I guess you're right. What do you want of me?"

"Do you see that man over there?" He pointed to an old man trying to carry a bag of feed to the chicken coop.

"Yes, I see him. Who is he?"

"His name is Mr. Wilhelm, Alec Wilhelm."

"Ok, and he is significant because?"

"He is significant because he is the man that you are going to free."

"Free? Free from what?"

"He needs your help, Tremaine, and only you can help him."

"I don't understand. Help him how? I can't help myself. After tomorrow I'll be homeless, thanks to you."

"Then the two of you can lean on each other. You have nowhere to go, and he needs someone to come."

"Look, I don't do charity work. Now, I'm sorry for the old guy, but it's not my calling, you know what I mean?"

"Yes, I know."

"Doesn't he have a family?" asked Tremaine.

"No, he is the last of his line and he holds the key," the man said.

"The key to what?" asked Tremaine. He watched as the man stumbled to the back yard because the bag of feed was too heavy for him to carry. He started to go forward to help, but stopped.

"Help him. He's an old man who needs someone . . . help him," said the man in such a solemn tone that it made Tremaine feel sad and guilty for hesitating.

They walked to the old cabin built in 1896 by Torrin Wilhelm. Most of the farm was gone, and newer homes circled the small patch of land, as if sheltering it from the world. The local people knew that Alec had no family and that once he passed, the land would be available for use by the local authorities. But, until then, no one bothered him about his land or his home. He was the only surviving descendant of the people of the original village.

He was his father David's only child, and David's father Michael had two children, Ethan and David. They both died horrible deaths, just like all of the descendants of the village, regardless of where they were in the world. Alec would often hear of a mysterious death where the life force was drained out of a body and left an empty shell of leather-like skin and bones. No one could ever find a cause for any of the deaths, but there had been many over the past one hundred years. Medical investigators had special teams working the cases. Paranormal scientists suggested that their body fluids were being drained by a supernatural force; and, of course, the religious zealots saw it as a punishment by God we could all expect to meet if we didn't change our ways.

Alec tried to carry the bag but couldn't; it was too heavy. He fell to the ground. Tremaine could hear him groan when his knee struck the ground.

The bag of feed fell from his arms and split open, pouring seed over the ground. As he struggled to get to his feet, he saw a hand reach out to him. He looked up into the face of a young Native American boy with hair as dark as coal. Alec took his hand and thanked him for his kindness.

"No problem. Let me help you with this."

Tremaine reached down to pick up the bag of feed. He gathered as much as he could from the ground and poured it back into the bag and tried to seal it as best he could. He walked to the chicken coop and leaned the bag against the fence. "There, now you can feed them from the bag. I can carry it back in once you're done."

"Thank you, young man, thank you," said Alec as he slowly walked to the coop and began throwing the feed all around. The chickens scurried around, clacking and fluttering their wings at the sight of the food.

Tremaine stepped back and turned around. "Ok, I helped him, now what?"

But there was no one there. The stranger was gone.

Tremaine walked out to the fence and looked all around. He walked back to the park and looked down the street, but he was gone. Tremaine didn't understand any of this. It seemed that the man led him there only to leave him.

What am I supposed to do now? he thought.

He stood near the well and wondered what this was all about. How strange it all was that he ended up miles away from home, helping a man that he didn't know, led by a man he had never seen before. He walked back to the cabin and checked on Alec.

"Mister, the man that was with me, did you see where he went?"

"I didn't see anyone, only you," Alec said as he attempted to pick up the feed bag with one hand while covering his back with the other.

Tremaine reached down and picked up the bag and carried it to the barn. Alec thanked him and walked toward the cabin.

The cabin was much larger than it was when Torrin built it for Melanie and his children. There were three bedrooms, indoor plumbing and a separate dinning area. Each generation modernized the home and kept it contemporary and comparable to the surrounding neighborhood, but the original cabin could still be carved out of the new logs and fresh paint. The cabin was twice its original size.

Alec stayed in the cabin after his father left. Alec's father David continued to run the farm after Michael left and never returned from his journey to find the rose. They both gave their lives to that horrible, wicked death that took all of the village people. Alec decided not to have a family. He lived alone his entire life. Just like Michael and David, Alec was told of the story of the evil by the well and shown the leather binder that told the horrid story of the pact made by Torrin. Alec didn't believe the story and felt that Michael and David gave their lives to a foolish tale. If it were true, Alec decided to end it with himself.

Michael tried to follow his father into the land that held the crystal rose, so did David, but Alec decided not to try. He could see the futility in it. He wasn't even sure he believed it, but he knew that something evil surrounded his family, and he wasn't going to pass it on to any future generations of Wilhelms. He was sixty years old and had a rough life trying to manage the farm alone. He knew that he would have no heirs to the farm, so he sold much of the land, a little at a time. His hair was so white, it nearly glowed, and his bushy mustache was mixed with the red hue of his original hair color. He wasn't a tall man, but it was obvious that he was once strong and virile from years of working the farm. His hazel-gray eyes were solemn and sad and told a story that seemed heartwrenching. Sometimes the loneliness was unbearable.

Torrin's story remained a family secret and was passed on to the elder male in each generation. That person was to make every attempt to find the crystal rose and break the curse. For the way to break the cycle was to have no children.

Tremaine took the feedbag back to the barn and placed it inside and walked to the porch, where Alec was waiting. Tremaine wasn't sure why he was there, but he felt that he was led to Alec for a reason that seemed insignificant. Now that his quest for money was interrupted by the stranger, he had nowhere to go, and deciding where to sleep through the night became paramount.

"Where you live, boy?" asked Alec.

"Nowhere, I guess."

"Oh, I see. That's a strange place for a boy to be . . . nowhere."

"I'm kinda in between jobs."

"In between jobs." Alec looked at him smartly. He knew that he was too young to have a full-time job. "You seem kinda young to be working. What kind of work do you do?"

"All kinds." Tremaine shrugged his shoulders, not knowing what to say. He had never had a real job. Working for anything was never a strong point for him.

"All kinds. Well, that's a lot for such a young boy. It seems as though you should be in school," said Alec.

Tremaine stumbled over what to say. "No, I—well, I was, but I graduated, you know. Because now I'm older. Old enough to take care of myself like a man."

"Yes, I can see that." Alec knew that the boy should be in school and wondered if he should call the authorities, but decided not to. He knew that the outcome could be disastrous for him. "Does your mother know where you are?"

"She decided that I should be on my own, you know, · like a man, taking care of myself. She said I was ready."

"Ok, that's a bunch of hogwash. Where is she, and what did you do to make her throw your butt out?" asked Alec.

Tremaine didn't like what Alec was insinuating. "What do you mean? I don't owe you any explanation for my situation. I'm a man, and I will take care of myself.".

"Well, thanks for your help." Alec turned and started to walk back inside.

Tremaine stood still and wondered what he was going to do. He couldn't go back to the apartment, and he didn't have any money. He felt as stupid as he did when he was standing in the living room watching his mother pack.

"She left and went back to the reservation. I guess I was more trouble than I was worth." Tremaine hung his head shamefully. He knew that Alec didn't buy the whole stand-on-my-own-two-feet-like-a-man story.

"Well, it does seem like parents got it pretty hard now days trying to raise a kid with all the crap going on in the world. I guess she did the best she could. I suppose you didn't help none."

"No, I suppose not."

Alec stared at the boy and wondered why he was

there. He knew it was not for money, and he also knew that he needed some help. It seemed strange that he would just show up out of nowhere, but he was there, and Alec saw no reason to turn him away.

"Well, you're welcome to stay as long as you're willing to help out around here. I'm quite a bit over the hill now, and I can't do like I used to."

"Thank you, sir. I will work hard, I promise. I won't need much," Tremaine said as he thought about the alternative of sleeping in the park.

"Come on in." Alec turned and walked inside.

Tremaine followed him into the three-bedroom cabin. The rooms were rustic and warm. The cabin had a feeling of family and children all around it. There was decor from all three generations, which produced a hodge-podge of themes throughout the cabin.

In the living room were old basins and pitchers that were used by Torrin and Melanie that now decorated corner walls. A rocking chair bought by Michael for his wife when she was carrying David sat near the fireplace, and a large cross was mounted to the wall over the fireplace by David to help shield them from evil spirits .

Tremaine followed Alec into the kitchen, where the massive stone fireplace built by Torrin still warmed the room. You could tell that this room was once the center of the house. Huge shelves lined one wall with all sorts of cooking utensils stacked on them. Some of the utensils dated back one hundred years. A wooden table and chairs centered the room, and barrels of oats and grains lined the opposite wall. Lanterns once used to light the room sat near the fireplace, boxes of matches and kindling piled against the wall.

"I always said I should throw some of this old junk away, but I never did. I guess, deep down inside, I never really wanted to. My father kept those lanterns from his

father. They haven't been used in fifty years, I'm sure."
Alec reached down and picked up one of the lanterns to
look at it, remembering a time gone by.

"Some of these things are antiques by now; they may
be worth something," said Tremaine.

"May be," replied Alec as he put the lantern down and
walked to the stove to check on his pot of stew. He
picked up the wooden spoon, removed the lid, and
began to stir. He took a good sniff and put the lid back
on. "A few more minutes yet. Let me show you where
you can sleep."

He walked Tremaine down a narrow hall and into a
small bedroom. The room was once a child's room. The
small bed barely fit, and the one window let in very little
light. It was very austere. He could tell that no one had
used the room for many years.

Alec walked to the dresser and pulled out a set of
sheets and a towel. "Here is some clean linen. You can
make up the bed. The bath is down the hall that way." He
pointed to the end of the hall. He put the sheets and
towel on the bed and walked toward the door. "I eat at
six. You're welcome to join me if you'd like."

"Yes, sir, I'd like to," replied Tremaine.

"Ok then," said Alec as he turned and walked out,
closing the door behind him.

Dinner was warm and filling. Tremaine was still a little
nervous about being there, but he knew it was better than
the alternative, which was to be nowhere. He sat quietly
and decided not to speak unless Alec spoke to him.

Alec had lived alone his whole life, so he was accustomed to eating in silence. He wasn't sure about the boy,
but he knew that he would not be able to stay on the
farm alone much longer, so he needed the help. He sat at

the table and wondered how he was going to get Tremaine back in school or even if he should care.

"Do you plan to finish school?"

"I told you I graduated."

"Ok, first thing, if you lie to me, I will throw you out, just like your mother did. Do we understand each other?"

Tremaine looked at him humbly as if he had been spanked. "Yes, sir, I understand."

"Ok, now, do you plan to finish school?" Alec asked again.

"I want to, but I just don't fit in. I never do well, and it's hard. I know I need to go to school, but I don't feel that I'm learning anything."

"That's because you're not. You're not learning anything. You have to pay attention to learn something, and you haven't done that."

"But, what good is it anyway? You never use most of that stuff anyway," said Tremaine.

"How do you know what you will use when you get forty or fifty years old? Just because you don't use it now doesn't mean you won't later. But, it's pretty hard to use it when you need it if you don't have it. Get everything you can get, you never know what life has in store for you. You have to be ready, and now is the time to ready yourself. If you wait, it'll be too late and you'll end up a broken-down young man that will grow into a broken-down, penniless, toothless old man, and there ain't nothing worse than that."

"Yeah, I guess you're right." Tremaine looked up into Alec's face. He stared at his hazel-gray eyes and wondered who this man really was.

"Hell, without schooling, your only option is a life of crime," said Alec.

Tremaine thought about the money he stole for the car, and the job he was trying to pull off when the stranger came along. He didn't have to say anything. Somehow he knew that Alec knew exactly who he was. He knew that he was going down the wrong path, and trying to pacify him with embellished stories of his plans and goals would only anger the man. He could tell that Alec was not your normal, everyday neighbor. He had a story himself that needed to be told, and whatever it was, it made him tough and strong. Alec could sense the will of the man and know his strengths and weaknesses. Tremaine felt humbled by him. He was glad to be there. He wasn't sure why.

The two continued to talk for another hour, learning about each other's lives and how they came to be where they were. Alec yawned and stood up to pour the remaining stew in a bowl and put it in the refrigerator. He removed the dishes from the table, washed them in the sink, and stored them in the tray on the counter. He wiped down the counter, closed the kitchen curtains, and walked to the front door and checked the lock.

"I'm off to bed. Turn the lights off when you're done," Alec said.

"Off to bed? It's just eight o'clock," said Tremaine.

"This is a farm. You rise early here," said Alec as he walked down the hall and into his room. He closed the door behind him, and silence besieged the cabin, making the atmosphere a little ominous.

Tremaine could hear the wood cracking, every window rattling, and every sound the wind made. He decided that it was time to go to bed.

"I guess you're right. We have an early morning." He turned off the lights and went into his small room, which he was so glad to have, and pulled back the covers. As guilty as he felt saying it, he thanked God for his blessings that night. He took off his clothes, got into bed, and went to sleep.

Tremaine heard the knock on the door that meant it was morning even though the sun didn't know it yet. He lay in bed, wondering what time it could be. He got up and went to the window and peered outside. He saw Alec walking toward the barn, carrying a flashlight. He walked back to the bed, put his clothes on and headed down the hall to the bathroom. He was ready for whatever Alec dished out to him today. He made up his mind that he was going to stay for as long as Alec would let him and try to make the best of things. He got cleaned up and walked outside.

The cool of the morning air was fresh and clean. There was moisture in the air as if rain was coming. He stood on the porch and looked up at the night sky and was amazed at the blanket of stars glittering in the darkness. *There are so many,* he thought.

The fall of the year was hard work for farmers. There wasn't much land left to grow upon, but it was enough to ensure a few hard days' work to bring the harvest in. Alec sold very little of his crop. He stored much of it for himself and the animals to get through the cold winter nights. He lived off the money from the sale of the land mostly, and the sale of the crop supplemented his savings. Harvesting the small crop was not enough work for day laborers, but more than he could do alone. All he needed was one helper.

"Damn, I knew farmers got up early, but this is ridiculous. Why would anybody do this?" Tremaine said as he stepped off the porch and walked toward the barn.

Alec was inside stroking his horse Tilly. Tremaine stood at the doorway and listened for a moment.

"Hello, girl. How are you today?"

Tilly nodded and nickered.

"I have a treat for you," said Alec as he reached into his pocket and pulled out a sugar cube. "I guess I need to get you your breakfast; you can't live off sugar alone." He smiled warmly as Tilly pulled at his pocket, where the sugar was. "Ok, one more, but that's it," he said lovingly.

Another farmer who decided to sell and move on twenty years ago gave Tilly to Alec. Their affection for each other was obvious. They shared their lives, and they'd both been through some hard times, but together they survived. Alec took special care to ensure that Tilly's stall was clean and that she always had hay and got her daily exercise. She was Alec's source of companionship. They shared a special bond.

Tilly let out a big snort when she realized that someone was nearby.

"It's okay, girl. It's just Tremaine. He's going to be helping us out for a while. You know we're not as young as we used to be. Come in, Tremaine, and let her see you."

Tremaine walked closer and stood in front of Tilly. Tilly looked into his eyes as if she were examining his soul. She needed to know that this new person would not harm Alec. Tremaine moved closer and began to stroke Tilly's mane. She nickered a bit.

"Ah, she likes you. That's good, girl. We'll get along just fine," Alec said as he walked to the pile of hay and picked up the pitchfork and began to toss hay into Tilly's stall.

"Let me do that for you." Tremaine reached out to take the pitchfork from Alec.

Alec stopped and stared at him. For a moment, he felt as if he wasn't needed by anyone any longer, not even Tilly. He had been tossing hay into Tilly's stall for twenty years, and now he had to accept that he may not be able to do it any longer. He sadly looked up at Tilly as if asking her for forgiveness. Tilly nickered and stomped her hoof in reply. She wanted Alec to know that she understood and that it was all right.

Tremaine took the pitchfork and tossed the hay. He was strong and full of life, and amazingly, he felt invigorated to be doing something useful.

Alec stepped over to Tilly and stroked her mane until Tremaine was done.

"If you carry the feedbag to the coop for me, I'll feed the chickens," said Alec.

"Sure," replied Tremaine. He picked up the bag of feed and walked outside.

Alec watched him and remembered what it was like to be that strong. He walked out behind him and looked at the horizon. The sun in all its glory peered just above the horizon. "There she is." Alec smiled. He walked to the coop and threw the food out to the rustling chickens.

"What do we have to do today?" asked Tremaine.

"We need to bring in some of that corn and heads of cabbage from the field today. That's going to take a few days, so we best get started. I'll fix us some breakfast, and I'll call you when it's done."

"Should I get started?" Tremaine asked.

"No, best not. I take it that you've never worked a farm before," said Alec.

"I helped my great-grandfather work his farm when I was younger. He had a small farm on the reservation. That's where my mother is now."

"Good, good, but I'd rather you wait for me on your first day. Just kinda hang out until I call," said Alec.

"Sure."

Tremaine started walking around, wondering what to do to occupy himself. He wandered back into the barn and started stroking Tilly. He moved around the barn looking for something to do when he saw an old wooden chest. It was layered with dust, had a lock on it and markings across the top. He swiped his hand across it and removed some of the dust. He did it two more times until he could clearly see the words DO NOT OPEN. He was intrigued. Tremaine was not the kind of person that you could tell not to do something and expect him to obey. He was curious and wanted to know what was inside. He couldn't imagine anything on this farm that could be so damaging that it needed to be kept a secret. He wondered about Alec and the way he lived all alone and wondered if the secrets of a lost love were in the box. He stared at it and wanted to break it open somehow. Just as he convinced himself that Alec would never find out, and he started to look around for a large rock to crack the lock, Alec called him to breakfast.

"Damn," he whispered. "Be right there," he yelled.

Tremaine didn't find the rock, so he had to leave it for another time, but he knew he wouldn't rest until he found out what was in the chest. He walked into the huge kitchen and sat at the table in front of a plate of food. He looked at it, amazed that anyone could eat all of it. "Do you eat like this every day?" he asked.

"You're going to need it when you're in the field working all day. Trust me, you'll burn it fast," said Alec.

"Ok," said Tremaine as he started forcing the food down and thinking that eating like this was a heart attack waiting to happen, but it sure was good.

They ate until they were full. Tremaine could barely move. He forced himself up and helped Alec put the dishes in the sink, and they headed for the field. He and Alec worked all morning in the field and stopped only to drink water and catch their breaths for the next round. Tremaine was energized. It reminded him of his great-grandfather's farm. He enjoyed working with his great-grandfather and watching him tender the land and cherish the bounty from it. His great-grandfather thought land was the Creator's greatest gift to man.

Halfway through the day, Alec let Tilly out to graze in an open field next to the cabin. Tilly ran around as much as she could and enjoyed the autumn sun. Alec went into the cabin and prepared sandwiches for lunch while Tremaine passed out under a tree near the cabin.

Tremaine couldn't believe how hungry he was when Alec came out with the food. He grabbed the sandwiches and ate like it was his first meal in a month. Alec sat on the ground with him and they both ate frantically.

When they noticed how crazy they were gorging themselves and then looked at each other, it was such a funny sight, especially after the enormous breakfast they ate. They fell over laughing at themselves and each other.

Alec laughed for the first time in months. There was very little in his life that brought joy and laughter. He had forgotten what it felt like to laugh. The feeling was so free and uplifting that it overwhelmed him and he started to cry.

"What's wrong? What did I do?" Tremaine moved closer to Alec to see what could be wrong.

"Nothing. You did nothing. I'm all right. I haven't had a reason to laugh in such a long time, and I guess I never thought I ever would again. It's been kinda hard, you know."

"Mr. Wilhelm?"

"Alec . . . call me Alec."

"Alec, why are you here alone? Where are your wife and children? Did they leave you?"

"No, no. I never married," he said solemnly.

"Never married, but why? Is there something wrong with you that you couldn't marry?"

"Yes, well, no . . . I mean, yes, yes, there's something wrong with me," he said as he tried to get up from the ground.

Tremaine grabbed his arm and helped him stand. "What's wrong with you? You seem perfectly fine to me."

"It's not something you can see."

"Are you sick? Have you always been sick?"

"No, it's not a sickness. It's just me," he said as he walked toward the field to start the second half of the day's work.

Tremaine followed him. He was curious and wanted to know more. He could look at Alec and tell that he was once a handsome man, so he must have had lots of girl-friends. For him to never marry was puzzling.

"Were you ever in love with anyone?"

"Yes." Alec stopped walking and took a deep breath.

He allowed himself a moment to remember the face of his only love, Gwyneth. She was petite and beautiful with beautiful green eyes, long locks of dark brown curls, an intoxicating laugh, and deep dimples that made her face glow. She was his life for many years, but he knew he could never have children and he knew how badly she wanted a family, so he had to let her go. She eventually married and had a family and moved on with her life, but Alec never did. He hated the choice he had to make, but knew it was the only choice for her. He lived with regret, but knew it was the only thing he could do with the ominous cloud that hung over his family.

Tremaine watched him and waited for his response. He could tell that the thought of someone pained him, and he felt guilty for bringing it up. But he wanted to know.

"Who was she?"

"Her name was Gwyneth."

"Where is she now?"

"She's gone, that's all. Just gone. Stop asking so many questions," Alec snapped.

"Ok, ok. It's just strange, that's all. Sorry, I won't ask again."

Tremaine looked into Alec's face and saw the anguish of a man whose life was troubled and whose past haunted him still. Tremaine walked back into the field and began the afternoon work. They worked until sunset and dragged their beaten bodies back to the cabin and inside. Tremaine went into the living room and stretched out over the sofa. Alec went into the kitchen and started dinner.

"My God, how does he do it? I can't move another muscle," whispered Tremaine as he lay on the sofa. "I guess he's used to it."

Alec washed up at the sink and started pulling food from the refrigerator for dinner. He made a pot of stew and some cornbread and a tall pitcher of lemonade.

Tremaine could smell the food from the kitchen and chuckled at the thought of eating yet again.

After about an hour, Alec summoned Tremaine to dinner. They sat at the table, too exhausted to talk.

Alec noticed that Tremaine did not have a change of clothes. "I have a few old clothes stored in the barn from when I was younger and thinner. Some of it may fit you. You are welcome to it, if you'd like."

"Is that what's stored in that old chest?" asked Tremaine intently.

"What old chest?"

"The one in the barn, the wooden chest."

"No, you stay away from that. It's none of your business. I won't have you snooping around into my personal things. You stay away from that chest."

Tremaine's prying into his personal life angered Alec. He knew he couldn't have anyone delving into his past.

"All right, all right. What's the big deal anyway? It's

not like you got a dead body in there or something. I'll
stay away. I won't touch it."

"See that you don't."

"I won't," replied Tremaine as he dropped his plate in
the sink and walked out of the kitchen. He walked outside and stood on the porch and stared at the night sky,
watching the sun set and the stars come out.

After a few minutes, he heard Alec walk down the hall
and into his room, closing the door behind him. Tremaine
thought about the chest and decided to see if he could
figure out what was inside. He walked to the barn and
looked around for the box of clothes Alec spoke of. He
found an old trunk with shirts, old pants, some hats,
gloves, and old boots. He tried the boots on and they
were a perfect fit. He pulled out the shirts and picked the
few that were in good condition. He found two pairs of
pants and an old army cap. He liked it and put it on.

There was a small metal box inside the trunk that
caught Tremaine's eye. He opened it and found old letters from Alec's father. The letters spoke of his journey
and how he was lost and cold but knew he had to continue for the sake of the village people. He read how
David found the skeleton of his father Michael on his
journey and dreaded the thought that Alec would have
to carry the same burden.

David wrote:

My son, it has been an unforgiving journey for me. I
walk alone, and the days are forever and the nights
forbidding. I stop frequently to ask about the crystal
rose, but most think that I am mad. I cannot stop my
quest, for I know failure would be devastating for all. It
pains me to know that if I fail, you will have to follow
and try to find the only known way to free our family of

the curse that lay upon it. We must free the souls of the well, so we must never stop trying to find the crystal rose. Your son shall follow, and so must his until it is done. If I should falter, please, my son, try, I beg you, and ensure that those that come after are aware of the dreaded day that evil besieged our village and took us from the arms of God. Make sure the children know what they must do.

Your loving father

Tremaine dug around in the box and found another letter. He opened the other letter and began to read.

My son, the years have taken their toll on me. I can no longer carry the guilt that lay upon my back, for it is heavy and worrisome. Age has decided my fate, and I too must lie down and take my last breath. As my father and his before him, I was unsuccessful in finding the crystal rose. I do not know that it exists at all; we move by faith and hope. The word of evil can never be trusted, and the Lamb of God struggles to find us under the cloak of darkness. I hope that you do not find me in your journey for, if you do, I fear that your path will be unfavorable. I followed my father and took the path opposite the face of evil, but it may not be true. Sometimes you have to walk toward what you fear and face it to conquer it. Walk toward him, my son, find your own way. I love you, son.

What the hell is this? These letters sound like Alec's family is cursed. I wonder where he is supposed to go and what is the crystal rose?

Tremaine had a lot of questions but no answers. He heard Tilly snort loudly and he saw a dark shadow scurry across the wall from the corner of his eye, leaving a foul stench in the barn. A burst of air blew through the barn and threw hay about the room, causing the shutters to clatter back and forth. He turned as fast as he could, and hoped to see who or what was in the barn with him, but there was no one. He looked all around, but he didn't see anyone.

He started to feel a little nervous and decided that he had seen enough for the night. He was very tired from working all day, and thought that his imagination was getting the best of him. He walked over and stroked Tilly to calm her. He said good night to Tilly and walked out. He didn't realize that he still had the letters in his hand until he was in his room. He laid them on the nightstand and got undressed and folded the covers back and got into bed. It felt good to be lying down, but his mind couldn't rest from thinking about the letters and what happened or didn't happen in the barn. He eventually fell asleep and slept well.

Morning came swiftly. Tremaine heard Alec's knock on the door. "Oh, please. It can't be true. It can't be morning already. I just got in the bed. Please, just a few more minutes," he begged.

"Up and at 'em. We got work to do," Alec yelled as he walked into the kitchen to start breakfast.

Tremaine pulled himself out of bed and got dressed. He saw the letters on the nightstand. He didn't want Alec to find them, so he put them in his shirt pocket with the hopes that he would make it back to the barn sometime during the day to return them to the box. He got cleaned up and met Alec in the kitchen.

"Good morning," said Tremaine.

"Morning," replied Alec.

Alec put some food on a plate and set it on the table. Tremaine didn't question the size of the meal this morning. He understood and knew he would need every bite to get through the morning. They ate until they were full and decided to start the day.

"You get the dishes; I'm going to check on Tilly," said Alec as he put on his cap and a light jacket, picked up the flashlight from the countertop, and walked out headed for the barn.

The air was crisp and moist. Alec knew the rain would come soon. *We won't get much done today*, he thought. *The rain will be here soon.* He walked into the barn and watched Tilly scurry around when she realized he was there. He tossed some hay into her stall and stroked her with her favorite brush. She was happy to see him. He could tell that she was disturbed by something, though. She seemed unsettled.

"What's wrong, girl? What's got you all stirred up?" He searched her eyes, hoping to see some reason for her restlessness. "It's all right. You're fine," he said. He gave her a piece of sugar, a big hug, and a pat on the backside.

Alec could tell that Tremaine found the box of clothes. The things he didn't want were left on the floor and tossed around inside the trunk. Alec noticed the metal box and remembered that the letters from his father were in there. He gasped when he realized the box had been opened.

"Oh no, I forgot all about this box. I hope the boy didn't find those letters." But deep down, he knew Tremaine read them. "That damn boy is going to nose around until he finds out things he shouldn't know."

Alec looked inside and noticed two of the letters were gone. He closed the box and put it back where Tremaine left it. He decided to wait and see if he would tell him that he had the letters. Alec walked outside and saw Tremaine coming outside.

"Can you get the feed for me?" Alec asked.

"Sure," said Tremaine as he walked into the barn. He stopped and spoke with Tilly. "I guess we had a scare last night, didn't we, girl? But it's all right now."

He stroked Tilly and looked around for the feedbag. He noticed the clothes thrown about and the metal box on the floor. He walked over and neatly put the letters back inside the box and put the box back where he found it and closed the trunk. It looked like it had never been disturbed.

He grabbed the feedbag and walked down to the chicken coop and laid the bag against the fence. Alec fed the chickens, closed the bag, put his gloves on, and walked into the field. Tremaine followed him.

"We'll have to work twice as hard this morning. It looks like a big rain is coming today. We're going to lose the better part of the day. Let's get started."

Alec worked beside Tremaine all morning, and they talked about all sorts of things, but never about the letters. Alec hoped that he would mention them, but he never did and Alec decided not to bring it up. It disturbed him that he would take the letters and then hide the fact that he had them. Alec was feeling a little invaded.

Who is this child, and why am I bothering with him, anyway? he thought, but was quickly reminded when he bent over to grab an ear of corn and could barely straighten up. He grabbed his back and moaned, "That's why."

"Are you all right?" asked Tremaine.

"I'll make it."

They worked desperately to get as much done as possible before the rain started. They worked through lunch and into the early afternoon before they felt the first drops of water.

"Here it comes," said Alec. He looked up at the dark

gray clouds and took a deep breath. "Well, I guess we did all right today. We put a dent in it. Let's get inside before it starts to pour."

"Yeah, I'm hungry," said Tremaine.

They walked back to the cabin and made it inside just before the rain started to pour. The cabin was nice and warm from the blaring fire in the kitchen, and the dark clouds cast an ominous shadow over the walls. Tremaine decided to help out with lunch. He searched the cabinets for bread and found some turkey meat in the refrigerator. He pulled out the mayonnaise and the mustard, pulled off a few pieces of lettuce, and sliced a tomato.

Alec watched him as he moved about the kitchen as if he'd lived there for weeks. Alec put his hat and jacket on. "I'm going to check on Tilly." He walked across the yard to the barn and found Tilly resting calmly. She'd seen many storms and high winds, so the rain didn't bother her.

Alec noticed that the clothes had been picked up and stored. He opened the trunk and checked the metal box and saw the two missing letters in the box. *He put them back, but he read them, I'm sure.* He closed the box, put it back inside the trunk, and closed it. He went over to Tilly and assured her that all was well. Alec stayed in the barn with Tilly while Tremaine ate his sandwich, turned on the TV, stretched out on the sofa, and went to sleep.

Alec and Tremaine worked with each other for months. The harvest was in and stored for the winter. The December wind was frigid and cold, which didn't allow for much outside work. Tremaine was concerned that Alec wouldn't need him and would ask him to leave, but he didn't. Tremaine tried to make himself useful in other ways. He became a real handyman around the cabin. He fixed things that were left unattended for years.

Alec realized that bringing in the harvest was his biggest job, but he knew that spring would come, and planting would be needed, so he was hoping Tremaine would want to stay. Alec would never admit it, but he was enjoying having someone to talk to and share a piece of his life with.

Alec never did much for Christmas, but Tremaine wanted to celebrate the season. He cut down a tree from Alec's backyard. Alec didn't mind. He said that the developers were going to cut them down after he died and the land would go to the county anyway.

The thought of it saddened Tremaine. He was comfortable there—more than he had been anywhere, even with his mother. He talked to Alec about things that he would never tell his mother. He enjoyed talking to another man, even if it was an old man. He told Alec about his life as a hoodlum and how he never wanted to end up that way, but didn't know how to do anything else. Deep down Tremaine was enjoying the company and the feeling of home and security that he never felt living on the streets and fighting to survive. He wanted to stay for as long as he could.

The Christmas tree was beautiful. Alec had a box of old decorations left from generations of Wilhelms celebrating Christmas in the cabin. He pulled the box out of the closet, and Tremaine decorated the tree. Some of the ornaments dated back to the 1800's. Tremaine marveled over them, and they brought back wonderful memories for Alec.

For the first time in years, Alec felt content. He wasn't happy, but he wasn't sad either, which was new for him. The feeling was so strange, he felt guilty for having it, as though he should apologize for abandoning his sadness. He knew it was crazy, but he couldn't help it. He was feeling light and free, and the thought of the well and the letters left his mind, at least for a moment.

Alec prepared a huge Christmas dinner, and unbeknownst to either of them, both of them bought presents for the other. Tremaine earned a share of the money from the sale of the crop, and he purchased Alec a back brace with a heating pad that provided relief from his back pain.

Alec was very pleased. "I didn't know they made these things," he said as he smiled and wrapped it around his waist. The warmth from the pad was soothing. He was very pleased. "Can I sleep in it?" he asked like a child with a new toy.

"I guess so," replied Tremaine.

"Nice." Alec walked to the tree and picked up a box and handed it to Tremaine. "Here you go. I hope you like it."

Tremaine took the box and opened it. The gloves and scarf were great. The new winter hat fit nicely. Tremaine needed these things; it got pretty cold this time of year.

"Great, this will go well with the coat I found in the trunk," he said and then hesitated to talk further about the contents of the trunk.

Alec looked at him and took a deep breath. A long sigh came out. "I guess we better talk about it," said Alec.

"Talk about what?"

"You know what I'm talking about. I know you read the letters."

"What letters? I don't—"

"Tremaine, stop. I know you read the letters. They were missing, and then they were put back in the metal box. Remember, I went into the barn before you had a chance to put them back? I saw later that you had, but not before you read them. So let's get this over with. What do you want to know?"

"Why did they leave? Where were they going? What happened to them? What is the crystal rose? Do you have to go? Who's in the well? I—"

"Wait, wait. One question at a time. I guess you've been thinking about this for months." Alec hesitated and waited a moment to gather his thoughts. "There is a story that there is a curse on my family that also affected the people in the village from the time of my great-grandfather. In order to rid the village of the curse, my father and his father went off on some quest and never returned."

"Is that what the crystal rose is for? To rid the village of the curse?"

"Yes, supposedly, this rose will free us from the Devil's curse that plagues the generations of the village people."

"When did all this happen, the curse I mean?"

"During the time when my great-grandfather Torrin Wilhelm settled here. He supposedly made a pact with the Devil for the life of my great-grandmother and my grandfather, her son. I guess this was around the late eighteen hundreds. It was Torrin who built this cabin, and all of the land belonged to him. It was over two hundred acres of land, until I started selling it off."

"Why? Why would you sell it?"

"I have no heirs. There's no one to leave it to, and besides, I'm too old to work it and I needed the income."

"Why didn't you marry, Alec?"

He wasn't sure how to answer that. He didn't want to lie, but he didn't want Tremaine to think that he believed in the curse story either.

"Is it because of the curse? Because if you didn't find the rose, your son would have to go and look for it and you didn't want that to happen? Why didn't you go look for it?"

"Because I don't believe any of it. I didn't marry because I just didn't, that's all," said Alec.

Tremaine looked at him strangely. He didn't believe him.

"Do those letters have anything to do with what's in that wooden chest?"

"No, absolutely not," demanded Alec, but his reaction told Tremaine that he was lying.

Alec's denial told Tremaine that the reason Alec was alone was because of what was in that chest, and that the reason his father left was in that chest. He never forgot about the chest and always wanted to know what was in there, but stayed away at the behest of Alec. But his curiosity was mounting, and he knew he would have to know and soon.

"These stories are just that, stories. No one believes in devils and ghosts and wishes being answered anymore. It's all nonsense," said Alec.

"Where is the well?" Tremaine stared into Alec's eyes.

"It's in the park near the gazebo," said Alec, "but, Tremaine, please don't waste your time searching for answers. You may not like what you find."

"There's something in the well, isn't there?"

"I don't know. I never went down there to find out. It's a simple wishing well. People walk by every now and then and someone throws a coin in and makes a wish, that's all it is. It was once hidden in the trees, but now it's part of the landscape. I can't buy into the foolishness. I won't."

"That's what the man said who brought me here."

"What? What man?"

"The man who stopped me from robbing the store that

night I came here. He said that the trees stretched out two blocks from where they are now, and the open area was hidden from the town. Do people visit the park a lot? Do they go to the well often?"

"No, not that much. I think the stories discourage a lot of activity, especially the stories of the horrible deaths of many of the townspeople."

"What stories? What deaths?"

"Well, it seems that right after Torrin made the pact, the village people starting dying in this horrible, unbelievable way. Their bodies dried up and turned to leather in an instant. Their lifeblood was sucked away. It was awful," said Alec.

"Did you ever see it?"

"Yes. Yes, I did, when I was a boy."

"What happened?"

Alec hesitated to talk about it. He didn't want to remember. He turned away from Tremaine and hoped that he would let it go, but he didn't.

"What happened, Alec?"

"There was an elderly man living on a farm a few miles up the road, Mr. Waterson. At that time, the store across the street wasn't there, and we could cross the field to get to his farm. One night we were playing around the well, doing nothing in particular, just throwing rocks and stones into the well, hoping to hear the water splash. Trent, one of the boys with us, threw a coin in, and we heard the saddest sound, like a woman crying. It frightened us, so we left, and Freddie and I started toward his grandfather's farm, Mr. Waterson. Freddie and I were playing along the way until we could hear screaming from the farm. We ran, and once inside, we saw Mr. Waterson's body sitting at the kitchen table like stone. His body dried up while he was holding a cup. It was the strangest thing I'd ever seen. Eventually, he fell over onto the floor. Freddie covered him with the table-cloth, and I ran home to get my father. My father left right after that on his journey. After Mr. Waterson's death he came to believe the curse was true."

"But you don't believe it?"

"No, I think it was just another death, and that whole story is an old wives tale," Alec said with some trepidation.

Tremaine didn't believe him. He could feel Alec's fear. He saw the sadness in his eyes and wanted to find out if it could be true.

Alec believes it, but feels helpless to do anything about it, he thought. "What if it is true? Does that mean that you will also die that way?"

"If it is true, I guess I will," said Alec in a thoughtful way. "But I just can't make myself believe it. It's too far-fetched."

"Yes, I suppose you're right, too farfetched." Tremaine stared at the floor in deep thought.

"So that's that."

Tremaine didn't say anything; he just stared at the floor in deep thought about Mr. Waterson's death.

"I'm going to get the kitchen cleaned up, and then I'm going to bed," said Alec.

"No, no, I can do that. If you're tired, go get some sleep. I'll take care of it," said Tremaine as he walked toward the kitchen.

"Fine, fine, I'll see you in the morning." Alec turned and walked down the hall. He wondered if he told Tremaine too much about the curse. He felt strongly that Tremaine would try to find out anyway after reading the letters, and he hoped that talking about it satisfied his curiosity.

Tremaine had no intentions of being satisfied. In fact, the story had just the opposite effect. Tremaine wanted to know all he could know, and he knew that part of the story was in that trunk.

He moved around the kitchen with ease as he put the cups and plates in their rightful places. He wiped down the countertop and the table, and grabbed the broom to sweep the floor.

Once finished, he had too much energy to sleep. His mind was moving a mile a minute with thoughts about the mystery curse. His first thought was how to open the chest without breaking the lock. He searched the kitchen drawers for a key or a small object that he could use to pick the lock.

After about thirty minutes of looking, he found a small key. He wondered if it would fit. He grabbed his coat and his new gloves and hat and walked to the barn.

"Tilly, it's me. It's okay, girl," he said so he wouldn't startle her. "Now, where was that trunk?"

He went to where he thought it was, but couldn't find it. It wasn't there. He looked all around for it, but couldn't find it.

"He moved it. He knew I'd find a way to look inside eventually, so he hid it. But it can't be far, because he couldn't carry it but so far, so it's here somewhere," whispered Tremaine.

He started looking around the barn. *It's not up there. He couldn't have done that by himself,* he thought as he looked up to the rafters. He searched behind boxes and an old tractor that hadn't been used in decades. He looked everywhere until he saw some scratch marks on the floor that looked like something had been dragged. He could tell that Alec tried to cover over them and wipe them out, but remnants of the marks were still visible. He followed the marks until he came to a pile of staked crates. Tremaine removed each crate one by one until he could see the wooden trunk.

Alec tried to hide it. He really doesn't want anyone to look inside.

Tremaine hesitated for a moment and wondered if he should consider Alec's wishes, but his curiosity overwhelmed him, and before he knew it, the key was in the lock and the trunk was open. He was shocked when he looked inside and found nothing but an old leather binder. He reached in and pulled it out.

"This is it? This is what he's hiding? It's just a book."

He found the flashlight Alec kept in the barn and began to read the most spellbinding story he had ever read. He couldn't put it down.

Alec stood at his bedroom window looking out at the barn and the hint of light seeping through the shutters, and he knew that Tremaine had found the binder. He wondered what would happen next. He knew the young man would not let it go.

Chapter Three

THE WELL

Tremaine couldn't sleep after reading Torrin's story. He paced around the room most of the night waiting for morning so he could talk to Alec. At five o'clock, Tremaine was dressed and in the kitchen. He started breakfast and waited for Alec to rise.

Before Alec could get into the room, Tremaine spoke right up. "I believe the story."

Alec stared at him and gave himself a moment to think about the answer. He knew Tremaine read the story and now he would start his own quest about something that didn't concern him. Alec made up his mind not to feed the child's fantasy by long, drawn-out conversations on the matter. He took a deep breath. "Why?"

"I just think it's possible. I thought about it last night, and I believe it can be true."

"It's not true," demanded Alec, "and I am not going to have a whole lot of discussion about it. I'm going into town today. You are welcome to join me if you'd like." Alec turned and walked to the closet and pulled out his coat.

He walked to the door and out to the barn to feed Tilly.

"Well, girl, it seems that the nightmare that we been avoiding our whole lives is back. I don't understand why this is happening or why this young man came into my life in the first place. It all seems so strange. I can't get drawn into believing this. I just can't. I'm an old man. I'd look like a fool going off on a useless quest. He's got to let it go."

Alec stroked Tilly's back with her brush and he turned to see where Tremaine put the crates back over the chest to hide any evidence that he found it. The whole ordeal saddened Alec deeply. He wanted to forget he ever saw Mr. Waterson, and he wanted to forget the day his father left. Tremaine reminded him of his lonely life and how he spent all of it regretting the loss of Gwyneth. He was reminded of how old he was and how he was becoming more and more useless. He turned his head and looked at Tilly.

"Tilly, what if it is true?"

Tremaine cleaned up the kitchen and left a plate for Alec.

Alec managed to feed the chickens without help and went back inside. He sat and ate his breakfast without much conversation.

"I'm going into town. Did you decide to come?"

"No, I think I'll hang around here," replied Tremaine.

Alec stepped out onto the porch and took a deep breath of the cold, fresh air. He looked up at the sky and said a silent prayer to God for wisdom on how to best handle this without alienating the boy. He walked to the driveway, got into his truck, and drove off.

Tremaine went back to the barn, removed the crates, opened the chest, and pulled the binder out. He opened it and read the story again. He had to go to the well.

He made sure the cabin was locked up and walked to

the park and stood by the well. He looked inside, but couldn't see anything. He reached inside his pocket and pulled out a coin and started to throw it inside to see if any water was there. He held the coin in his hand, but hesitated. He didn't know why, but something was wrong, and he couldn't do it. He thought about Alec and remembered the story that suggested that every time someone throws a coin in the well, a member of the village would die.

"That's why Mr. Waterson died. Trent threw the coin in the well."

He looked around and found a stone and tossed it in. He heard nothing. He walked back to the barn and found some long rope and the flashlight. He walked back to the well and tied the rope securely to a tree. He tugged on it several times to make sure it would hold his weight. He looked around to see if anyone was nearby, but saw no one.

It's still quite early, he thought.

Tremaine strapped the flashlight to his belt, grabbed hold of the rope, and lowered himself into the well. He was so afraid he could barely keep from shaking. His teeth clattered together from the cold and the fear, but he had to find out. He reached the bottom much sooner than he thought he would.

"That's strange. With the bottom this close, I should have heard something when I threw the rock in," he whispered.

He turned the flashlight on and noticed the coins all over the ground. He picked them up and wondered if there was something unique about them. The coins were from the late 1800's to 2006. He marveled at the differences between them. He was studying them when something caught his eye. It seemed like something moved.

He looked up to see if someone had cast a shadow over the well, but he didn't see anyone.

He moved the light down slowly to see the contour of the wall and he couldn't believe his eyes. It was the wall that was moving. Shadows moved back and forth, and faces of anguish and despair showed through. Tremaine was shocked. He could tell that they were human faces. He could see the outline of heads and bodies, hands and feet. He tried to rationalize it, but couldn't. He dropped the coin he had in his hand and he saw the face of a woman scream through the stone.

"That coin was her," he whispered.

He picked up another coin and dropped it and saw the anguish of an old man press against the wall as if he were trying to push himself out.

"Oh my God, every time a coin was thrown in, a person was drawn into the wall. The coin pulled them into the wall. There's a soul for every coin, and there are hundreds of them. If someone throws a coin in, Alec will be pulled into the wall. I can't let that happen. What can I do?"

As he moved around, he shuffled the coins and the souls in the wall reached out to him for help. He wanted to help, but how?

"They know I'm here, what can I do?"

His body shook with fear. He couldn't control the fear or the helplessness he felt to do anything to release them from the wall.

He pulled himself together and decided that he couldn't help anyone standing there. He pulled himself up and out of the well, knowing that what he thought were rock formations in the wall as he came down were really the protruding forms of bodily souls pressing against the wall.

He climbed out and sat on the ground for a moment, trying to accept what he just saw as reality. He told himself it was fiction and that he made the whole thing up somehow. But the problem was, it tied back to Torrin's story, so he couldn't dismiss it as a hallucination.

"When the evil took their life force, he took their flesh and they dwell in the wall forever."

He couldn't believe it. He started to run. He felt the same way he felt when he ran to the park six months earlier. He started to run back to his old apartment, but realized it was gone.

He didn't want to go back to Alec's cabin, but he had nowhere else to go. He wasn't thinking straight. He ran into the barn, sat on the floor, and cried. He was so exhausted from not sleeping all night that he eventually cried himself to sleep, lying in a stack of hay.

When Alec couldn't find Tremaine in the cabin, he checked the barn. He found him asleep not far from Tilly's stall. Alec knew something had happened, and wasn't sure that he wanted to know what.

"What happened, girl?" He walked over to Tilly and stroked her mane.

She nickered and stomped, which woke Tremaine. He stirred around and tried to get his bearings. He saw Alec standing in front of Tilly's stall and wondered how he was going to tell him what happened when he was told to stay away from the chest. Now he wished he had.

"Alec, I have something to tell you," he said.

"What? That you read the binder?"

"Yes. How did you know?"

"I knew you wouldn't let it go, so I knew you'd find a way eventually."

"Alec, it's true. The story is true," Tremaine said frantically.

"How do you know?"

"I saw them. I saw them, Alec."

"Saw who?"

"The souls, I saw them in the well. It was horrible." He cringed at the thought.

"What's real and what you thought you saw may be very different things," said Alec.

"No, it's real. I don't want to believe it either, but it's real, and deep down inside you know it. That's why you didn't have any children. You didn't want to pass this curse on to anyone else. It would end with you. But, Alec, what about the rest of the descendants of the village people? What about all of their children and the souls that are trapped down there? You can't just think of yourself," said Tremaine.

"You don't know what you're talking about. There are no souls trapped anywhere."

Tremaine barely heard him, because he was thinking about what he saw. "There are souls. They are living and are trapped in an eternal hell. They never really died. Oh my God, they kept their bodies and they are alive living in torment. They can't live or die. We must help them, we have to," Tremaine demanded.

"I knew this would happen. I won't let you pull me into this nightmare. It's not real, Tremaine. It's not real!"

"The next coin could be you, Alec. It could be you," Tremaine said sadly.

"I won't believe any of this, I won't believe it," yelled Alec. He walked out of the barn and into the front yard. He stopped and looked toward the well and wondered if any part of Tremaine's story could be true.

"Come with me, I'll show you," said Tremaine as he grabbed Alec's arm and pulled him toward the well. The rope was still there and Tremaine pointed to it. "Go down," he said.

Alec stared at him and knew that Tremaine was telling

the truth and he really didn't want to see it. He grabbed the rope and started to climb down. Tremaine followed, and they both stood inside the well and wept.

Tremaine helped Alec climb out of the well.

At his age, that was no easy task. Alec couldn't stay in the well long; he couldn't watch it. He reached the top and climbed out. He fell on the ground to catch his breath and gather his thoughts.

Tremaine climbed out and waited for Alec's response.

Alec said nothing. He sat on the ground and stared out into space. He didn't know what to say or what to do. The feelings building up inside of him were overwhelming, and he felt out of control. He knew that nothing he could say could make this right.

"We have to free them," said Tremaine.

"Spoken like a naïve child with no idea what that means, even if it could be done at all," said Alec.

"I can. I know it. We have to find the rose," said Tremaine.

Alec stood up and started walking toward the cabin. He didn't say anything, he just kept walking as if he were unaware of everything around him. He couldn't think straight. His thoughts were all scrambled and jumbled up. He never thought that the pact that Torrin made would have resulted in the horror inside the well. He couldn't talk, he couldn't think.

"What are we going to do?" yelled Tremaine.

"Nothing," replied Alec as he kept walking. He didn't want to look back; he couldn't face it.

Alec entered the cabin and went into the kitchen and sat at the table. He was numb. He couldn't move. The faces in the wall kept running through his mind, and no matter how hard he tried to erase it, he couldn't. He felt angry. He was so angry for what Torrin did, but he knew that if Torrin hadn't made the pact, he wouldn't be here, because Michael would have died at birth.

Better not to be born than to live with this torment, he thought.

He started shaking and crying. He came to his feet and screamed in desperation and anguish as loud as he could. He fell to his knees and cried.

Tremaine stood in the doorway and watched Alec suffer. He knew he could not let Alec's soul end up in that wall. For the first time in his young life, someone else's life was more important than his own. He felt strong and energized to do whatever needed to be done to free them and save his friend Alec from that fate.

"That's what the man said when I came here. He said you were the man that I am going to free." He knew what that meant and why he was brought there. He knew it with certainty that this was the job he was chosen to do. He didn't know how, but he was going to find a way or die trying.

"What can we do? I'm an old man. I can't make the journey," said Alec.

"Yes, you can. Knowing what you know now, can you spend the rest of your life doing nothing and waiting for someone to throw a coin in the well? Can you really do nothing?"

"You're right. If not for myself, I must try to help them. What should we do?" asked Alec.

"First, we are going to read Torrin's binder and figure out what the evil one was trying to tell him. What the riddle meant. We need to do this while the weather is cold, because by summer there will be people in the park and the potential for someone to throw a coin in the well will be greater. Alec, we have to try. What if you are the last descendant and we fail? Your soul and everyone else's will be trapped forever. You have everything to gain and nothing to lose by trying."

Tremaine went into the barn, uncovered the chest, and

pulled out the binder. He walked back inside and placed it on the kitchen table, where Alec was sitting.

Tremaine took a deep breath, opened the binder, and began to read. He deciphered each word. He asked twenty questions and took notes about every aspect of the riddle.

"Crystal rose, what could that be? Let's think about that for a moment. It could be light crystallized into the shape of a rose."

"How do you crystallize light?" asked Alec with a puzzled look on his face.

"Can light take shape?"

"I don't know," said Alec.

They looked at each other, frightened that the answer may not be obtainable.

"Okay, let's focus on what we can figure out. Number one, we know that a descendant must find the original coin. Second, we can see that the sun will dissolve the coin, and third . . . and third is that we know we can't figure this out by ourselves. We need some help."

"It did say to seek those who know the wind. He could have been talking about you," said Alec.

"Oh yeah, in those days we did talk to the wind, sky, rain, and all that sort of stuff. I don't think anyone does that," said Tremaine.

"You mean you don't know about your heritage?"

"No more than you know about yours. Besides, no one believes in devils and spirits and talking to the wind anymore. I mean, most of us assimilated too. We go to college, like everybody else."

"But, Tremaine, look at what we saw today. What we need is someone who still does believe in devils and spirits and talking to the wind. That may be the only person who can help us understand this. You have to know somebody," said Alec.

Tremaine thought about it for a few minutes.

"My great-grandfather."

"Yes, you mentioned him before. That's where your mother is," said Alec.

"Yes, my mother's grandfather. He is over one hundred years old and he lives on the reservation. That's where my mother is now, with him."

"What happened to your grandfather?"

"My mother's father was killed when she was young. I never knew my father, so I don't know his people," said Tremaine sadly.

"Well, if he is over one hundred years old, he may be able to help us. If he still has his wits about him, he may remember the old ways," said Alec. "Do you know how to get there?"

"Yes, I know where he is," said Tremaine. He was not looking forward to seeing the look on his mother's face. She would think he followed her because he couldn't make it on his own, but he would have to deal with it. "What about Tilly and the farm?"

"Yeah, I'll have to get someone to care for her. I still know a few farmers a few miles down the road who may take her for me, and I'll give the chickens to whomever will take them. We should be back by spring to plant, I hope."

"Ok, let's get as much done tomorrow to ready ourselves to leave by the end of the week," said Tremaine.

"I did everything I could not to take this journey, but I guess God has decided that I must. I dread this, but I have no choice. I can't live another day knowing what I know now and doing nothing." Alec stood, walked to the living room window, looked out toward the well, and held back the tears.

The next few days were very busy. Alec sadly hitched Tilly's trailer to his truck and drove her to Mr. Crowner's farm. Jake Crowner was one of Alec's closest friends. They both were third generation farmers in the area. Jake lived several miles from the town. His grandfather was one of the many who sold their farms and bought property further out as the town encroached upon them.

Jake watched as Alec pulled the truck up to the barn and parked. He watched as Alec guided Tilly out of the trailer and walked her inside. Tilly knew something was wrong. She was very fidgety and restless.

"It's all right, girl. I won't be gone long. It's only for a short while, I promise."

Alec hugged Tilly's neck and laid his head upon her. He knew he would never see his friend again, and he found it hard to say good-bye. Tilly's mood became somber, as she seemed to realize that her friend was leaving and life would never be the same.

Alec handed the reins to Jake and turned and walked away.

"When will you be back?" Jake asked.

"I don't know. I don't know if I'll ever be back. Please take good care of her. I suppose I spoiled her some, so she will have to get used to you now. Please be patient with her; she'll come around. She really is the best."

"Don't worry. I lost my mare a few years back, and she was my companion after Julie died. I know how much you'll miss her. I promise to give her whatever she needs." Jake gave Alec a puzzed look. "I know this is none of my business, but why now, Alec? Why leave now?"

Alec thought about the answer and decided to tell Jake just enough of the truth that he wouldn't be lying, but not enough to cause him to venture out to the well.

"There's a curse on my family, and I have to try to make things right before I die. I tried not to go, been living in denial, but I have to. I just have to."

Alec looked at him, hoping that he would be satisfied.

Jake was an older man and didn't need much to satisfy his curiosity. He knew when to pry and when it was best to leave things alone. This was something he really didn't want to know about. He gave Alec a concerned look.

"I wish you luck in your search, Alec. I don't believe in curses and things like that, but if you do, I wish you the best and hope you find what you are looking for," he said.

"Thank you . . . thank you."

Alec reached out to Jake, and they shook hands and said good-bye.

Tremaine had rounded up all the chickens and put them in crates by the time Alec returned. He had checked the cabin to ensure that everything was turned off, locked up, and secured.

Alec dropped checks in the mail for six months advance payment for his utilities, lawn care, and taxes. He wanted folks to think he was on a long vacation, in the hopes that he may return someday. *If I'm not back in six months, I'll probably be dead and none of this will matter,* he thought.

"Did you gas up the truck?" asked Tremaine.

"Yep, I think we're ready," replied Alec.

They threw their belongings in the back of the truck, climbed inside and headed down the driveway. Alec stopped for a moment and looked back. He tried to imagine what the cabin must have looked like from the outside when Torrin built it. His face saddened. He wanted to go inside and sit by the huge fireplace in the kitchen, where he was comfortable and safe from the world and all the madness that he was about to confront.

"You know what your fate will be if you don't try," said Tremaine.

"Yeah, but what I don't understand is why you care.

Your family is not affected; it isn't your fate. Why would you go through this?"

Alec wasn't sure he wanted to know the answer. He was afraid that Tremaine might think twice and back out. He needed Tremaine's help, but he felt that he was putting the young man in harm's way for matters that didn't concern him.

This is my problem, and he shouldn't sacrifice himself for it. It's not right, he thought.

Tremaine thought about it. A very strange feeling came over him, and he wasn't sure how to answer him. He hesitated, but not for the reason Alec thought. He wasn't having second thoughts. He hesitated because he couldn't describe the emotion he was feeling. He had lived his whole life hating so much, other feelings were foreign to him. He began to realize how much he loved his mother and great-grandfather and how empty his life was without them, and he realized that he loved Alec too. Alec was his friend, and he wanted to be a friend to him. He wanted to be somebody other than the man he had always been. Someone needed him.

"It is important to me because you are my friend."

His sincerity rang through Alec's heart.

For the first time, they both finally understood what it meant to stand with someone through the worst of times and sacrifice pieces of themselves for someone else.

It took two days to get to the Navajo Nation in Arizona. The great seal of the Navajo Nation dominated the entrance into the reservation that sat in the Arizona, New Mexico, and Utah deserts. Alec was in awe. He expected to see an old, worn-down desert town isolated and destitute, but the nation was thriving. Much of the land was pristine, but it was obvious that through some twist of fate, the Navajo people found a way to survive and thrive into a prosperous nation.

"How many people live here?" Alec asked.

"About two hundred fifty thousand, I think," replied Tremaine.

"How did they manage to create all of this?" asked Alec.

Tremaine took offense to his suggestion. "Because we are smart, that's how," he replied with a little agitation in his voice.

"I didn't mean . . . well, I guess I always thought that Indians were poor, you know," Alec stumbled.

"We are not Indians. We are Navajo, and, yes, some native people are poor. Many do live impoverished lives, but they found oil here, and that made all the difference. We were smart enough to use their need to our advantage."

"Excellent," Alec said as he continued to drive through the town.

It wasn't unlike any other town or city. Homes, schools, shops and businesses lined the streets. The vast desert that surrounded the reservation was magnificent. Much of the land was pristine and was only looked at from afar. It was still wild and reminiscent of the time when horses and buffalo roamed the country.

Alec never took the time to understand anyone outside of himself and his closed unicultural world. This was big for him, but he wanted to be open to it. He never had prejudices about people; he just didn't know much about anyone other than White people, except for what he saw on television, which wasn't good most of the time.

He tried to be polite. "I saw *Dances with Wolves*. It was good."

"Ok, I saw *Gone with the Wind*. What is your point?" Tremaine knew what he was trying to do, but decided not to let him get away with stereotyping.

"I'm just saying I thought it was good, that's all."

"Yeah, well, I'm glad you enjoyed it." Tremaine stared out the window and tried to move on to another subject. "We're almost there; just a few more miles."

They drove a little longer, and the landscape changed from semi-urban to rural. Huge farms spread out over the landscape. Horses and livestock grazed about, and the sounds of tractors and barking dogs lingered in the distance.

"Turn here. My great-grandfather's cabin is over there," said Tremaine. He pointed to the small log cabin surrounded by acres of land that was once green and alive.

Except for a small patch of land that Alaya maintained for them, most of the farm was in disrepair. The condition of the farm saddened Tremaine. His great-great-grandfather always wanted him to stay with him and take care of the farm that had been in his family for generations, but Tremaine couldn't be bothered. He was too busy stealing and conning people out of money to give of himself. He felt ashamed just being there, and now having to ask for help.

The farm reminded Alec of his home and made him a little homesick.

"He doesn't work the farm anymore?" Alec asked.

"No, he's too old to work it, and it costs too much to hire people."

Alec pulled into the driveway and followed the long, narrow road that led to the front of the house. The few animals that scurried around scattered when the truck drove up and stopped. Alec climbed out of the truck and stretched his body to work his joints loose. He stiffened badly when he sat too long.

Tremaine sat in the truck and wondered what his mother would think of all of this. *She will probably think I'm using this as an excuse to get back home*, he thought. *I wish I didn't have to do this, but I have to speak to Great-grandfather. I have to.*

He climbed out of the truck and waited for Alec to come around. They both stood at the entrance and stared at the large wooden door and wondered how they were going to make anyone believe this story.

Tremaine walked up and knocked on the door, and within moments, it opened.

Alaya stood on the other side staring back at him. She didn't know how to feel about seeing him. She was so thankful he was alive and well and that he managed to stay out of jail. But was he here because he was running from the law or from someone trying to kill him? What trouble had he brought to her grandfather's house?

"Hello, Mother," he said hesitantly.

"Tremaine . . . are you all right?"

"Yes, Mother, I am fine."

Alec noticed the distance between them. He stood back and waited.

She looked up at Alec.

"Oh, this is Mr. Wilhelm. Alec Wilhelm. We need to speak with Great-grandfather."

"What do you want of him, Tremaine?"

"Please, Mother. I did not come to argue. This man is my friend, and he has a problem that Great-grandfather may be able to help him with. I swear, this has nothing to do with me or anything that I've done."

She looked at Alec and hesitated. She wondered why an elderly White man would become friends with Tremaine. They did seem like an unlikely pair. *Maybe Tremaine has finally found someone to focus on. We'll see*, she thought.

"Come in," she said as she stepped back and allowed them to enter.

They entered the small home decorated with all sorts of Navajo artifacts and memorabilia. Upon entering, there was a large foyer table with pictures of Tremaine's great-grandfather's children, grandchildren, and great-grandchildren. There was a large picture of the Navajo tribe the way it was around the 1700s when they lived in teepees, grew corn, and herded horses. The picture was reminiscent of another time. The living room had a large handmade rug that was woven by his mother fifty years ago of rust, green, and soft yellow colors. He had a beautiful wooden sculpture of a herd of horses running across the mantel. A Navajo headdress worn by his great-grandfather rested in a special place next to the fireplace.

"Have a seat," Alaya said. "I'll see if he is up to talking to anyone right now." She walked into a back room.

Alec sat on the sofa and stared all around. Tremaine watched him and wondered what he thought of all of this.

"So, what do you think?"

"I don't know. You know the closest I've come to knowing anything about native people is through television, mostly old westerns, and you know what they were like. I never thought . . . I mean, I guess we're all the same, aren't we?"

"Yes, we all want the same things. What we think will bring us peace or war."

Alec thought that was a strange way to state that, but there was truth to it. He looked at Tremaine surprised that the young man could have such profound thought.

"Actually, I find this fascinating," Alec said as he continued to look around as if he were in a museum admiring the antiques of a time long past.

Tremaine noticed his great-grandfather entering the room. "Great-grandfather, sir."

Tremaine paused at the stature of the man. At one hundred years old, he was still striking. His hair was completely white and very thin on the top. It was long and pulled back into a ponytail. His face told the story of his life and ageless strength. He was a man who stood between the past and the present, a world that once was and the world that is. He was old enough to have witnessed the kind of life his people lived at the turn of the twentieth century. Much of the old ways were gone, but he had the stories from his great-grandfather and grandfather to hold on to.

John Scott was named after John the Baptist. His mother, Kai, was converted to Christianity in the late 1800s. She learned to read English and taught John from the Bible. But with all his strength, he tried to stay true to his Navajo roots and the ways of his father, who never embraced the Christian faith.

John walked in silently and took a seat in his favorite chair. He didn't speak. He stared into Tremaine's eyes. He studied his face to see the face of his son and grandson, to see where he was in the young man, to know that through Tremaine, he would exist beyond death.

His frail voice whispered, "You are afraid."

Tremaine looked into his eyes and pondered how to tell this story without appearing to be insane. He hesitated as he tried to form the words that would best tell what he saw.

"Great-grandfather, I saw—I mean, I met Alec, here"— He pointed to Alec—"and his family is cursed, and there are people in the well, and we have to find a rose and—"

"Wait, be still," John said. "Come here and sit beside me." He beckoned to Tremaine.

Tremaine took a seat on a stool next to his great-grandfather. He took deep breaths as he tried to calm himself. Alec sat on the sofa and watched.

Alaya stood in the doorway and wondered what her son had gotten involved in.

John took Tremaine's hand and held it. His calming nature made Tremaine relax and focus. "How is your life, son?" John asked.

"I am fine, Great-grandfather."

"Where do you live?"

"I live with Alec."

John looked up at Alec. "How did you come to know this man?"

"It's strange. I was walking the streets one night and I met a Black man with blue eyes and he kept following me. I ran from him and found myself at Alec's house."

"What happened to the man with the blue eyes?"

"He was there too. I never figured out how he was always there," said Tremaine, a puzzled looked on his face.

"What did this man want from you?"

"I never figured that out either. He pointed Alec out to me and told me to help him. He said that he was the man I was going to free. I didn't understand what that meant, but I helped Alec around the farm and he invited me to stay. I was alone, so I did." He looked into his mother's eyes.

She sadly turned away from him. It hurt her to remember the day she left her child alone and helpless. But she felt it to be the only way to help him.

"Do you like living with Alec?"

"Yes, it is a great farm with chickens, and a horse named Tilly, and corn. I didn't realize how much I missed it until now."

"What else is there?"

"In Alec's barn, his great-grandfather left a binder that told a story about a pact he made with the Devil that caused all the people of his village and their descendants to die a horrible death, and their souls live inside the wall of the well forever."

John looked into Alec's eyes, hoping that he would have a mature twist to this farfetched story.

Alec simply stared back at him. He didn't know what to say.

"There are souls trapped in the wall of a well, is that true?" John looked at Alec again and waited.

"I know this sounds bizarre, but I saw them too," said Alec. "I saw the souls of my family in the well. I didn't believe the story, not even when my own father told it to me and left the family to find the rose, or maybe I didn't want to believe it. I didn't believe it until Tremaine forced me into the well and I saw them, all of them. I'm so sorry."

"You should not carry the guilt of your fathers. It was not your fear that made the pact, it was your great-grandfather, and he will carry that burden through time. I will admit that I am having a hard time believing that this could be true. But life has taught me that all things are possible when the mind makes it so. Are you sure that this is not something that comes from within your own subconscious?" asked John.

"I wish it were," said Alec, "and if Tremaine had not seen it too, I would think that I was delusional. But unfortunately, it is real and I have ignored it all of my life. I guess I thought that it would only be true if I acknowledged it. But ignoring something doesn't make it go away. It's real."

John took a deep breath. He stared at Tremaine. "It seems that you have been chosen to bring peace to the lost souls."

"But why? Why me? I haven't done much right in my whole life. I don't understand that," said Tremaine.

"I do not know that I believe you or that I can help you. I think that you believe it, so it is real to you. Today, the world is beyond ghosts and lost souls. No one practices rituals and rights and praying to spirits and ancestors anymore. We live in modern times, and this would does not fit modern logic," said John.

"There must be something that you remember from the old ways; something that your grandfather taught you about the spirit world. You are our only hope. There's got to be something that will help us," said Tremaine.

"Do you have the binder with you?" John asked.

"Yes, I have it." Tremaine stood and walked to the sofa where his bag sat. He reached inside and pulled out the leather binder and handed it to his great-grandfather.

"Read to me about the rose. Tell me what the binder says," said John as he closed his eyes and listened.

Tremaine opened the binder and began to read.

"Torrin wrote that the crystal rose is in the world beyond. He said it lies beyond the highest place and into the lowest place. It is not of this world and only those with the faith of a thousand angels can ever get close to it. He said it has been among the angels forever. It is what gives hope and joy to all that believe in goodness and light. He said that it was the only thing that would free the souls, but once the rose is removed from its rightful place, the world will began to deteriorate. The evil inside of man will manifest itself, and goodness will not walk upon the face of the earth."

Tremaine stopped. He watched his great-grandfather sit in silence with his eyes closed. The silence was nerve-racking.

Tremaine and Alec looked at each other and wondered if John was asleep. Moments passed in silence. Just as Tremaine was about to speak, John acknowledged his impatience.

"Did you know, you can not hear if you are talking?" asked John.

Tremaine stopped and walked back to the sofa and sat by Alec and waited.

"If I interpret the words correctly, this journey cannot be taken in this life. You will have to transition into the world beyond," said John.

Alaya walked to the center of the room, looked at Alec, and firmly rejected the idea.

"No!" she said. "No, it's too dangerous. You cannot ask him to do this."

"He did not ask me, Mother. He is my friend, and I will not live knowing he is trapped in that well and I did nothing to help him. I must try, I must." He looked at John, and with fear gripping his heart he asked, "What do I need to do?"

"This choice that you make takes great courage. It is the choice of a man, a man with strength and character."

"What do we have to do?" asked Alec.

"You have to die," said John emphatically. John looked into Tremaine's eyes and waited for him to flinch, but he didn't. He stared back and waited for whatever John would say next.

"I do not understand. How will dying help us fine the rose?" asked Alec.

"Death is a transition from one existence to another. The rose that you seek is not in this existence; it is in the world beyond, in the highest place and the lowest place. It is not of this world. It does not dwell in any existence that the body can enter into," said John.

"Can't we just meditate like you guys used to, with the smoke and the pipe and dancing or something?" Tremaine asked.

"Meditation takes you into your subconscious, but you are still earthbound, still of this world. Nothing will materialize there. What you seek is beyond the subconscious."

Silence befell the room.

"If we die, we cannot fix anything. We can't bring the rose back from death. How does this help?" asked Alec.

"Just as this life is a temporary state of being, so is what we know as death. The two existences can cross one another and can open portals to and from," said John.

"How will we know when their paths meet?" asked Tremaine.

"Your guide will know."

"Guide? What guide?" asked Alec.

"When you cross over, there will be someone there to meet you. He will know when the gate will open."

"But when we cross over, won't we already be there?" asked Tremaine.

"Yes and no. Just like in this dimension, there are several there. He will help you to your final destination," said John.

"I don't like this. I don't want you to do this, Tremaine. This is not your problem. It is not your sacrifice to make," cried Alaya.

"Great-grandfather, if we do not come back, what will happen?"

"Alec's soul will dwell in the well for eternity, and your life force will transition to another existence. You will cease to exist in this life. If the crystal rose is moved and you do not make it back, the world will fall into darkness. What you are proposing to do can have far-reaching effect, much more than just saving Alec. Be sure. You must be sure." John stood up and walked to his bedroom.

Alec and Tremaine sat on the sofa in silence.

Alaya followed John to help him settle in to rest. She was so disturbed by this, she couldn't stay inside. After getting John settled in, she walked back to the living room where they were sitting.

"I have to leave. I need some air."

She grabbed her sweater and walked out. She didn't know where she was going. She got into her truck and started driving. She drove for a while until she saw the local library. She pulled into the parking lot and stopped. She got out of the truck and stood for a moment, staring at the building. The small adobe-style, rust-colored building seemed to be calling her.

She walked inside and looked all around. It was a small library, and she could see the entire library from where she was standing. She noticed the circular information-counter in the center of the room and watched the people moving about. She walked to the computers that lined the wall directly in front of her and typed in "dimensions."

Numerous titles showed up, but one stood out for her. A book by Kathleen Cho called *Crossing Dimension, Beyond Time and Space*. She wrote down the location and started to search for the book. She found it, found a seat, and started to read.

She stayed for a few hours, until she saw darkness falling outside the library window. She gathered her books and took them to the desk to check them out before making her way home.

Tremaine was frightened by what his great-grandfather said, but felt strongly that this was his destiny, regardless of the outcome.

"Alec, you can take the guest room, and I'll sleep on the sofa. I think we should give this some thought tonight," said Tremaine.

"Okay, but, Tremaine, your mother is right. This is not your problem, and the risks are too high. I would like for you to reconsider. I will take the journey alone."

"We should sleep on it," said Tremaine. "We'll talk in the morning."

He and Alec walked down the hall, and he looked upon his mother's face and lost the words to say.

There was nothing he could say to make this better. She turned, stepped into her room and closed the door. The sadness in her face was profound. She knew he was going to do it. He never backed away from anything, no matter how dangerous it was. She knew that she was going to lose him, and letting go was hurting already.

The night dragged on forever. Tremaine lay in bed and stared at the ceiling for most of the night. He couldn't stop thinking about what his great-grandfather had said. He knew deep inside that he was right and that something drastic had to happen to find the crystal rose, even if it existed at all. Tremaine felt deeply that the story was true, and that if the story was true, that the solution must also be true.

Alaya barely slept all night. She rose early and pulled herself together. She picked up the book from the nightstand that she got from the library. She opened it and thumbed through it for a moment and closed the book in anger.

"This can't be happening. None of this is real. This is like time travel or something. I bet she really don't believe this either." She glared at the book, wondering who could write such nonsense.

She walked to the kitchen and decided to start breakfast. Without realizing it, she still had the book in her hand. She laid it on the table, walked to the refrigerator, and pulled out the eggs and butter. She placed them on the table and walked to the cabinet, pulled out a bowl, walked back to the table, and stopped.

For a moment she couldn't move. She took a deep breath and closed her eyes and sat down to keep from falling. She began to cry. She couldn't stop thinking about what was about to happen. She wanted to convince Tremaine not to try this, but she knew he would. She knew that he had to prove to her and himself that he was a man and that his word meant something.

He will want to show his courage and strength, and in the process he could lose his life, she thought. *Oh God, I shouldn't have left him. If I had stayed, he would have never met this man. What am I going to do? I never meant for anything like this to happen. I just wanted him to grow up and take responsibility for himself and now I will lose him forever. Why couldn't he just join the Army or something, like normal children? This is too hard. I don't know what to do.*

The tears rolled down her face. She heard someone enter the room.

"Don't worry, I will stop him. I won't let him do this," said Alec.

She stood and walked to the sink. She washed the bowl and began to dry it. She never looked back at him, but she knew he was still standing there.

"There is nothing you can do," she said. "Tremaine will not be stopped. You don't understand. He thinks he was chosen to do this. I don't know . . . maybe he was. When he spoke of the man with the blue eyes, it does seem that he was sent to you, and even if he wasn't, Tremaine believes he was. He considers you his friend, and he will do whatever it takes to help you. He has no fear, no limitations. He will never see that it can not be done." She turned and looked into Alec's eyes.

Her sadness was heart-wrenching to him. He knew he had endangered her child beyond anything he could imagine, and he didn't know how to fix it, to stop it. He couldn't make it all just go away. It was real, and he believed that John was right—it wasn't something that could be fixed in this world. But he was uncertain how to die and return to free the souls from the well, to free himself from that awful fate and save Tremaine. He walked over to her and held her in his arms and let her cry. He knew she was right and they had no choice but to try. He decided to deal with it, no matter what the outcome. If he loses his life, so be it, but the thought of an eighteen-year-old boy losing his life was harder to cope with. But it seemed the choice was made.

"Don't cry, Mother," said Tremaine as he entered the kitchen to see Alec comforting her. "It will be all right. I know it will."

"You speak with the mind of a child, Tremaine. No matter how much you believe you are grown, and in some ways you may be, but you do not have the experience to deal with something like this. This is beyond anything you could ever imagine, and I fear that you will not be able to cope through the ordeal."

"Maybe you're right, Mother. Maybe I will die and lose my life, but it will be for something, rather than being shot in the street like some gangster over drugs or stealing something. Maybe how you die is just as important as how you live. This is how I want to live the last days of my life, pursuing something greater than myself, giving myself to something of value. I know I'm young, and you're right, inexperienced, but I'll just have to grow up fast."

He walked into the living room and picked up the binder that was lying on the sofa. He opened it and began to read.

Alaya looked at Alec and nodded her head. She had to submit and accept the reality of the situation and do what she could to help. She turned back to the table and cracked open the eggs, pulled a fork from the drawer, and began to whisk the eggs around in the bowl.

Alec stepped into the living room and sat down just as John entered the room. Alec reached over to help him to his chair. As Alec slowly moved John through the room, he saw his future if he should live to be so old and dreaded the thought. He looked at the pictures of John that canvassed the room when he was a young man, so vibrant and strong. He had been a handsome man, and now he was old and tired, worn out from age and illness. His mind was still sound, but the vitality was long gone.

"How are you today, Great-grandfather?" asked Tremaine.

"It is a good day. I am alive," he said.

Alec smiled at his response. He went back to the sofa and sat. He didn't know what to say, so he said nothing.

"I think I understand what you mean when you said we would have to die, but I can't figure out how it can be done. How can a person die and return?" asked Tremaine.

"This is where you need the guide because he will have the link between life and death that will keep you attached to this world as you cross into the next," said John.

"Where can we find a guide?" asked Alec.

"He also lies in your subconscious."

That confused Alec even more.

"Breakfast is ready. Tremaine, help your great-grandfather to the table."

"Yes, Mother." Tremaine helped John stand and walked him to the table.

They all sat and joined hands to pray.

"We thank You for our food today, Lord. We thank You for our lives and our loved ones. We ask for Your blessings. Watch over us and keep us from harm. Lord, today my child makes a decision that should be left to men, and so today is the day he becomes a man. He and his friend will come to You for help and guidance and we ask that You do not forsake them in their time of need. Give us all the strength we need to do what must be done. In Your Holy Name we pray, Amen."

John opened his eyes and pulled the plate closer to him. He began to eat as the prayer rang in everyone's ears over and over again. They all remained silent.

CHAPTER 4

In the Mind's Eye

John sat in his chair and waited for Tremaine to tell him his decision. John knew the risk involved in either choice, but was determined not to influence Tremaine or Alec one way or the other. This had to be their choice, because the consequences were theirs to bear.

Alaya stood by the doorway that led from the living room to the dining room and watched her child struggle with the biggest decision of his life. She didn't want him to do it, but she knew she had to let him make the decision. She felt strongly that he would lose his life before he had a chance to become the man she'd always wanted him to be.

She held her breath when she heard him say, "Grandfather, we are ready."

"I cannot guarantee you success. Do you understand this? I am taking my cues from what I remembered my grandfather performed during one of his ceremonies when I was a boy. My memory is not sharp, and my ability to perform this isn't very good. It may not work at all."

"We must try," said Alec.

"You know that you could die?"

John stared into Alec's eyes and waited for him to flinch at the thought of death, but he didn't, he only smiled and said, "Death is not my greatest fear, eternity in Hell is. I cannot imagine existing in that well for an eternity, and now that I know, I can't let those souls continue to exist in such anguish. I must try."

Alaya clutched her chest. Her heart ached and she pleaded, "Nooooo, please, Tremaine, please don't do this."

He walked over to her and hugged her. He let her cry on his shoulder.

"Mother, I have not been a good son. I have done everything that I know how to screw up my life, and in the process, I made your life miserable. I don't know why I was chosen to help Alec, but I was, and maybe in the process, I may find my own way. If I do not survive this, you should know that you are a good mother. You did all that anyone could have done, and I thank you for it. I love you and, no matter what, I will always be with you." He kissed her on the forehead and turned toward John.

"I am ready." He looked at Alec.

"I am ready too," Alec said.

Alaya turned and walked down the hall and into her room. She closed the door and decided that she did not want to see the end of her son's life.

"Tremaine, place two chairs here, in front of me." John pointed to a spot on the floor where he wanted the chairs to sit.

Tremaine got two chairs from the dining room and placed them in front of where John was sitting.

"Alec, turn the lights off and close the curtains," said John.

Alec worked his way around the room, turning off all lights and closing the curtains so that no outside light entered the room.

"Come and sit," said John.

They both took a seat on the chairs and waited. They were both gripped with fear, but they pulled from deep inside to find the strength to take the next step.

John took their hands and softly said, "You will have to join one to the other in spirit and soul. You will travel beyond the subconscious and exist between death and eternity. You will cross over, but you will not commit to the death journey. It is a natural course that once a person crosses over, their journey leads them to the next existence. Your reluctance to this will upset the natural order of things, and the spiritual forces will try to tempt you to enter, but you cannot. You will meet yourself and all that you carried with you into the spiritual plane. If you carry fear, it will haunt you; if you carry guilt, it will cripple you; if you carry hate, it will destroy you. Your self will be your greatest enemy. You must search deep within yourself to hold onto the love and grace that will give you strength. We have it within ourselves to know the goodness of God, but we cannot see it because of want. You must find it and hold onto it, or else you will perish.

"Your guide will meet you and carry you into the dimension of time and space that lies just across from our subconscious. It is a world unlike what you know to be true. The laws that govern this world will have no meaning there. Think beyond the limitations of the body and the cardinal mind. Take heed to the wisdom of your guide, and he will see you through."

"How will we know him?" asked Tremaine.

"He will know you," answered John. "Now, let's get started. We have no time to waste; he will know our plan soon and will try to stop you." He stood and walked to the basement door. He opened it and stared down the dark stairwell. "Come," he said.

Tremaine held John's arm and helped him maneuver his way down the stairs. Alec joined them at the bottom of the stairs.

John reached up and pulled the chain that turned the overhead light on and walked to the center of the room. He pointed to two cots that lay against the wall. "Bring them here and place them side by side over here." John pointed to the center of the room.

Tremaine and Alec grabbed the cots and put them in place.

"Get those candles from the shelf and place them around the cots. Find the matches and light them."

Alec grabbed the candles, and Tremaine found the matches. As Alec placed the candles around the cots into a circle, Tremaine lit each one.

"Now, inside that box on the desk is various types of herbs. Look inside and find the herb that is yellow in color."

Alec and Tremaine walked over and opened the box. They looked at each other when they realized that they would be consuming the herb. They each picked up two pieces of the yellow plant and walked back to John.

"Sit on the cot and eat the herb and then lay down."

They both did as John said.

"Hold hands." John took a leather strap from a table and tied their wrists together. "Keep your hands together so that you will pass through time and space together. If this works, you will arrive in the spirit world together."

They lay on the cots with their eyes closed and listened to John chant a sweet, melodic sound. They knew they were holding each other's hand, but they could feel their bodies relax as if they were going to sleep. Their thoughts were scrambled, and their hearts raced. They could hear the sound of their hearts beating so loudly, they thought it would burst. Tremaine became frightened.

After what seemed like minutes, he opened his eyes and looked around.

"Great-grandfather, nothing happened. We are still here."

Alec could hear John chanting and wondered what, if anything, happened. He looked at Tremaine and saw nothing different. He was disappointed. He really needed for this to work. It was his only hope of freeing himself and his family from the well.

John continued to chant until Tremaine sat up and yelled, "Great-grandfather, something went wrong. We are still here."

Alec sat up and untied the leather strap from their wrist.

John kept chanting.

"Something's wrong," said Alec. He turned and looked upstairs. Everything seemed the same, but different. "Maybe it did work." He stepped off the cot, walked to the bottom of the steps, and stared upstairs.

Tremaine followed him. "What's going on, Alec?"

"I don't know," he said as he started to climb the stairs. He reached the top and looked around. Everything was the same.

Tremaine followed him. They could still hear John in the basement chanting and movement from outside.

Alec walked to the kitchen and noticed the book on the table. "What is this?" he asked.

"I don't know. I don't know where it came from." Tremaine picked the book up and began to read. "Listen," he said. " 'The possibility of moving from one dimension is becoming more and more real to the subconscious mind. If a person can occupy the subconscious for periods of time, the more accessible other spaces that are coexisting in time are.' What does that mean?"

"I'm not sure, but I think we should find out. Where can we find this person?" asked Alec.

"Her name is Kathleen Cho, and she teaches at the university," said Tremaine.

"Let's go. We have to find her and see if she can help," said Alec.

"What about my great-grandfather? Should we let him know?"

Alec thought about it for a moment. Somehow he knew not to disturb him. He started to walk downstairs, but stopped.

"He needs to continue doing what he is doing. Tremaine, I'm not sure, but I feel that we are not in the same place that we started. I just don't know what's different or where we are. Maybe this woman can tell us. Let's go."

They walked outside, where everything looked just like it did yesterday and the day before. They got into the truck and headed toward the university.

They seemed to have reached the campus faster than expected, and they parked the trucked, walked inside the administration building, and noticed a counter with a large sign over it that read ADMISSIONS. They walked toward it.

"May I help you?" asked the woman behind the counter.

The room was filled with students and administrators working to sign students up for the summer session.

"We are looking for Professor Kathleen Cho. Do you know where we can find her?"

"Professor Cho's office is closed for the summer. I can leave a message in her mailbox and she will check it periodically," the lady said.

"No, no, you see, we must speak with her now. It is an emergency," said Alec.

"Well, I don't know how I can help you. She's not here, and I cannot give you her information."

"Tremaine, do you have one of those cell phones?"

"Yes, I have it," he said.

Alec wrote the information down and handed it to the young lady. "Here, take this number and you call her and tell her that she must contact me. It is a matter of life and death." His heart sank when he realized that she would never make the call. He knew when he handed the paper to her that he would have to find another way to find this woman.

They left the building feeling a little defeated.

"What do we do now?" asked Tremaine.

"I don't know," said Alec with a big sigh. "Maybe we can find her through her publishing company. You know, the people who published her book, they should know how to reach her."

"But will they tell us?"

"No, but they may contact her for us . . . maybe." Alec looked all around, hoping the answer would present itself, when he heard a voice from the bottom of the steps.

"Are you looking for me?" a woman yelled.

They looked at her strangely and wondered if she was talking to them. They looked at each other and wondered if it could be her. They began to walk down slowly and hesitated to respond.

"Are you deaf? Did you not hear me? Are you looking for me?" she asked again.

"That depends upon who you are." Alec stared at her and waited for her response.

They stood at the bottom of the steps and studied the woman intently.

She looked puzzled at the questions, as if it was obvious who she was. "Why, I'm Kathleen Cho. I understand that you are looking for me."

"Yes, we sure are," said Tremaine with a sense of relief that they found her without struggle.

"Wait," said Alec hesitantly, "how did you know we were looking for you?"

She looked at him strangely and took offense to his tone. "I got a call. Does it matter? What do you want?"

"Yes, it does," said Alec.

"No, it doesn't," inserted Tremaine quickly to squelch the attitudes and get on with it. "We need your help," he said as he began walking with her across the campus.

Alec was still hesitating to embrace her as an ally. He wasn't sure, but something didn't feel right to him. He watched as they walked away from him and wondered if this was the right thing to do. He decided to let his fears go and get as much information as he could and hoped that she would not lead them astray. He started to walk behind them until he caught up. He heard Tremaine ask about the afterlife.

"Is there a way to enter the afterlife and survive?"

"Survive what?" she asked.

"Survive death," he said.

She stared into his eyes. She could feel the intensity in his voice and saw the weight of worry on his face. She knew he meant every word, so there was no need to ask him to repeat it. It was obvious that he was sincere in his request. The question was how to answer him.

"You came to me because of the book, didn't you?" She hesitated and took a deep breath.

It almost seemed that she felt a sorrow for writing the book, as if it brought her sadness and distress. She waited to gather her thoughts and realized that she had no choice but to be honest with them.

"I know what you are asking. I know that in that book it seemed that it is possible to cross into other planes of life and exist there without letting go of this life. It all sounds great, but it is just theory. Of course, no one has tried this and survived to come back and say, 'Yeah, it works.' I'm not sure what to tell you, because I can see that you really have a need. Tell me what is so important that you would go to this length for an answer."

Tremaine looked at Alec and wondered if he should tell the story.

"Let me," said Alec.

He began to talk to her about Torrin and the pact he made with the Devil. He spoke of the well and the horrible way the people died. He told her of their quest for the crystal rose and how they believed that they had to die to retrieve it and bring it back to this world to save his family and himself from the well."

The look of amazement on her face made Alec step back. He couldn't tell if she believed him or not. For a moment, she couldn't speak.

"Wow . . . now that's . . . wow, I don't know what to say to that. I don't know if I can help you or not. No, I take that back, I'm sure I can't help you."

"Then this is hopeless," said Tremaine.

"Maybe not," she said as she looked up at the sky and closed her eyes and thought deeply for a moment. She took a deep breath and rubbed her eyes. "There may be a way. The question is how to get to him."

"Get to who? What are you talking about?" asked Alec.

"Ok, listen, well wait, I'm hungry, and if I'm going to tell this, I need to do it on a full stomach." She looked around and saw the food stand at the end of the street. She started walking toward it while checking her pockets for money. She found a few dollars and stood in line for a few minutes.

Alec and Tremaine followed her.

"What do you think?" whispered Tremaine.

"I don't know. She seems a little weird to me," said Alec.

"Yep, you're right. I guess I am a little weird." She looked back at Alec. "I guess I have to be to get involved in this nightmare you got going on. A sane person would have walked away the moment you said 'pact with the devil.' " She turned back around and looked at the guy behind the counter. She smiled at his expression.

He wasn't sure if he had already heard too much, and he just wanted them to go away.

"Let me have a dog and a Coke," she said.

The young man pulled the bun from the bag and grabbed a hotdog from the rack. He placed it in the bun. He filled the cup with Coke, topped it, and placed it on the counter. "What's on it?" he asked.

"Mustard, relish, and a few onions."

He topped the hot dog with the fixings and wrapped it in foil. He handed it to her while she handed him five bucks. "Keep the change," she said as she picked up her Coke and walked back toward Alec. "Now, where were we?" She took a bite of the hot dog and wiped the mustard from her chin. She walked toward a bench under a huge maple tree and sat down.

They followed her and she began to speak about a place where it was believed that men lived within their subconscious minds and moved crossed into parallel worlds.

"Through my travels I've heard of a place that sits on the highest mountain range. It is so isolated that no one really knows if it exists or not. Few people have ever found it, and those who claim to have found it could never prove anything, so most thought they were mad. Much as with most stories, some truth lies behind, but how much is truth and how much is legend is unknown."

"Where is this place?" asked Tremaine.

"Well, I'm not sure. I heard it was near Mongolia, but since most people think it's a myth, a location will be hard to pin down. I don't really know if it exists at all, but if it does, it may give you the answers you seek," she said.

"How could we ever find a place that may not exist at all? The whole thing sounds farfetched to me," said Alec.

"More farfetched than your story?" She looked at him in total confusion at his response. "The first thing we have to do is dispel any notion of what we believe to be right or wrong, real or false. Truth for you is different than it is for anyone else, because by virtue of your circumstances, you have already moved into the world of metaphysics and beyond. You will have to believe that it is so, and therefore it is. Do you understand?" She looked at both of them, inquiring to their willingness to put all that they knew as reality behind them to move into a world where natural laws did not apply.

"That's going to be hard to do. How do I decide that the tree that I am looking at isn't really a tree, or better yet, isn't there at all? That's not possible," said Tremaine.

"It will have to be, and somehow we will have to get both of you to a place where you can see beyond the physical," she said.

"How do we do that?" asked Alec.

"I guess we will start by learning to meditate. You've got to make a connection with your higher consciousness, your true self. Do you understand?" She looked firmly at both of them.

"No," they both said in unison with a resounding tone that assured her that she was working with true novices.

She took a deep breath, looked into their eyes, and thought about her next step. "I guess we'll have to start from scratch. I'm hoping the two of you are open-minded enough to grasp the concept, because if you're not, this may not happen. For where we are going, you have to prepare the mind as well as the body."

"Ma'am, I'm not a young man. I may not have a lot of time to spare, and as far as I know, I could be the last of my family. So if someone throws a coin in that well today, I die today. There is a sense of urgency here. Please understand that while we are preparing," said Alec.

"Yes, yes, I understand." She meandered around awkwardly for a moment in deep thought. She wandered back. She could tell from the look on their faces that they were worried about her credibility. She smiled and took Alec's hand. "We'll figure this out. Don't worry." She took a deep breath and looked all around as if she was soaking up the world as she knew it today, because it may all be different tomorrow or she may not be there to embrace the beauty of it all. "I guess all you have are the things on your back."

"Yep, this is it," said Tremaine.

"Ok, let's get started," she said as she started to walk away.

"Get started? how? Where?" asked Alec.

"My house . . . we will stay at my house until we are ready," she said. She kept walking, knowing they would follow. She knew that she really was their only hope and that the burden they had now laid on her shoulders would consume her for a long time. She wasn't really sure she could help them, but they landed on her doorstep, so to speak, and now she felt obligated to try. Her mind was swirling around with the question, "Try what?" She unlocked the doors to an oversized black truck.

Alec laughed.

"What are you doing trying to drive this bus? Can your feet reach the gas pedal? Can you see out the window?"

Tremaine laughed when she jumped inside and seemed lost in the big cab of the truck. It did seem that her face barely reached the console. She had the seat pulled up so close to the steering wheel, neither of them could sit in front. They laughed for the first time in months. It was a funny sight. She looked like a twelve-year-old trying to drive Daddy's truck.

She inserted the key and started the engine. It roared, and when she put the truck in DRIVE, she hit the gas pedal and forced them back in their seat.

"Whoa, little lady, this isn't a toy," said Alec.

She sneered. "I beg your pardon, sir. I've been driving this truck for years, and I know how to handle it, thank you very much."

"Okay, okay, I hear ya."

Alec sat back, and he and Tremaine enjoyed the ride, knowing that it could be the last thing they enjoyed for a while.

She drove for about thirty minutes then she slowly pulled onto what appeared to be a long road, but turned out to be her driveway. She drove for a few minutes until she stopped in front of a beautiful cottage. It was something right out of a storybook, all the way down to the white picket fence. The quaint house was surrounded by acres of land and beautiful, tall trees. Her garden was colorful and filled with flowers of all kinds. It was truly amazing to see.

Tremaine became very skeptical. He didn't know why, but something about this picture was alarming to him. It was beautiful, but maybe a little too beautiful.

Alec noticed the look on his face. "What's wrong?"

"I don't know. It just seems strange for a place like this to be sitting in the middle of a town." He looked all around. "It's very quiet and still, don't you think?"

Alec looked around and wondered about it. He did not have the same concern that Tremaine had, but he didn't want to just blow his concerns off either.

"I think it's okay. I mean, it looks like the kind of place she would live in. I think it's perfect for what we need to do." Alec walked toward the fence and held the gate open for Tremaine.

Tremaine shook off the feeling and smiled. He walked inside to the coziest, warmest place he had ever seen. The colors of green and blue moved throughout the house, and she had soft lighting everywhere. The rooms were small, but there were many of them. The living room had a vaulted ceiling with huge wood beams stretching across it. The furniture was green and the walls were a soft blue. The fireplace centered the room with large stones of gray and white. The kitchen was large and led to an all-glass sunroom that opened the back of the house to a panoramic view of acres of meadows and trees.

"Have a seat." Kathleen pointed to the sunroom.

They walked inside in awe of the breathtaking view before them. They found a comfortable chair and sat in silence.

Kathleen went into the kitchen and put a pot of water on the stove to boil. "I'll make us some herb tea that will help us relax."

While Alec was mesmerized with the view, Tremaine was watching her every move. She got the cups from the cabinet and poured the hot water and placed a tea bag into each cup. She grabbed a bottle from a corner shelf and a spoon from the drawer. He watched her pour one teaspoon of the dark liquid into each cup of tea.

"What is that?" he asked.

"It will help you see," she answered.

"See what?" he asked.

"See what path we have to take."

Alec began to notice her and the conversation they were having. "What is it?" Alec wished he had been paying attention.

"It's an herb that will help you to relax and concentrate on what we have to do. We don't have much time, as you said, so I don't have months to teach you how to relax and meditate and how to get in touch with your inner self. We need to move now, and this is the only way I know how to do it."

"What will it do to us?" Alec asked.

"It will open your mind to a world beyond anything you have ever known." She noticed the nervousness in each of them. She didn't want them to be scared, but she knew she didn't have time to do a whole lot of explaining and training. "I will drink it first. It will not harm you, but if you decide that you don't want to do this and try another way to find the rose, we can stop now. But once you take this, we move forward, no matter what." She stopped and waited for their response.

"You are going to go with us?" asked Tremaine.

"Well, I guess it's time that I find out what the hell I've been writing about all these years. I've always wanted to do this, but was afraid. But now I have a reason, a cause, so to speak, and it's now or never. Besides, I think you will need me."

Tremaine and Alec looked at each other, and without a word they reached for the cups of tea and began to drink. Kathleen took a seat and drank her tea. She reached out and took their hands and started to chant. It sounded like John's chanting but stronger. The sound was relaxing and soothing. They could feel the effects of the tea. Their legs and arms seemed to weigh a ton, but they knew not to let go of each other's hand. They hung their heads from the weight and passed from this world into the next.

At first glance they seemed to be in a white room with people moving about. People of all races and creeds were there, and they didn't seem to notice each other.

"This is odd," said Kathleen as she looked all around.

Things were hazy and a little fuzzy, but they knew that they were no longer in Kathleen's house, but where they were, they didn't know.

"What?" asked Alec.

"There are no doors, but people are coming and going," she replied.

"Coming and going from where to where?" Tremaine looked out as far as he could see, but everything was a blur. He couldn't find an end to the room, so he tried to focus on a man sitting in front of him on what appeared to be a contour in the space around him. It was just white space everywhere. He stared at the man and watched as he phased in and out. His body would appear in front of him for a moment, and then he would slowly become invisible, and within minutes he would phase back in.

Tremaine walked toward the man and reached out to him, but just as the man looked into his eyes, he phased out. Tremaine stepped back. "What is this place?"

His frightened voice caught Alec's ear. "I don't know, but somehow we have to find out what this place has to do with our journey," he said.

People were phasing in and out of time and space all around them. One man phased in, dressed as if he had been in a great war. His uniform was gray and laced with medals and ribbons. He carried a weapon with teeth like a saw but shaped like a sword. His face was bloody from a head wound, and his blue eyes filled with tears from the pain and death that seemingly was all around him. He phased in and looked into Alec's eyes.

"The war on Talus 5 was devastating. All was lost, all was lost," he said.

"How long was the war?" Alec asked.

"Seven years, seven years long," the man said as he phased out.

Alec reached for him, but he was gone. He stood in awe and wondered how this was happening.

Tremaine saw the man that was sitting in front of him phase back in. Tremaine immediately reached for him and touched him. "Where are we?" he asked.

"Fifteen years on the Aria Space Station was grueling, but I would do it again, if I had to."

"Fifteen years? You've only been gone for moments."

"Moments here are lifetimes there."

"What do you mean?"

"A life is but a moment in the eyes of God," he said as he began to phase out again.

Tremaine stepped back. He watched as the man smiled as if to say good-bye and was gone.

"What is this place?" Tremaine was frightened. He felt trapped, and he wanted to get out, but couldn't figure out how.

"This is the place where life and death meet. Linear time does not exist here. There is no past or future, no yesterday or tomorrow. Everything begins anew with every phase. Each of these souls died and phased in and phased out to begin again," said Kathleen.

"This is where life ends and begins. Nothing ever ends," said Tremaine.

"Life eternal," said Alec.

A young girl phased in and walked toward Tremaine. She was dressed as if she were from the 1950s. Her button-down sweater and knee-length straight skirt was complementing. Her long dark hair was pinned back, and her twenty-something brown face was young and fresh. Her dark eyes were piercing as she smiled at Tremaine. She walked straight toward him as if she knew him and wanted to say hello. He wasn't sure how to react. His first thought was to run, but she seemed so pleasant and comforting. The young African American girl was not familiar to him. His heart started to race as she reached out to touch him.

"Hello," she said. She looked into his eyes and touched his shoulder. "You were here before."

"Before what?" he asked.

"Before my last existence," she said.

"I don't understand."

"That's all right. I haven't phased, so I think that my next existence is here with you," she said.

"Where is *here*?" asked Alec.

"It is where your questions can be answered," she said.

Alec looked confused as he tried to decipher the riddle.

"Is this Heaven?" asked Tremaine.

She gently touched his face and smiled. "If it gives you what you need, then, yes, it is for you."

"Heaven is the same for everyone," said Kathleen.

"Are you sure?" she asked as she firmly looked over at Kathleen and waited for her response.

Kathleen stared back at the girl and wondered who she was. She decided not to answer, since she wasn't sure if her assumption was right. She looked away, hoping it would end the exchange.

"We need to move on," the girl said. She turned and walked away toward nothing.

They didn't move. They watched her and wondered if they should trust her. Where would she take them? She stopped and looked back. She smiled so sweetly.

"We all have guides along our paths," she said as she reached out her hand, beckoning them to follow.

They looked at each other and decided to take the risk. Without saying a word, they understood each other and took the first step toward the unknown.

"Are you our guide? My great-grandfather spoke of a guide. Is that you?" Tremaine asked.

"We all have many who guide us," she said as they phased out of the white world where time did not exist into a pasture of green grass, wildflowers, birds, and soft breezes.

The bright red sun was ominous, yet warm and soothing. Deer moved around in the distance, and young wolf cubs played at the base of a tree. The yellow-red horizon draped over the mountain range like a warm blanket, causing a beautiful glow in the evening sky. It was serene and calming. Their clothes changed into khaki pants, boots, long-sleeved shirts, and a backpack that contained winter wear, first-aid kits, food, and water.

"Where are we going that we would need these things?" asked Alec.

She pointed to the top of the snow-capped mountains. She didn't look back as she secured her backpack to her shoulders and started walking.

They were stunned. "What the hell are we doing?" seemed to be a singular thought.

She walked ahead of them.

Tremaine ran to catch up with her.

"Excuse me, but can you be just a little more specific about what you are doing and why and who are you? Do you have a name?"

"My name, my name . . . well," she thought, "my name from my last existence was Clara."

"Where was your last existence?" Tremaine asked.

"I was on earth. I was born in nineteen thirty-eight, and I died in nineteen fifty-nine."

"How did you die?"

"I was poisoned," she said.

Tremaine stopped walking. She stated it so profoundly with such ease and insensitivity that it took his breath away for a moment. She never stopped walking. He caught up with her.

"How? Who? What happened?"

"My lover poisoned me because he thought I was going to leave him."

"Were you?"

"Yes."

"Wow, you were so young. That had to be hard," he said.

She laughed. "Hard on whom?"

"Why, you, of course."

"No." She giggled. "Death is death. We all have to do it. It doesn't matter how you die, the point is that you do. Sometimes it's a long life, sometimes it isn't; your spirit doesn't know the difference. It's only moments in what you call time."

"You sound like my great-grandfather," said Tremaine.

"Your great-grandfather is a wise spirit. Angels hover around him all the time."

"You speak as if you know him."

"Our paths have crossed before, somewhere in time," she said. She looked back over her shoulder at Alec and Kathleen. "We need to reach the foothills before nightfall. We should move faster."

Tremaine studied her face. *She is very pretty*, he thought.

"I think I want a different name," she said.

"Like what?" asked Tremaine, thinking how strange it was to just arbitrarily change your name?

She thought for a moment.

"What about *Isadora*?"

"Isadora." Tremaine thought about it. "Yes. I like it. We can call you *Issi*," he said.

"Or Dora," she said. "Yes, Isadora it is."

They smiled at each other and enjoyed the first moments of building a new friendship.

"What is this, Kathleen? Who is she?" Alec looked at Kathleen, hoping that she could shed some light on what was happening.

"I don't know. The things that I thought don't seem to be true about this existence and the realm of the unknown. I guess I really had no idea what I was talking about. I am surprised that I've been allowed to participate in your journey. I wasn't sure if I would be allowed to cross over, but now that I have, I have an uneasy feeling that I won't make it back."

He looked at her. What she said frightened him because he knew that she meant it and that her fear was real. He felt helpless to do anything about it. He felt horrible that he had pulled another innocent person into his nightmare. This was his burden, and now the lives of three other people were threatened because of Torrin's act over one hundred years ago that now seemed like yesterday. He was frustrated and felt that he should have been more adamant about doing this alone.

"I should have taken my punishment and lived in the wall of the well with the rest of my ancestors for eternity."

"What would make you say such a thing?" She looked at him, amazed at his willingness to give up. "You bear no guilt for this. This is not of your doing."

"It affects me and me alone. I should not have involved all of you," he sadly said.

Suddenly there was a foul stench in the air. Everything became still and lifeless. The wind stopped blowing, and the sounds of nature that filled their evening walk were gone.

"What are you thinking?" Isadora turned and looked back at Alec and Kathleen. "What are you thinking about? Stop it. Don't allow yourself to bring the ugliness of physical life into this realm. What is wrong?" she yelled.

Alec and Kathleen were startled by her reaction. Neither of them knew how to respond. Their silence was frustrating to her.

"Can one of you tell me what your conversation was about, please?" she asked. "This is important."

"I was telling Kathleen how I wish I had not involved the three of you in this mess that was caused by my fore-father. I was simply saying that this should be a burden that I should carry alone. I—"

"Quiet. We must hurry. We don't have much time. We must get to the foothills and find shelter now. It's not much farther. Come, we must hurry."

Isadora started to walk very fast. They worked to keep up with her. There was fear on her face, and they could not understand why.

Alec knew he had done something, but didn't know what, which made him feel even more guilty.

They had walked for another ten minutes when they started to hear a thunderous sound in the distance. The sound was faint, but notable. They looked back beyond the horizon but couldn't see anything. The sound was getting louder and louder. It was coming toward them, but what was it? Where was it?

Isadora was visibly scared. "We must hurry." She started running toward the mountains as fast as she could.

They ran with her without really understanding why. The sound got louder and louder. It was if they were being chased by thunder.

A herd of buffalo would make such a sound, thought Kathleen. She looked back, and still there was nothing.

Suddenly, the mountain range was upon them. Isadora ran all around looking for an opening, a cave, some kind of shelter.

"Here, come over here," she yelled.

The sound was upon them. The sound of their heart-beats was deafening.

Alec tried to keep up, but at sixty-five years old, it was-n't easy. He found himself still outside when Isadora and Kathleen entered a small opening in the rock.

Tremaine looked back and saw Alec struggling. He started stepping over rock to reach him when he saw Alec brutally attacked by something. It tore at his flesh and ripped his clothes. Tremaine yelled Alec's name at the top of his lungs and screamed for help. He ran to Alec and worked to pull him free. He looked into the evening light, hoping to see whatever it was that was violently attack-ing his friend, and images of ferocious wolves phased in and out of view. Alec couldn't see them, so he couldn't fight nor run.

Isadora found a large stick and some loose brush. She picked up the brush with the stick and blew upon it, and the dried brush burst into flames.

Kathleen stood back and watched Isadora throw the flame into the emptiness, causing the onslaught to cease. They heard the sound of what were obviously animals backing away, panting and breathing, and moving about.

"Get him inside now," Isadora yelled.

Tremaine pulled Alec's lifeless body up the slope. Kathleen ran down and grabbed Alec's legs, and they carried him into the cave. The narrow opening was per-fect to keep out whatever was out there.

Once inside, the cave opened up to a wide area that al-lowed them ease of movement.

"Lay him over there," said Isadora as she pointed to a flat space by the wall.

They laid Alec's injured body on the cave floor.

"Tremaine, help me put this rock at the opening."

"Why? Do you think they will come back?"

"Just in case, just in case," she said as they grabbed a large rock and rolled it to the cave opening. Except for a slight opening to let air in, the rock blocked out all light.

"We won't be able to see," said Tremaine.

"She can start a fire. I saw her," said Kathleen.

Alec moaned horribly from the pain. It was agonizing.

"Stumble around and find whatever will burn," said Isadora.

They gathered what they could and placed it near Alec.

"Stand back." She softly blew the warm air from her mouth and the brush and twigs began to smolder.

Tremaine stared at the smoke, completely stunned by what he saw. He watched the smoke turn into a fledgling fire and then into a roaring flame. The shadows of the cave came to life as the cave walls lit up. Isadora searched her backpack for her first-aid kit.

"How did you do that?" Tremaine asked.

Isadora found some bandages and medicated cream. She poured some water from her bottle and began to clean Alec's wounds. She could hear the agony in his moans, but all she had was aspirin, and she knew he needed more.

She stroked his brow with a wet cloth. "He's in so much pain. I wish I could do something else."

Tremaine was still waiting for an answer to his question. He couldn't stop thinking about it and was feeling a little out of control.

"I have these," said Kathleen as she approached Isadora with a bottle of pills. "I take them for back pain. They may help some."

"Yes, thank you." Isadora took the bottle and poured two pills into her hand. She forced them into Alec's mouth and gave him some water. She took the winter coat from the backpack and covered him and placed the backpack under his head to make him more comfortable.

"What was it?" Alec's voice quivered from the relentless pain. He struggled to open his eyes. He reached out and grabbed her arm. "What was it?"

She looked at him and sat down beside him and held his hand. She could see the terror in Tremaine's and Kathleen's eyes. She took a deep breath and tried to explain the best she could.

"In this place things exist that cannot exist in your world. Your world is governed by the laws of physics, the laws of nature, but here in this place, those laws do not apply, so you may have capabilities that you would not have in your world, and you may also manifest what is real to the subconscious."

"What does all that mean? Are you some kind of a magician and the invisible pack of wolves came from our subconscious? What does it mean?" Tremaine's fear was evident. He didn't want to hear a whole lot of sci-fi double talk. He wanted to know in layman's terms what he was up against. He didn't want to leave the cave, but he also knew he couldn't stay. He wondered what he had gotten himself into and knew now with certainty that he would never see his mother again.

"Yes, Tremaine, what you are saying is correct. What attacked Alec was a product of his subconscious, wasn't it?" asked Kathleen.

"Yes. He must have seen something that made him think of wolves. Maybe it was the cubs we saw when we entered this realm. I don't know, but whatever he saw, his subconscious manifested the image as those wolves," said Isadora.

"But why? Why did they attack him?" Tremaine remembered something his great-grandfather said about the baggage we carry. He started to pace around.

Isadora looked into Alec's eyes. He could barely see her. He tried to focus and listen.

She caressed his hand and whispered, "Guilt is an awful thing. It can eat way at you a little at a time for years and years. It can rob you of what is most precious to you: your joy. You cannot go through life wishing for what you could have done, or blaming yourself for what someone else did. You have been in denial about the pact Torrin made for your entire life, and when Tremaine forced you to see it, you began to wonder if there was something you could have done to fix it before now. You wonder if there was a way to erase what your grandfather did to free all of those people. You carry the burden of all of those people as if you did something to them. Deep down inside, you think this journey is hopeless and that the souls of those people, including your own, are lost, and you fear that Tremaine, Kathleen, and me will lose our lives because you carry this awful curse. The guilt you carry is what attacked you, and it is what will keep you enslaved long after your death, for eternity. In this world, what your subconscious fears the most will become real, and what it loves the most will be true. Until you let it go, it will haunt you. It will kill you. It will never stop. You cannot kill it without killing yourself, because it is a part of you."

"What can I do?" Alec murmured. A tear rolled down his face as he accepted the hopelessness of it.

"You have to free yourself of it. You have to come to terms with who carries the blame, and even if it is you, forgive yourself as you would another," she said.

"I don't know how. I've had it all of my life. It's who I am," he said.

"Then it's time you become someone else," she said as she heard the scratching of animals at the rock that was blocking the entry into the cave. "They are back."

"Oh God, what do we do?" Tremaine asked frantically.

"I don't think we will be able to stay here much longer.

It's just a matter of time before they force that rock out of the way. Tremaine, let's find something to brace it with to buy us as much time as possible," said Kathleen.

"I'll look for something that we can use as a stretcher for Alec. We may have to carry him," said Isadora.

"No, leave me. I don't want anyone else to get hurt because of me," said Alec

"You don't understand. It will not harm us, it will kill you and you alone. Once you are dead, it will go away. We are going to save your life," said Isadora.

"Don't bother."

"What? Without you, all of those people will stay locked in Hell for an eternity. All of this would have been for nothing. What is wrong with you? You need to work this out. You need to see who you are as a man and not as the great-grandson of Torrin. Stop this, stop it now," yelled Tremaine.

He was so angry. He turned away from Alec, furious with his disregard for everything they had been through together. He heard the scratching at the opening and looked up to see the rock move a little. "We don't have much time. What can we do to keep that rock from moving?"

He and Kathleen looked all around and found three flat pieces of wood that would have been used in a mining shaft. They were sturdy enough to push against the rock and brace against the floor to reinforce the rock for a while. The sound of the pack of wolves scratching at the surface was terrifying. Tremaine and Kathleen weren't so sure that the horror on the other side of the rock wouldn't harm them as well as Alec. They feared for their lives as much as his and wanted to do whatever they could to stay alive.

Isadora found two longer pieces of the same wood. "Let's stretch a coat over these two pieces of wood and create a stretcher," she said.

Tremaine opened his coat and laid it down and they place the wood on top of the coat and closed the coat by buttoning it over the wood. By separating the wood to opposite sides, it created a hammock-like stretcher that, if the buttons hold, should carry Alec.

They lifted Alec and laid him on the coat, and Tremaine lifted the front end and Kathleen lifted the back end, and they carried Alec down into the cave.

Isadora took a piece of clothing and stuffed it full of twigs and sticks and wrapped it around a long stick. She brushed it by the fire and lit the cloth. She knew the flame wouldn't last long, but hopefully, it would last long enough for them to find a way out. She knew the evil on the other side of that rock would break through and when it did, Alec would die.

They walked farther and farther down into the cave. Soon they began to notice remnants of tools, equipment, and debris used for mining this cave for coal. The old mine must have been closed fifty years ago. You could see old shoring and used lanterns and tracks used to carry the coal in and out.

Isadora tried to light the lanterns, because the flame she was carrying would burn out soon. She tried three or four with no luck, but soon she found one with enough oil left in it to keep the wick burning. She lit the lantern and tossed the stick aside. She got in front of them and used the light to guide them through the shaft. Alec was semi-conscious and was talking in his sleep. He called out Torrin's name and spoke of his father. He cursed God for letting this happen and cried at his own helplessness. Every so often, Isadora would yell at him to let it go.

"Who are you, Alec?" she would ask.

"I am a murderer," he would respond.

"Then you shall die," she would say.

"Then I shall die."

They kept walking. Isadora felt a breeze, but the cave was dark and closed. *Where could that have come from?* she thought. She stopped and held the lantern up to look around, and just beneath her was an abyss that melted into infinity. She could hear rushing water. She held the lantern up higher and saw the downhill slope that the water must have been going toward.

"What do you see?" asked Tremaine.

"There's a bridge here, and I think a river runs through the bottom of the chasm." She walked toward the bridge and held the lantern over it to see how badly worn out it was and just how unsafe it would be to cross it. She was about to decide that the path was too dangerous when she heard the sound of the wolves beating down upon them.

"Alec, who is to blame? Alec, whose fault is it?" she yelled.

"I don't know, I don't know. There was nothing I could do. Nothing. I wanted to, but I couldn't, I just couldn't."

"What do we do?" Kathleen asked. "If we stay on this side, Alec will die. If we attempt to use the bridge, we will all die. If Alec dies, the quest is over and the souls trapped in the well are lost to an eternal Hell." There was no good choice.

Isadora needed to find a way for them to see. She found some oil in a can and two dried paintbrushes and decided to light them as torches. She doused the brushes in oil and blew a breath of warm air upon them until they burned steadily. She positioned one brush at the starting point, and she carried the other with her as she stepped onto the bridge and slowly maneuvered her way across. She found each stable plank and cautiously stepped on each one while holding onto the ropes tightly. If it broke she'd hold the rope and pull herself back up. She held her breath as she took each step. She took a piece of coal and marked each plank that was sturdy enough to hold her weight. From the middle of the bridge, she yelled back at Alec, "Alec, who's fault is it? Who is to blame?"

"I don't know," he cried. "It isn't me. I did nothing. I did nothing. But I didn't try either. I didn't try. It's my fault. I could have tried."

"Tried to do what?" she yelled.

"Why are you torturing him?" yelled Tremaine. "He can't take it. Can't you see he's in pain?"

"He has to believe he is not to blame. He has to let go or he dies tonight," she said.

She stepped off at the end of the bridge. She placed the makeshift torch at the end of the bridge and lit up the path that they should take.

Kathleen could hear the wolves getting closer. "Tremaine, hurry, hurry, they are coming," she yelled.

Tremaine looked back. He could hear the rustling sound, but he saw nothing. He and Kathleen moved Alec slowly across the bridge. Tremaine would step to the right, directly on the crosses marked by Isadora. Kathleen tried to see around the stretcher to find the marks and she would follow his lead.

The horrible sound was getting closer and closer. Kathleen got very scared. If they entered this bridge, it would crumble from the weight and they would all die.

"Please hurry."

The terror in her voice was sickening to Tremaine because he was moving as fast as he could, but he knew it might not be fast enough. Just as the sound was upon them, Tremaine stepped onto the other side. He and Isadora held the stretcher while Kathleen maneuvered those last few planks. Just as she was about to make the last step, the bridge began to sway back and forth. It shook underneath from the movement of the feet from the horror that tracked them.

Kathleen lost her footing and reached for the rope, but

she could not grab it and she fell. She fell over the side, and her scream made Tremaine's heart stop. He moved to the edge to see, but the image of the wolves fading in and out of space was lurching at him.

Isadora stood back and blew a burst of flames that caused the animals to squeal. She aimed at the bridge and set the ropes on fires. The bridge burned and the ropes gave way with the wolves falling into the darkness below.

Tremaine ran to the edge and wondered about Kathleen. He looked all around and hoped that she could have survived somehow, but he knew better. "Oh God, she's gone. Alec will die when he realizes what happened. He will never let go, never." Just as he was about to walk away, he heard a faint sound from the cliff.

"Help me," the voice softly cried.

He got down on his knees and leaned forward as far as he could. Isadora held onto him as he searched the underside of the cliff and he saw her.

Kathleen had grabbed onto a branch and crawled onto a ledge. She tried to cover herself from the fire and the wolves as they fell to the bottom.

"Are you all right? Can you climb up?" yelled Tremaine.

"I think so. I may have broken my leg, but I'm alive, I think."

He smiled at her comic relief at an awful situation.

"I'll come down for you." He started looking for something, anything that could be used as a rope. He walked around for a while until he found pieces of the rope from the bridge. He found the longest piece and tied it around a nearby rock. He dropped the other end over the side to see how far it would extend. It made it. It was long enough. He grabbed the rope.

"Issi, I am going to tie the rope around her. Do you think you can pull her up?" He looked at her with hope in his eyes. He knew that Kathleen weighed more than Isadora, but he needed her to have more strength now than she ever had.

"I will try my best."

She braced herself against a rock and held the rope. She watched as Tremaine grabbed the rope and hoisted himself down the side of the cliff toward Kathleen.

He tried not to look down. It made him dizzy. He kept his eyes on the rock face in front of him and moved himself slowly downward until he reached the landing, where Kathleen was sitting and pampering her injured leg. He swung onto the landing and walked over to her.

"Well, nice of you to visit," she said smugly. "Now, how do you plan to get me up there? I'm no featherweight."

He looked around, and his eyes glanced at the bottomless pit that lay beneath them. He knew this was going to be risky. He was afraid that Issi would not be able to hold Kathleen's weight, but he knew he had to try. It was the only way he knew to get her off this ledge. He kneeled down and took her leg in his hand.

"How is it?"

"It hurts."

He moved her ankle back and forth and got a loud piercing scream from her.

"It's not broken. May be a bad sprain."

"How do you know?" she asked.

"If it was broken and I did that, you would have knocked me off this cliff. It wouldn't have moved. Let's see if you can put any weight on it."

He helped her stand and she tried to put her leg down, put couldn't completely, but she could limp a little.

"What I need for you to do is going to be excruciatingly painful, but it's the only way to get you up there." He tied the rope around her waist and made sure it was tight. "Now, Issi is going to help pull you up, but you will have to climb. Your leg is going to hurt like hell, but I need for you to do it anyway. Understand?"

"Yeah, I got it. You want me to swing out over the abyss with one leg and no upper body strength and climb up the side of a cliff."

"Yep, that's it," he proudly said, as if he was glad she understood.

"Okay," she said as she grabbed the rope and found the starting point.

"Okay, Issi, here she comes," yelled Tremaine.

Kathleen grabbed hold of the rock and started to climb. Isadora braced herself and pulled the rope as Kathleen made her ascent. She groaned horribly every time she had to use the bad leg. She was halfway up when putting any weight on that leg became unbearable, which put more weight onto the rope, and poor Isadora was struggling to hold on.

Isadora screamed in agony when the rope burned her hands as it started to slip away. Kathleen felt the slack in the rope and felt certain that Isadora would not be able to hold her and that she would fall. She looked down at Tremaine as if to say good-bye.

Just as Isadora was about to let go, Alec's hand grabbed the rope and held it steady. He braced himself behind Isadora, and the two of them pulled Kathleen to the surface.

She grabbed hold of the edge and pulled herself over. She lay on the ground for a few minutes thinking about what could have happened. She looked over and saw Alec and smiled.

"Thank you," she whispered.

He slowly walked over to her and helped her up. They hugged in genuine happiness to see each other alive.

"Hello, I'm still down here." Tremaine looked up in anticipation of seeing the rope drop at anytime.

Alec helped Kathleen take the rope from around her waist and tossed it back down to Tremaine.

"Wait until we yell *ready*," said Alec.

"Alec, is that you?" yelled Tremaine.

"Yes, I'm here," he said.

He walked back to the rock, where Isadora was examining the burns on her hands.

Tremaine was glad to hear the sound of Alec's voice.

Alec saw Isadora flinching over the pain to her hands and searched the backpack for a bandage. He wrapped her hands so she could help pull Tremaine up. He positioned himself behind her, and they both grabbed the rope.

"Tremaine, are you ready?"

Tremaine tightened the rope around his waist. "Yes, I'm ready."

He grabbed the rock and began to pull himself up the cliff. It was easier on Alec and Isadora, because Tremaine did most of the work. He made it to the ledge quickly and pulled himself over. He immediately went over to Alec to see how he was doing.

"Man, I'm glad to see you." He hugged him and smiled. He removed the rope and went to check on Kathleen. "I guess we've gotta find something to help you walk." He reached down and helped her stand.

Alec pulled the coat from the made up stretcher and folded it into his backpack. They walked a few feet away from the cliff. Tremaine found a piece of wood and used some gauze to create a splinter for Kathleen. He wrapped her ankle and found a long stick that she could use to help her walk.

She took a few of the pills for the pain and readied her self for a long and painful journey.

Tremaine looked around at everyone. "Wow, we look pretty beat up. How are your hands?" he asked Isadora.

"I'll live," she replied.

"Maybe we should just stay here for the night and get some rest," said Tremaine.

"That sounds good, but I don't want you to think that this is over," said Isadora. "Until Alec completely lets go of the guilt, they will be back, and they will kill him." She was very forthright in her statement. This was not a game, and she wanted them to understand it clearly. They could not let their guards down.

"It's dead. I saw it fall to the bottom. There's no way it survived," said Tremaine.

"You say that like it was alive. Don't think that way. It isn't living, except in Alec's subconscious. His subconscious can recreate it or something even worse at any time," said Isadora. She worried about Alec's ability to shed this horror from his mind. "Alec, I knew you would let it go, if you could, but it took you a lifetime to weave this nightmare, and you've been carrying it forever and now I'm asking you to let it go just like that. It's a part of you. I know it won't be easy, but you must try."

"I'll try, but you're right, it is a part of who I am, and I'm not sure who that is anymore," he said.

"You are this guilt, and you've got to think of yourself differently or you will never see your life again, and the reason you came here will be lost," said Isadora.

"You have to try," said Tremaine.

"Don't push him. It will only make him feel even more guilty, and we don't want that," said Kathleen as she positioned herself on the ground in a cozy spot to rest for the night.

Alec and Tremaine followed her lead and found a place to rest on the cold, hard ground. Isadora sat at the base of a large rock and stared into the night as if waiting for the inevitable.

Alec tossed and turned all night. He never really slept,

lingering somewhere between asleep and awake. He was afraid that his guilt could manifest those horrible animals again.

Kathleen slept fine. She was afraid that tomorrow would bring a whole new set of challenges that may be worse than today. She was concerned about Alec and his ability to purge the guilt from his mind. *I'll not think about it tonight*, she thought.

Isadora reluctantly closed her eyes and slept.

Tremaine could feel warmth on his face. It felt good as he dreamt about happier times when he was a boy playing on his great-grandfather's farm. The hot summer days and warm, pleasant nights were some of the best times of his young life. As he smiled from the thought, he realized that he was in a dark cave. He remembered the events of yesterday and wondered where the warmth was coming from. *It's a dream*, he thought, but he felt so nice and comforted. He slowly opened his eyes to a point of light shining in his face. He stared up at the source of the light.

"Outside . . . it's a way outside," he said. He stood up and tried to get as close a look as he could. "Yes, yes . . . Alec, Alec, wake up, wake up, man." He shook Alec's leg.

"What? What is it?"

"Look." Tremaine pointed to the light from the sky.

Alec sat up and smiled. "Do you think it's a way out?"

"I don't know, but that light has to be coming from outside. I'm going to find out what's up there." Tremaine walked to a point just beneath the light and looked up. He noticed an old ladder made of dried rope and rotten wood. "This was another way in and out," he shouted. He woke Isadora and Kathleen.

Isadora looked up at Tremaine with great concern. "What are you doing?" she asked.

Kathleen stood up and watched as Tremaine pulled on

the ladder to see how strong it was. He gave it a couple of big tugs and then allowed his weight to hang from the rope.

"It seems sturdy," he said.

"What are you doing, Tremaine?" Isadora asked again.

"Issi, this looks like a way out." He pointed to the top.

She walked over to see the stream of light shining through. "I don't know, Tremaine, it looks dangerous," she said.

"More dangerous than this?" replied Kathleen as she looked around the cave. "I think we should try. The question is, can Alec make it? He's still hurting."

"I can make it; we have to try," Alec said.

Tremaine took hold of the rope. He started to climb the ladder. But the first piece of rotten wood gave way and he stumbled. He gathered himself and yanked on the rope again. *It seems ok*, he thought.

Isadora had a terrible feeling about this. This was not going to be an easy climb, and she feared for his life. She stood back and watched as Tremaine climbed the wall holding onto a piece of dried rope.

Tremaine was careful to place his feet onto solid rock as he ascended the wall. The three-story climb was slow and fearful. The closer he got to the top, the more nervous he became.

Alec's heart started to pound when Tremaine stepped on some loose rock and almost lost his grip.

"I'm all right," he yelled as he regained his footing. He looked up at the light. *Just a few more feet,* he thought. The rock was looser the closer to the top he got. It became more and more difficult to anchor himself steady. He held onto the rope and pulled himself up until he reached the top.

"There are wood planks closing off the entrance," he yelled. He anchored himself against the wall and pushed upward to loosen the wood from its base. The planks were rotting and came away without much effort.

Alec, Kathleen, and Isadora could see the sky. They were happy to see the outside, but they were all frightened about making that climb.

Tremaine moved all the wood out of the way and decided to climb outside. "I'm going to take a look," he yelled.

Isadora got a strange feeling. "No, Tremaine. Wait," she yelled, just as he stepped onto some loose rock and began to fumble.

He tried to hold onto the rope, but felt his hands slipping away. His body thrashed against the rocks and caused great pain. His scream was alarming, and Alec moved closer to the rope.

"Hold on, dammit, hold on," yelled Alec. He held the rope steady to keep Tremaine from swinging around, but it didn't help. He lost his grip and he couldn't hold on.

Tremaine knew that this was the moment of his death. He knew he would not survive the fall. He freed his mind of all worldly things as he fell toward the ground. He looked up at the sky as it got farther and farther away. His heart said good-bye to his mother and great-grandfather and his friend Alec.

Alec panicked. He wanted to catch him, but knew he probably couldn't. "No, no, no," he yelled. It seemed to Alec that his heart stopped. He seemed to be looking down at Tremaine from the top of the cave and willed him to stop. He closed his eyes because he couldn't watch. "STOP," he yelled in a tone so demanding that the walls vibrated.

Kathleen looked around and saw stones crumbling apart and falling from the wall.

Isadora never took her eyes off of Tremaine. She was shocked when she saw him hanging in mid-air. Alec's inner strength had stopped him from falling. He lay suspended about two feet from the ground.

Tremaine waited for the impact and his last breath, but it didn't happen. He was alive and scared. He opened his eyes and was amazed at the feeling of weightlessness. "What the hell happened?" he asked.

Kathleen laughed and danced around. She was so happy. "How did you do that?" she asked as she giggled and laughed.

Alec could not speak. He was holding onto Tremaine with his mind until he was sure he was safe. He was motionless and quiet.

Isadora placed her hand on his back, and he took a deep breath, which released his hold on Tremaine. Tremaine fell the two feet and lay on the ground wondering what just happened.

Alec fell to the ground. It drained him of all his energy. He couldn't stand. Kathleen helped him to a cool spot out of the sunlight.

Tremaine was still gathering himself when he realized that something was wrong with Alec. He ran to him and watched him slip away. "Is he alive? Is he?" cried Tremaine.

Kathleen checked his pulse and his eyes.

"Yes, but he's unconscious. We'll have to wait and hope that he'll be all right. There isn't much we can do for him in here," she said as she walked over to the light where Tremaine hung like a puppet on a string and wondered how Alec did that.

They knew they couldn't go anywhere until Alec regained consciousness, so they tried to rest, knowing they would need it to take the long climb to the top.

After a few hours, Alec began to move around. He was regaining consciousness and didn't remember the event that saved Tremaine's life. He opened his eyes and screamed when he remembered that Tremaine had fallen to his death.

Kathleen ran to his side and knelt down beside him. "It's all right, Alec, it's all right," she whispered.

He cried helplessly until he looked up and saw Tremaine standing in front of him. He couldn't believe his eyes, but he was so happy, he didn't care how it happened. "You're alive," he cried.

"Yes, thanks to you," he said as he took Alec's hand.

Kathleen helped him sit up, and they all took a deep breath and gave thanks to God for seeing them through this ordeal.

They waited a few more hours and decided to make the climb.

Tremaine took the lead and told them, "Step where I step, and don't look down."

One at a time, they slowly followed him up the cave wall and out onto the hard, dry dirt that never felt so good.

The night air was brisk and cool. The stars in the night sky hung low and vast. They appeared so close, it seemed they could reach up and pick one like an apple from a tree. A solemn mood hovered around them. The journey had just begun, and already it had taken its toll on them.

Alec's leg pained with every step, and his arm hung in a sling made from his belt, which was wrapped around his neck. Kathleen's ankle was still swollen, so she limped along as best as she could. Tremaine tried to help her whenever he could.

They walked for several hours. The uphill climb became harder and harder as the mountain became more steep and the air more thin. Tremaine and Alec wondered where they were going and if there was another way to get there. They made eye contact with each other every so often, as if they could read each other's thoughts.

Kathleen stopped and looked back at Alec. "So, are you going to talk about it or not?" she asked abruptly.

"No," he said without looking up from the ground.

"No? No . . . what do you mean no? I think it deserves some explanation. I mean, where did that come from? Could you do it all the time? What else can you do?"

He never looked up. He walked past her as if she wasn't there.

"Alec," she yelled.

He stopped and looked back at her. He wanted her to stop, but knew that she wouldn't until he spoke of it. "Look, I don't know. What do you want me to say? I don't know, Kathleen. I really don't remember what happened. I know I wanted him to stop falling, and I must have willed it. I didn't see it. I was there, but wasn't. I can't explain it. I wanted him to stop, and he did. I only know what you told me. I can't remember." The wrinkles in his forehead evidenced his agitation.

He just wanted to forget about it, but she wouldn't let it go. "Kathleen, I don't mean to be cross with you, but this is all just a little overwhelming, don't you think? And I'm scared to death about what could happen next. Remember, Issi said that things are different here and there may be things we can do now that we couldn't do before. Let's just get past it," he said as he turned and continued the slow, arduous uphill climb.

"Where are we going?" Tremaine looked at Isadora, hoping she could explain the purpose for such a hard and tiring journey. He knew the higher they went, the harder it was going to be on Alec. He was very concerned, and he wanted to know if there could be another way.

"There are stories that a village of people live atop these mountains who have the power to move through objects and space and time like light through a prism.

They can exist here and there simultaneously. They may be able to find what you are seeking," she said.

Alec stopped and looked back at Isadora with concern. Tremaine saw him and stopped.

Kathleen, being in her own world, kept going a few feet before she realized that she was alone. She stopped and looked back. "What's going on?" she asked as she walked back toward Alec. She looked in his face and could see his bewilderment about something. "What is it, Alec?"

He looked at Isadora. "I don't recall telling you what we were looking for. In fact, I don't recall any of us telling you that we were looking for anything. How do you know these people can help, when you don't know what we need help with?" He waited for her response.

She stared back at him and began to smile. "Well, it seems that you do not trust me. That's okay; I wouldn't trust me either under the circumstances. But you see, it does not matter if I know, only if *they* know. I know that you are looking for something, or why else would you be here? I don't need to know what it is."

"How do you know they can help, if you don't know what it is?" asked Kathleen.

"They are very close to the source of knowledge and wisdom. They are not like us, and there will be little you can hide from them. Their source of knowledge will lead you to what you seek. They will know where it is and what it will take to get it."

She looked into Alec's face as she walked past him. She didn't look back because she knew that Alec was not happy with her answer. She wanted to move away from the question and any curiosity about her.

They walked for a while longer until Kathleen's ankle was hurting so badly, she couldn't go on. "I have to stop. I have to let this leg heal a little." She limped to the base of a rock and sat down.

Isadora stooped down beside her and checked her ankle. "It's really swollen. We may have to figure out a way to carry you like we did Alec. It could be days before this heals."

"Let's put an ice pack on it and wait out the rest of the night. We need to find a place to settle in," said Alec.

Isadora looked ahead and found an open area away from the edge of the cliff. Tremaine helped Kathleen climb, and they all found a spot on the ground and tried to rest. Alec pulled an ice pack from his backpack and wrapped Kathleen's leg with it. She cringed a little from the cold, but she knew it would help the swelling.

"Alec," said Isadora, "you know you still have to face your fears. I don't want you to get too complacent about it. You have to work this out, or you will never be free."

"You don't think those animals can come back, do you?" asked Tremaine.

Isadora's eyes locked onto Alec's.

Alec knew she was right, but also he knew he couldn't just let go of years of guilt overnight. He didn't want to dwell on it. He had managed to control his thoughts and was hoping he would keep them away until this journey was over. He didn't say anything. He looked at Isadora sadly and turned and walked back to check on Kathleen.

"How are you doing?" he asked.

"I'll live," she said. She understood his fight with himself and wished she could do something to help, but she knew she couldn't. He was trying, and she knew it. "I'll be all right, Alec. Somehow we'll deal with it, but for now, try not to think about it."

"Yes, I guess that would be best." He found a spot and sat down.

"Yeah, man, don't think about it," Tremaine nervously said.

He was obviously frightened, but the look on his face

was so funny, Alec and Kathleen looked at each other and burst into laughter.

Isadora looked back at them and couldn't figure out what was funny, but was pleased that they were laughing.

"What? What's funny? This isn't funny," said Tremaine. He couldn't understand what they were laughing at because none of this had been funny so far.

"Let's try to rest. We'll have a long day tomorrow," said Isadora. She found a spot on the ground and settled down for the evening.

The nights were starting to get cool. The further up the mountain they climbed, the colder it got. Soon there will be snow to deal with, and none of them were experienced climbers.

Alec was really concerned about being able to make this journey, and he was even more concerned about Kathleen. He knew they had a long way to go, and he wondered if either of them was really up to it.

They were exhausted, so falling asleep was easy. They all slept soundly.

The sound of thunder roaring through the morning sky woke Isadora. She sat up and looked around at the trees swaying in the cool breeze and the gray clouds moving by. The sound of thunder cracked through the sky again.

Alec and Kathleen looked and saw a huge dark cloud moving toward them.

"What is that?" Alec asked.

"I don't know, but it doesn't look good." Isadora tried to distinguish the dark cloud from the others moving through the sky. "What was everyone thinking about? What's on your mind, Alec?"

"It's not me. I don't think. Unless I dreamt something crazy, but I can't control that," he said.

"No, no, it's happening now. Someone is—" She looked at Tremaine, who was still fast asleep. "Tremaine," she yelled. "Tremaine." She walked toward him.

He turned over and sat up and looked into her face. He knew it was bad, and looked over at Alec.

"What were you dreaming about?" she asked.

"My father, I was thinking about my father."

"Tremaine, you hate your father. I've never heard you say a kind thing about him," said Alec.

"Oh God, not hate, please don't let us have to deal with hate. We have to move, we have to move now."

Isadora looked up and saw the cloud getting closer and closer. It was dark and ominous. She knew this was the worst of all emotions. It would be the hardest one to destroy.

Tremaine never knew himself without this emotion, so he had no idea who he was without it. He didn't know what his life would be like without it. He had to forgive his father, just like Alec had to let go of the guilt.

Guilt would destroy whoever harbored it, but this hate was something different. Isadora had hoped desperately that this would not be one of the emotions that she would have to deal with, but there it was, and it was strong. It could not only kill Tremaine, but possibly all of them in their effort to save him. It was the cruelest of all, and would not stop until Tremaine let it go or died.

They grabbed their gear and tried to get a head start to the horror that they knew would be upon them soon. They started to run. They weren't sure if they were going up or down, but it didn't matter. They ran aimlessly until they heard the foulest sound they'd ever heard. The deep, gut-wrenching sound was bone-chilling.

It was the most frightening sound Tremaine could hear, the most evil side of him. He knew it was him. He could hear the tone of his own voice underneath the growling animal that chased him.

"I am here," it said as he began to follow them furiously.

He did not run, he did not try to catch them. He walked with the will of a thousand men as if going into battle, a battle he knew he could win. Tremaine looked back to see the hideous creature. He screamed at the sight of it and fell to his knees.

Alec ran to him. "No, Tremaine, we have to go. Please don't falter on me now. We need you, I need you. Please, Tremaine, please come on," Alec pleaded as he pulled Tremaine to his feet.

The horror was gaining ground and would soon be upon them. Alec knew he could not leave Tremaine, so if he died today, so would Alec.

Without realizing, they ran downhill. The terrain turned more green and wooded. As they came off the mountain, an open field lay ahead of them. They did not see any place to hide. The forest was on the other side of the field, and somehow they had to get there before the creature got to them.

Without saying a word, they all started running for the trees. It seemed to be an endless struggle. Tremaine felt such hopelessness. He wondered if he should just let it take him. He was so tired of being miserable and afraid of what the next day would bring until it seemed a fitting way to end his life.

Isadora looked back and could see it gaining on them. She knew that Tremaine was feeding it and making it stronger with every step. Its face was scarred with life and disfigured from carrying the weight of hate, disappointment, and dismay. It gained strength from Tremaine's weakness. It fought Tremaine for its very life. It taunted Tremaine for his whole life, and now he had an opportunity to kill it and be free of the weakness and pity that held him back.

"Tremaine, think of something pleasant. Try . . . think of your mother, girlfriend, anything. You have to try, or it will kill you," yelled Isadora.

The frightening sound came from behind them. "That will not free you. I am more than a thought. I am more than an emotion, I am who he is."

They reached the forest and darted inside, hoping it would give them some cover. They kept running. Tremaine could feel his heart pounding. He felt as if he were lifted from the moment and could see beyond the world that surrounded him. Everything seemed unreal and dream-like. He felt as if his body was looking down on the events taking place. He recognized it as the moment of his death. He was not afraid and wondered if he would go to the white room with no time, where he met Isadora. *Maybe we can be together forever*, he thought.

Without realizing it, he began to slow down. He found himself behind everyone else and decided to face his self. Tremaine turned, and suddenly the horror stood before him. Its bulging eyes and crooked teeth snarled beneath its disfigured face and malformed body. The creature resembled Tremaine, and he could see that he and it were one, but the horror of looking into those hollow eyes and that desperate stare brought fear to his heart. Not a fear of dying, but the fear of its survival.

If I die, does this die too?

The creature's gnarled hand reached up and grabbed Tremaine's neck and lifted him from the ground. Tremaine gasped for air and tried to free himself when the creature flung him twenty feet against a tree. Tremaine cringed from the pain. He didn't think he could take another hit and survive.

He managed to stand and could see the creature coming toward him, when a hand grabbed his shirt and pulled him forward. He was in excruciating pain, but when he saw Alec's face, he knew he had to try. He kept up as best he could while they ran through the forest. The trees were thick, and climbing over fallen trees and through the underlying brush made the struggle twice as hard. But the worst was yet to come, for when they reached the edge of the forest, it was a few feet from what seemed to be the edge of the world.

The gorge was long and deep. They could barely hear the ranging water at the bottom that probably carved out the huge gap millions of years ago; the gap that stood in between life and death.

He turned and saw the creature coming toward him. Tremaine was more afraid for his friends than himself. He thought about how beautiful this place was and how clear the sky seemed. He was taking it all in as if it would be the last thing he would ever see. He looked at Alec and Kathleen and smiled and studied Isadora's pretty face. He smiled and moved close to the edge.

Alec could tell that something was wrong. The look on Tremaine's face was calm and peaceful, and Alec knew that look meant trouble. He looked back and saw the creature getting closer, and he looked back at Tremaine, knowing Tremaine was planning to give his life to save theirs. He couldn't let that happen. He had to stop this creature somehow. He positioned himself in between the creature and Tremaine and made a stand. He heard Tremaine yell his name just as the creature effortlessly lifted him from the ground and tossed him aside. He came back and pushed his body into it full force and managed to shove him back a little, but not enough to make it stop.

"Run, run," Alec yelled as he felt the creature's hand around his throat. He struggled to breathe, but he wanted to buy them some time to get ahead of it. The creature threw him again. He knew he would not have too many more chances at this.

"Hurry," he yelled. He could see them rushing to find a way down as he made one last attempt to stop the creature. His body ached from head to toe, but he managed to pick up a large stick and strike the creature across its back.

It yelled horribly, but it was not deterred. It turned toward Alec, agitated by his persistence.

Alec backed up as the creature came toward him. He couldn't watch behind himself, so he eventually backed up until he fell over a fallen tree. He lay on the ground looking up at this horrible creature, hoping that they had gotten away.

The creature leaned over him and raised his arm. Alec tried to gain his footing, but he was struck so hard across his face that he fell against a log and passed out.

Kathleen stopped running. She looked back. "Nooooo," she yelled. She knew Alec was hurt, and she also knew it was all in vain because the creature would never stop, no matter what they did. She started to run back, but she stopped when she saw the creature coming toward them.

Tremaine and Isadora stopped and watched as it passed Kathleen and walked toward them.

Kathleen turned to Tremaine and yelled, "Tremaine, you've got to let it go. You've got to forgive your father. You can't hate him anymore. You've got to let it go."

The creature stopped to listen to Kathleen's pleading.

"Is that what you think I am, hate for his father?" The creature turned and looked into Kathleen's eyes. It smiled and then laughed loudly. "It's not only about his father. Forgiving him would mean nothing. This is about the hate he carries for himself. He loathes himself, and as long as he does, I will exist and I will continue to destroy him long after this life." It looked into Tremaine's eyes.

"You see, I am the best part of you. I am the part you have been feeding your whole life. I am your reason for living. Without me, you are no one."

"Don't listen to it," cried Isadora. "It's not true, and deep down inside, you know it's not true."

Tremaine backed up as far as he could. He looked behind him at the river that looked like a tiny stream rushing below and looked back at Isadora and Kathleen.

"If I die, will it die too?" he asked Isadora.

"Yes," she said, "but that's not the answer. It's not what you want to do. You have to let it go, Tremaine. If you die without forgiving, it will live through eternity. You will carry it from one existence to the other. You have to let it go," she pleaded.

The creature laughed. "But you can't." It reached for Tremaine and swung to grab him just as Tremaine stepped off the cliff and fell.

The creature laughed. "He will die hating, and I will live eternally." It turned and walked past Isadora, who stepped back. The creature stopped and stared at her. She stepped back again, hoping to distance herself from its wrath. "I have no more need of you," it said as it turned and walked past Kathleen and Alec. It looked down and watched Kathleen care for Alec's injuries and wondered why it mattered.

"Let him die. He deserves it just like you do." It snickered and walked by.

Isadora walked over to Kathleen and kneeled down. "Something's wrong," she whispered to Kathleen as they both watched the creature meander around.

Kathleen couldn't stop crying. "It was all for nothing, for nothing," she cried.

"No, Kathleen, listen. It should have disappeared as soon as Tremaine died. It should be dead too, but it's not. Why not?"

"Yes, you're right. I don't understand, it should be—oh God, he's not dead." Kathleen realized what Isadora was alluding to and was delighted at the thought of Tremaine still being alive, but worried about the extent of his injuries and what would happen when the creature realized it.

"Tremaine," Alec moaned.

"Alec, Alec, lay still, don't move," said Kathleen as he leaned over him and tried to keep him calm. She wiped his forehead.

He opened his eyes and tried to focus. "Tremaine, is he—"

"Don't talk, just rest for a moment," she said. The worried look on her face deepened his worst fear.

"Is he dead?" he asked as he struggled to sit up.

"I don't know," she answered, "but I'm going to find out. Now lay back."

She walked toward Isadora and watched the creature move about. It seemed harmless now, as if it too was uncertain of its next move and was waiting for something to happen.

"I have to go down there," said Kathleen. "I have to find out."

Isadora looked into her eyes intently and held her hands tightly. She knew that Kathleen probably wouldn't make it down the cliff before the creature realized that she was missing and why.

"Maybe it should be me. Isn't your ankle bothering you?" asked Isadora.

"No, no, it's much better now. I'll do it. I'll go," insisted Kathleen.

"All right, you go and I'll stay with Alec. Please be very careful," said Isadora.

Kathleen smiled. She could tell that Isadora was genuinely worried, but she also knew it had to be done. She never trusted Isadora completely. She always felt that there was something too mysterious about her, but now, she seemed so caring. *Maybe I was wrong and she really is looking out for us*, she thought.

"I know I'm no spring chicken, but I feel that I have to try," said Kathleen.

Isadora gently touched her shoulder as she slipped out of sight unnoticed. Isadora went to Alec and tried to make him comfortable while Kathleen tried to maneuver herself down the cliff. She had to walk dangerously close to the edge in some places. She clung to the wall of rock that was between her and the edge as she inched her way down. She held onto whatever was in her path that provided some stability. She stepped carefully and prayed with every step. She was more worried about Tremaine than herself. She tried to stay focused on what she was doing and why, no matter how hard it got. She came to a very narrow ledge that stopped her. Her heart pounded as she studied the gap between where she was and where she needed to be.

How do I get across? There's got to be a way.

She looked all around and saw a large notch in the rock. If she could hold onto it, she may be able to reach the other side. While she was thinking about it, she knew her chances of making it were slim to none. As fast as she talked herself into it, she talked herself out of it.

She looked up, closed her eyes. "Please God," she whispered and reached up and felt the notch in the stone. She got a good grip. She opened her eyes and grabbed the notch with her other hand and came up onto her toes. She slowly tiptoed across the uneven ledge and took a deep breath with every step. She held onto the notch as tightly as she could while she slid her hands and feet until she reached the end of the notch and couldn't go any farther. She had about three feet left to bridge before she could let go. She started to panic. Her heart was racing as she became more and more afraid. She stretched her leg as far as she could, but it wasn't enough; she couldn't reach the other side. She could jump, but she didn't think she would be able to land steady, and the slightest mistake would be deadly. She leaped to the other side and tried to get her footing. She grabbed the rock wall and held on so tight that her fingers bled. She cried for help just as she lost her footing and the ground beneath her gave way and she fell. She knew that this was it, and she wanted to be at peace with it. With her back to the wind, she stretched out her arms and soared through the air.

Isadora's heart sank. She knew something was wrong when she heard the faint cry. She ran to the edge to look for her, but she saw no one. She knew Kathleen was in trouble, but how or why, she couldn't tell.

Kathleen fell into the wind. She seemed to be floating as the wind wrapped around her as if to protect her from the fall. She closed her eyes and let the wind carry her. She didn't know if she was imagining the experience as part of her death journey or if it was real. She seemed to see the light of angels around her phasing in and out of existence, just like the wolves did that attacked Alec. It was so beautiful, she was not afraid. She didn't want this feeling to end.

Just as she accepted that the angels had come for her, she hit the water and started to sink. She swam to the surface and caught her breath. She was elated that she was alive and had a chance to find Tremaine before the creature did. She swam to the river's edge and pulled herself out of the water. She lay on the ground and tried to catch her breath. She knew she didn't have much time, so she forced herself up and started looking around for Tremaine.

What if the river took him downstream? she thought.

She walked along the shore of the river for more than an hour before she saw him. He was lying just at the river's edge, and she could see that he was breathing, but barely. She ran with all her might to get to him, but then she heard the scream, the scream of the creature when it realized that Tremaine was not dead.

She looked back and saw the creature leap from the cliff as if it had wings to fly and landed on the ground feet first without wavering for a second. It started to walk toward her, and she knew it would kill her to get to him. Fear was not the answer right now.

Just as it lurched toward her, she waved her hands in front of it and stopped it. It seemed to be behind some kind of force field or glass wall. She could see it as clear as day, but it could not reach her. It tried earnestly. It scratched and clawed at the invisible wall, but could not move it. It ran up and down, but could not get around it. It was powerless, and that made it more and more angry. Hate is usually in power. It usually determines your every thought, and now the creature was trapped and helpless. "Hate, my God, it's a horrible thing."

She turned her attention back to Tremaine and walked toward him. As she got closer, she saw a man standing nearby. She didn't know if he meant Tremaine harm or not. He didn't appear angry or cruel; in fact, there was something serene about him. She slowed her pace and watched intently. She looked back to make sure the creature was still secured, and it was, so she kept walking toward him.

The man was tall with black hair. He kneeled down beside Tremaine and stroked his brow. "Tremaine, my son, please do not hate me."

Tremaine opened his eyes and looked into the face of his father. This was the man he had hated all of his life, and now he kneeled beside him and lovingly spoke with the tenderness of a father.

"Father . . . father, is that you?"

"Tremaine, you cannot hate me without hurting yourself. It is not right that you carry this burden. The fault is not yours. I was not a good man. The best thing that I could have done for you was to leave you. I would have caused great pain to you and your mother, and you would be a much different person had I stayed."

The tall, fair-skinned man with dark green eyes helped Tremaine to sit up.

"You could have tried. You could have loved us more. I am your son, why didn't you love me enough? You didn't want me, why?" Tremaine cried.

"I will always love you, but I was not as strong as you. I was not half the man you are. I love you, still I just could not give you what you needed to become the man that you are," he said.

"The man that I am? I'm a thief. I steal whatever I can. I grew up horribly because of you," cried Tremaine.

"No . . . you are the man I have always wanted to be. What you are doing for your friend takes great courage. You needed to find your way, but your heart always held the courage that would make you strong and powerful. I am sorry that I could not be who you wanted me to be, but it's not your fault. I wasn't worth much before you were born, so you can't blame yourself. It is because of me that you hate yourself, and you shouldn't. You are everything I hoped you would become. Please, son, forgive me, forgive yourself, and let it go." He held Tremaine in his arms and let him cry. "I have to go, but I am never far from you. Remember that I had to be who I was, but you don't have to be me. You must be of your nature, not mine. Let it go." He tried to stand as Tremaine held onto him.

"No, Father, please don't leave me."

"Tremaine, I am always with you," he said as he stood and started to back away. "I am always with you."

Tremaine stood and reached out to him.

"I love you, Father."

"I love you too." He faded into the trees just as the last piercing scream was heard from the creature as it phased out of existence.

"Tremaine," Kathleen cried as she ran to him. She threw her arms around him and hugged him. "Boy, you scared us half to death. Don't you ever jump off cliffs like that again."

He laughed. He looked into her eyes. "It's gone, the hate is gone. My father was here. He spoke to me, and he's proud of me. Isn't that something? He's proud of me. Maybe I'm not such a bad person after all."

"I know. I saw," she said as he laid his head on her shoulder. "Are you all right? Can you walk?" she asked.

"Yes, I can walk. Can we get back to Alec? How is he?"

"Don't know, but he wasn't looking too good. He's been through a lot. We won't make it back tonight. We've got to find a way to let them know that we're all right," said Kathleen.

"I don't know how." He looked around. "We need to find a place to rest for the night," said Tremaine.

"Let's stay out in the open, near the river. We can rest right here," said Kathleen as she found a spot close to the trees and sat down.

Tremaine followed and found a spot nearby and lay down and watched the sunset turn into a blanket of stars.

Isadora sat beside Alec and watched him sleep. She knew she couldn't leave him to go find Kathleen and Tremaine, so she decided to settle in for the night. She found some brush and sticks and made a pile for a fire. She gently blew over the pile and watched as a small flame began to grow into a warm glowing fire. She looked at Alec and laid her hand on his forehead.

"You have suffered enough," she said as she closed her eyes and let her warm healing powers flow through her hand into Alec's broken body.

His broken bones and bleeding cuts began to heal. His scars and bruises faded away, and his vital signs returned to normal while he slept. He was unaware of what was happening to him. She knew he would not survive the night, and without him, the journey was all in vain.

"You rest now, and we will begin again in the morning." She walked to the edge of the cliff and looked down. "They are fine. I know they are. I can feel it." She walked back to Alec, who slept soundly, and found a spot nearby to lie down. She looked up at the stars for a moment as she drifted to sleep.

The night moved by swiftly, and Tremaine wanted to sleep longer, but Kathleen kept poking him and demanding that he get up.

"Come on, Tremaine. We have to go."

"I'm coming," he said as he turned over and tried to grab one more minute.

"I know you're tired, Tremaine, but Alec is hurt and we need to get moving."

"Alec." Tremaine jumped up. "I forgot, he's hurt. I'm ready." Tremaine brushed himself off and started walking.

Kathleen followed until they reached the bottom of the cliff. Tremaine started up the same path she came down.

"We can't go that way," she said.

"Why?" He looked back at her.

"I came this way. I didn't make it."

He wondered how that could be, because she was standing right in front of him.

She could tell from the look on his face that he didn't understand. "There's a huge gap along the ledge that was too wide for me to cross, and I couldn't jump it."

"So, what did you do?"

"I tried, but I didn't make it and I fell."

"Kathleen, if you fell, you should be dead."

"I know, but somehow, I was carried down by the wind, or—"

"Or what?" He looked at her suspiciously

"Or angels held me."

"Ok, that's good. Angels." He took a deep breath and turned and started uphill.

"No, Tremaine, we can't go that way."

"If the angels took care of you once, maybe they'll do it again."

"I don't know. I don't think I should take that chance, and besides, the angels probably saved you too. How do you think you survived the fall? Hell, you're the one that should be dead."

"Maybe you're right. I wondered that myself, but decided not to look a gift horse in the mouth. Isadora said that we have powers here. Maybe flying is one of them."

"No, I didn't fly. Someone or something helped me, and I don't want to test them, so I'm not going to try it again. I'm going up the other side." Kathleen started walking toward the other side of the large cliff that protruded out from the mountainous wall.

"How did you stop the creature? You knew I was going to ask sooner or later." Tremaine walked beside her, but didn't look up from the ground. He wasn't sure that he really wanted to know, but obviously, something miraculous happened.

"I wanted it to stop, and I raised my hands in front of it, and my mind just kept saying, 'No, you will not harm him, no, no,' and the next thing I knew it was trapped behind this invisible wall. I suppose I willed it."

"Wow. I guess I owe you one."

"Yeah, I guess so." She grabbed his arm and held on.

They smiled at each other and prepared themselves for the long uphill climb and the possibility that Alec didn't make it through the night.

Alec awoke feeling fresh and revived from a good night's sleep. He didn't understand why or how he was still alive, but he was glad. He stood and could see that Isadora was already up and planning their next move.

"Good morning," he said .

"Hello, Alec. Are you feeling better today?"

"Much, much better, I'm not sure why. I should be dead." He looked at her, hoping to get an answer, but she said nothing.

She turned and looked out over the cliff. "There's been no word about Tremaine," she said.

"Where's Kathleen and the creature?"

"She went looking for Tremaine. We realized when the creature didn't disappear that Tremaine may be still alive, so she went downhill to find him. The creature soon figured it out and jumped the gorge to find him."

"What happened?"

"I don't know." She stared down, hoping to see any movement.

"Well, then I guess we are going to find out." Alec started down the same path that Kathleen took.

"I don't think we should go that way. I think Kathleen had problems."

"What kind of problems?"

"I don't know, but I heard her scream, or at least I thought I did."

"Either way, we will find out," he said as he started walking downhill.

It wasn't long before Alec and Isadora came across the same gap in the ledge that Kathleen encountered.

"We'll make it," he said. "I'll go first."

Alec's long legs were barely able to bridge the gap. He stretched his tall frame across the rock face and held onto a branch protruding out of the rock to stabilize himself. He was frightened, but he couldn't let her see it. He pulled himself to the other side and leaned against the cliff wall. He caught his breath and looked across the gap at her.

"Are you ready?" he asked as he reached out his hand.

She nodded. "Take my hand and jump. I will hold onto this branch and it will help to keep me stable. I won't drop you, I promise."

She looked into his eyes and jumped. She grabbed his hand, and he pulled her to the other side. She had made it.

Alec held onto the branch and looked up at the sky. He was thankful she'd made it without a problem. He was shaken and was getting tired of this struggle. *Too many lives*, he thought. *Too many lives.*

"What was that?" Tremaine stopped when she heard what sounded like a scream. "Did you hear that?"

"Yes, I don't know what it could be," said Kathleen.

"It sounded like Issi. She's in trouble. I have to help her." He turned and started to walk back down the hill.

"What about Alec?" Kathleen stared at him.

He looked back at her and saw the concern in her eyes. Isadora had touched his heart, but Alec was his friend and had risked his life for him more than once. He was reminded quickly what should come first. He turned back and started back uphill.

"You're right, let's check on Alec first." His heart was torn, but he knew that this whole venture was about Alec and if anything happened to him, everything would be lost.

They walked for thirty more minutes and finally reached the location where Isadora and Alec should have been. They looked around but there was nothing.

"Where are they?" Tremaine asked.

"I don't know, but there was no way Alec could have walked out of here. He was badly beaten. He never could have made it down," said Kathleen.

"They must have tried somehow," replied Tremaine. "They went this way." He looked down the same path that Kathleen took and, through the grace of God, survived.

"Oh no. Then that was Isadora that you heard. There's no way she made it across that gap . . . no way, she's shorter than me. She didn't make it."

"If she fell, maybe the wind carried her down too. She may be all right," he said.

"So, what do we do?" she asked.

"We go back down." He turned and started the long walk back down.

Kathleen looked at him and saw that he was headed for the same direction she took. "You are such a man, so hardheaded. Read my lips, we are not going that way. We may not be as lucky this time. I'm not taking any chances." She headed for the longer but safer path down the other side.

As Tremaine and Kathleen made their way down, Alec was trying to hold on to Isadora as they made their way downhill. Alec was determined that her death would not be on his hands. He was carrying enough guilt with all the deaths caused by Torrin, he couldn't bear to lose Tremaine, possibly Kathleen, and now he held Isadora's life in his hands too. It was too much. He knew his emotions were getting the better of him. He tried, but all he could think about was his responsibility for everything. All of this was because of his family, his need to set things right, his problem, and now, as far as he knew, Tremaine and Kathleen could be dead.

Isadora could feel that something was wrong. She could feel his emotions raging. "No, Alec! You can't go there, not now. Do you see where we are? Do you think we will have any chance of survival if your demons show up now? Please, Alec, please. Let it go. You have to know that this is not your fault. You did not cause this; you are trying to correct a long-standing wrong that was caused by someone else. He was your ancestor, not you. You are not Torrin. Let it go," she demanded.

She couldn't be firmer with him, and in his mind he knew she was right, but his heart was hurting. When he finally saw the bottom, he started to calm down. He thought about Tremaine and Kathleen, and finding them became paramount. They looked all around. They searched up and down the shoreline, but they didn't see anyone.

"Do you see anything?" she asked.

"No, maybe the river washed them downstream a little," said Alec as he started walking down the river's edge.

They didn't say anything, but they were both thinking that Kathleen could not have made it down the ledge and that she may have fallen into the river and was washed away. And Tremaine, well, the creature probably destroyed him. They wanted to believe the impossible, but it was hard, and no matter how much Alec tried, he could not let go. The fear of losing them gripped his heart, and he became more and more scared the farther they walked down the river. He stopped and turned and looked back at Isadora.

"I'm sorry," he said. His sadness was overwhelming, and Isadora knew she could not stop him, but she tried.

"Whose fault is it, Alec?" she yelled.

He started backing away from her, to separate the onslaught from her.

"Whose fault is it, Alec?"

He couldn't speak. He could hear the sounds in the distance. It was a familiar sound, and he knew the outcome. He didn't try to run this time. He wasn't going to fight. He accepted the outcome and kept separating himself from her.

"You coward, you coward, how dare you? We put ourselves through all of this so you can accept defeat. What was all of this for? You know this isn't your fault, but you readily accept it because you want to live in the misery of it. You have lived with it for so long, you don't know how life could be without the weight and pain of it. You would die and leave us alone."

"Us, what us? You're the only one left, and if anyone will survive, it will be you. There is no us," he cried.

"And what about the souls in the well? You intend to join them? Well now, that's just heavenly, don't you think, to live your eternity trapped in a wall? Well, if you don't care about yourself, care about them. Stop thinking of yourself for once and think of them," she yelled.

"I am thinking of them, that's why I came in the first place."

"Then why are you giving up now? It's all about you and how you feel. You like being in this horrible place; you are comfortable there. That's why you never tried to find out about this years ago, because it would have freed you from your blanket of misery that you love so much. If you really accept that this isn't your fault, you won't have that woe-is-me factor to lean on. Stop victimizing yourself and let it go. WHOSE FAULT IS IT?" she yelled.

The sounds were getting closer. Alec kept backing up farther and farther.

Kathleen and Tremaine could hear the sounds and knew that Alec was alive and that he was allowing himself to feel the unrelenting guilt that had plagued him forever.

They began to run downhill and finally made it to the bottom. Tremaine could see the enraged gray-and-white wolves phasing in and out of existence, forming horrible images of grimacing teeth and fierce red and yellow eyes. They were ferocious, and their intent was deadly.

Tremaine started running, and Kathleen followed and tried to reach Alec first, but it was too late. They stopped when they saw Alec standing against a cliff, as if waiting to be violated.

They could hear Isadora yelling, "WHOSE FAULT IS IT, ALEC? WHOSE FAULT IS IT?"

"NOOOOOO!" yelled Tremaine as he watched the wolves leap toward Alec in a mad frenzy.

When Alec heard Tremaine's voice, he dropped to his knees and yelled, "IT'S NOT MY FAULT, it's not my fault, it's not my fault. I didn't cause this."

He kneeled on the ground and watched as the wolves leaped toward him. He prepared himself to die, but instead he watched the wolves phase in and out and suddenly out of existence. They were gone, and he had this overwhelming feeling of peace. For the first time he felt that this really was not his fault and that he did not have to carry the shame for Torrin's actions ever again. He forgave Torrin. In that instant, he realized that Torrin had been deceived and that he would have made a different choice if he had understood the truth.

"I understand now. It wasn't your fault either. You didn't know. You made the only choice you had, and you didn't know. I'm sorry," he whispered to Torrin as he embraced the memory of this great-great-grandfather for the first time.

"Alec," Tremaine yelled.

They ran as fast as they could. Tremaine was so frightened. When he saw the wolves, he was certain that he had lost his friend forever.

When Alec heard Tremaine he could not contain his joy. He walked toward them and fell to his knees. He couldn't take another step. He was so relieved to hear the sound of his friend's voice that it made all of what just happened seem distant and small. He was so thankful, he threw his arms around them and cried.

Isadora stood back and watched.

Tremaine looked back at her and realized that he was just as happy to see her alive, because he was afraid that she had fallen from the cliff. He walked to her and gave her a big hug.

"For a moment, we thought we had lost you too." He smiled.

"For a moment, I thought so too." She looked into his eyes and gently kissed his cheek.

He smiled and held her close, and knew that his heart was losing this fight.

They decided to rest at the river's edge for the night.

Alec was exhausted and just wanted to hear himself breathe. He couldn't help thinking about Torrin and what he must have gone through when he realized why the people of the village were dying so horribly. They all started out on this same journey, his father, grandfather and great-grandfather. But they never realized what the true path was. They never realized that it couldn't be achieved in the present tense. He thought about Tremaine and wondered why he was brought into his life.

It was for this. Without him I would have never figured this out. I wouldn't have even tried. He brought me to this place, but why now? Why couldn't a person of understanding have approached Torrin or Michael? Why now? I guess I shouldn't question it. At least I have a chance to change things. In those days, they wouldn't have been open to the idea anyway—living in the realm of death to find life—my God.

The evening moved into the night slowly. They didn't speak much, didn't know what to say. They all thought about what they'd been through and worried about what was yet to come.

Kathleen stood along the river's edge and studied the moving current and the calming nature of the water. She watched Tremaine and Isadora stare at each other. She remembered what it was like to have a new love, the euphoria of it and the feeling that all is right with the world.

To be young and naïve, what a wonderful place to be. It seems so long ago, I've forgotten. It's shameful that we lose it. The joy of life is replaced with the fear of death. How sad.

She looked at them holding hands and wandering around engrossed in each other's every word, and she smiled. *Enjoy it, children. Enjoy it while you can.*

"What do you think will happen next?" Tremaine asked as he looked into Isadora's beautiful brown eyes and thought, *How lovely.*

"I don't know. I hope we are done, but I doubt it," she replied.

"You doubt it? What else can happen?"

She looked up at him and smiled at his naïve boyish charm.

"Humans carry a lot of waste. Our minds are full of unnecessary junk that we've collected over the years. Some people think we collect it over many lives. I don't know. But we have it, and it controls us and makes us do some terrible things to each other. There's always something worse, always."

"What can we do about it?"

"Nothing."

"Nothing? That can't be the answer. There's always a way."

"No, there's good and there's bad. Sometimes the good outweighs the bad, sometimes the bad outweighs the good, but either way, they are both always there. It is the nature of things; one does not exist without the other. What we hope for is that the good will prevail, and mostly it does, but there are times when bad makes a horrible noise that leaves a scar so deep that it can not be repaired. You will need to remember this, for at some point you will be confronted with your fear and you will have to choose to surrender or fight."

Tremaine's heart sank. He could tell from the tone of her voice and the look in her eyes that the worst was yet to come.

PART TWO

Courage

"Courage faces fear and thereby masters it. Cowardice represses fear and is thereby mastered by it."
—Rev. Martin Luther King, Jr.

Chapter Five

Your Deepest Fear

There was calmness in the air as they moved about. Everything was still and silent. They decided to try the uphill climb again, hoping to reach this mystical place that Isadora spoke of. Tremaine was a little uneasy about what Isadora spoke of, but he never let anyone see his concern. He tried to find some comfort in the moment of peace that they had and to keep his fears to himself.

They walked from sunup to sundown and would find open spaces and caves to rest in during the night. Their measurement of time was off track. Sometimes the sun would shine for what seemed like days, and other times it seemed to rise and set within hours. Some nights the stars were so bright, they were like beams of flashlights all around, and some nights the sky was pitch-black, without a star or moonlight. It was so dark, you couldn't see your hand in front of you.

It was strange. It seemed that they moved between time and space without knowing. As if they were in different worlds from one day to the next. Nothing seemed the same as they moved up what they believed to be a mountain. The farther up they went, the colder it got. They pulled out their winter gear and bundled up. They walked slowly as the deep snow slowed them down considerably. It was white everywhere, and they couldn't tell what direction they were going, only that it felt like an upward movement.

"Are we on the same mountain?" asked Alec.

"Of course. Why do you ask?" Kathleen replied.

"Yesterday all we could see was snow, and now there is a line of trees just ahead that wasn't there before," he said.

"Maybe we just missed them yesterday, just didn't see them," said Tremaine.

"Do you think all of us could have missed seeing a forest?" Alec was concerned. He looked around and couldn't help but feel a little disoriented. He couldn't get his bearings, and he couldn't understand why.

"I feel it too. I have no sense of time. I can't tell what day it is or how long we've been walking," said Kathleen.

"And it seems that no matter how far we walk, we are never any closer to the top. I feel like I've been going in circles," said Tremaine. "Issi, where are we going?"

She looked back at them. "Why are we stopping? We are almost there."

"Almost where?" asked Alec.

"When do we get to the top, or near the top? We've been walking forever." Tremaine looked all around and all he could see was white. There was something wrong, but he couldn't figure out what it was.

"We can't stop now," said Isadora as she turned and continued the arduous uphill climb.

The others looked at each other and wondered if they should follow, but what other option was there? When they looked behind them, there was an emptiness that faded into a white cloud. They all kept walking uphill and hoped that this would end soon.

As night fell, they took refuge at the base of a snow bank. They seemed to be sitting in a cloud. They could barely see each other. They wore dark shades and large parkas with thick gloves and padded boots. They were so well insulated that their movements were horribly restricted, but as night fell, they would need every layer of clothing they could find. The nights were treacherous. The wind thrashed around like the sharp end of a whip, endlessly blowing wet snow. The wind had no mercy. The piercing cold and the howling wind left them numb and helpless.

"I can't . . . I can't do this anymore. I can't do this. I have to go, I have to go back. This is too much. I can't, I just can't," Kathleen said.

She tried to stand. The wind forced her back. She stood again and tried to brave the storm. "I can't, it's too hard. I just can't." Tears rolled down her face and froze to her skin. She fell.

"Kathleen, Kathleen," yelled Tremaine. He forced his way to her and tried to help her back to the mound.

"No, leave me alone. I can't do this anymore. Leave me alone," she yelled.

Tremaine pulled her along and forced her back to the mound.

She sat on the ground and covered her face with her coat and cried.

Alec held her and tried to comfort her. "It can't last much longer, Kathleen. It will be over soon," he said tenderly. He didn't feel the guilt anymore. He knew it was her choice to come, but he didn't want her or anyone else to suffer anymore. He was ready for this to end too.

The night was long and no one slept, but by sunrise the storm had passed, and they pulled themselves out from under mounds of snow and tried to get their bearings. They still had some food left in their backpacks, if you could call the military-like rations food.

Alec stood and looked all around and couldn't see anything. "The trees, the trees are gone."

"Maybe they were covered by the snow," said Kathleen.

"The entire forest?" Tremaine wondered. He walked around, but all he could see was white. God, I'm tired of looking at this. When will we reach the top?"

"Top? There is no top," said Isadora, as she seemed puzzled by the question.

"Wait. What do you mean, no top? What does that mean, Issi?" asked Tremaine.

"Yeah, I thought we were going to this place where people moved through time and space, to the people that could help us find the rose. What is this, Isadora?" demanded Alec

"We are lost forever," Kathleen whispered. She fell to her knees. She couldn't take another step.

Alec started moving around and touching the white mist that lingered around them.

"Where are we? What is this? At first we could see the snow, but now it's just this white mist-like stuff. I—oh my God, this is cloud. Are we in a cloud? Isadora, where are we?" Alec firmly looked into her eyes. He was determined that he was not going to take another step until he got some answers.

Isadora looked at each of them and smiled. "The highest place." She turned and kept walking.

Alec and Tremaine looked at each other and remembered the quote from Torrin's binder. The rose can be found in the highest place and the lowest place. They stared at each other, wondering what was to be found in this place.

"The highest place—that's from Torrin's journal. But where is the rose? What happens here?" asked Tremaine.

"It is where you find yourself," she said.

"Find myself? I've already seen myself and I didn't like it. I don't want to see any more of me." Tremaine laughed. "Oh no, I'm done with me."

"What do you mean, Isadora? What do we have to do?" asked Alec. He waited intently, but feared her answer.

She hesitated and stared deep into their eyes. She was calm and reserved as if she was holding something back. As if she held the secret that they longed to know. She looked into Tremaine's eyes and smiled warmly. There was a strange calmness that moved through each of them that gave them an eerie feeling that they couldn't explain.

"What is your deepest fear?" She smiled, turned, and walked into the cloud and out of sight.

Tremaine ran after her. "Issi, Issi, where are you! What's going on? Where are you?"

He looked all around. Visibility was no farther than arm's-length, so he couldn't see anything. His heart sank when he realized that she was gone. He felt abandoned, but more than that, he was hurt. He was starting to feel a connection between them that could have grown into something special. He was hurt and angry.

Kathleen could see the sadness in his eyes. She walked to him and held him close. "What was she? Was she a ghost or something? I thought she was our guide. Damn, now what?"

"We can't trust anything in this realm. Nothing is real," said Kathleen.

Tremaine looked over at Alec. He was so confused and sad that he couldn't think straight. "What do we do?"

For the first time since they started this journey, Alec

saw the boy in Tremaine. He had been masquerading as a man thus far, but now he was truly lost and helpless. Alec knew he couldn't falter, not now. He could tell that without Isadora, he became the leader, and God knew he had no idea what to do.

"Standing here isn't the answer. I say we start back down and start over," said Alec. He turned and started walking in the opposite direction and he could only hope that it was down. He had come to realize that just because it felt right, didn't make it so. He could be walking in an angle, and may not know it.

They followed him. Kathleen was so glad to be getting off that mountain, she walked at a pace they hadn't seen before. Alec understood this had been hard on her, and he wanted it to be over as much as she did.

They walked a few miles, and suddenly they were out of the thick fog that blinded them for so long. They could see the evening sky and the snowcapped mountains around them. Finally, they could clearly see each other. A sigh of relief came over them as they stared out over the mountain range and took a deep breath.

"It will be getting dark soon. Let's stay here for the night," said Alec.

"Yeah, I'm exhausted." Tremaine removed his backpack and stretched out on the soft warm ground. He was so glad to be free of snow, he didn't care where he was. He put the backpack under his head and closed his eyes.

Kathleen sat down nearby. She looked out over the landscape in deep thought.

"What's on your mind?" Alec asked as he found himself a spot on the ground to rest for the night.

"I was thinking about what Isadora said. She said that we were in the highest place. What did that mean? What was supposed to happen there? I was sure that the highest place was where God would be, but there was nothing." She seemed disappointed and a little disillusioned.

"Something did happen—at least to me," he said.

"What?"

"What is your deepest fear? Ever since she said that, I have not stopped thinking about my greatest fear. It's a little debilitating."

"What is it?" she asked.

He looked at her almost too frightened to say it. He turned away from her because he didn't want her to see his weakness, his fear.

"Ending up in that damn wall, the wall of the well. Deep inside, I always knew the story was true, but I thought that if I never saw it, that it wouldn't be real. That it was only real if I made it so, and I was determined to never do that. But now, now I know, and the thought of living eternity in that wall is devastating. The worst part is, I'm starting to think that there is no rose and no way out for me. I'm going to end up there, and I will have failed every soul that's been trapped in that well over the past one hundred years."

She reached over and held his hand. "I know what you mean. I can't stop thinking about my worst fear either. When she said it, I shuddered at the thought and wanted to scream. God, I pray that I don't have to live it."

"What is it?"

"When I was a child my mother took me to Hawaii and we flew over the big island and saw the active volcano. You could see down in there and see where the hot melting lava flowed out onto unsuspecting villages and burned people and destroyed homes. The agony of it must have been unbelievable. I imagined being tossed into a lava flow and my skin melting away. I would burn in agony and pain, but I would not die. I would become grotesque and hideous and the pain would be unbearable and it would never end, never ever." She started to cry.

Alec held her in his arms and wondered what could be in store for them now. He looked over at Tremaine and wondered if he was having the same relenting thoughts about his deepest fear.

"It's only a thought. It can't hurt you."

"For now," she whispered as she lay back onto her backpack and tried to sleep.

Tremaine could feel the little creatures on his heels. He ran as fast as he could. He didn't know what they were, only that they were evil. His heart pounded with fear, and he struggled to climb up as far as he could. He knew that going up was important, but he didn't know why. He just kept climbing and tried desperately to keep them off his heels. He knew if they ever caught him, he would never see the light again.

He ran through trees and streams and crossed deteriorating bridges over deep canyons. He was exhausted, and he knew he would not be able to run forever. He had to figure out how to outsmart them, how to conquer them. The little demons that tugged at his heels were like small toys that moved in packs, like ants canvassing the desert floor. Their grotesque faces and malformed bodies were demonic and evil. They squealed when struck, and some lifeless, yellow, murky substance would flow from their damaged bodies.

Tremaine used a large stick that he managed to pick up in the forest to fight them off. He turned and swung his stick, throwing some of them more than fifty feet into the air.

They screamed a horrible sound that pierced his ears and made him shudder. He knew he could not let them catch him; his soul would be lost.

Sweat poured off of him, and he knew he was beginning to falter. His legs felt like rubber, and his lungs
burned as they struggled for air.

"WHAT'S HAPPENING TO ME?" he yelled as he ran.
He ran so hard, his heart almost jumped out of his chest.
He knew he would die. He fell into a deep hole and into
a dark cave. It was surreal. Everything seemed to be moving in slow motion. He seemed to be looking down at
himself fighting off the horrible creatures from hell. He
struggled as the tiny creatures grabbed his heels and
pulled him deeper and deeper into the ground.

"THEY GOT ME, HELP ME!" he screamed as he
grabbed hold of whatever he could, but there were too
many of them and they overwhelmed him. He couldn't
fight them all. He calmed himself and surrendered and
let the awful, hideous creatures pull his soul into the
bowels of Hell.

"NOOOOOO!" Tremaine screamed. He jumped up
and looked all around. He was sweating and muttering,
"No, no, please don't let that happen, please don't be
true."

Kathleen woke up and went to him quickly. Alec sat
up and watched.

"Tremaine, what is it? What's wrong?" She stroked his
forehead and saw that he was shaking and his eyes were
moving back and forth. He was so frightened it scared
her. "Tremaine, it was a dream, a dream." She pulled a
cloth from her bag and began to wipe the sweat from his
face. He was staggering around.

Alec walked over to him and held him still. "Tremaine,
focus. Look at me. Look at me, Tremaine," Alec demanded.
"Breathe slowly, slowly."

Tremaine stared into Alec's face and began to calm down.

"Deep breaths, deep breaths . . . now, you had a dream,
that's all, just a dream. Calm down."

Tremaine realized that it was a dream, but it was so real that he couldn't let it go. He sat down and held his face in his hands.

"My deepest fear," he said.

"What?" Kathleen kneeled down beside him and stroked his hair. "What did you say?"

"My deepest fear. I kept remembering what Isadora said just before she left. I couldn't get it out of my head my deepest fear. I didn't know what it was until now."

"We had the same experience, only we talked about it last night. You went to sleep, so yours came out in a nightmare," said Alec.

"What does it mean? Will I have to live it?" Tremaine looked up at Alec, hoping the answer was no.

"I don't know. I do think we will be confronted with it and we will have to deal with it. We should talk about it so that we all understand and can maybe help each other through it," said Alec.

Kathleen told Tremaine about her fear of burning eternally in a pit of scorching hot lava. Alec talked about his fear of living eternity in the wall of the well, and Tremaine told them of his nightmare, where his soul was pulled into Hell by relentless demonic creatures.

"They all seem to have a common theme, Hell."

The earth beneath shook as if an earthquake were ripping the planet apart. They knew they were near the epicenter, but where would the earth divide? Below them or behind? They stood still and watched as a gorge as wide and deep as they had ever seen materialized before them. Massive boulders and chunks of earth fell away into an abyss. It was impassable. They were scared beyond belief. They couldn't go back up the mountain, and now they couldn't get across either.

Alec walked over to the edge and looked down. It was endless. The pit was black and empty.

"My God." He turned and walked back. He was solemn. This was more hopeless than he could ever imagine.

Tremaine looked down into the gorge and knew that was where he had to go to confront the creatures of his dream. He turned and looked up the mountain that they descended from.

"The highest place," he said, and then he turned and looked down into the crack in the earth and said, "The lowest place." He looked back at Alec and Kathleen and saw the fear in Kathleen's eyes.

"N-no, Tremaine. You can't mean that we go down there," she stuttered.

"Yes, Kathleen."

He walked over to her and kneeled down. He took her hand. "Don't you see, if we don't conquer our fears, we will never get close to the heavenly place. We have to go down there."

Alec knew Tremaine was right, but he hesitated. He couldn't imagine what he could be confronting, and he didn't want to find out. Without realizing it, he started walking backward. He wanted to distance himself from the pit of Hell and remove it from his sight.

"Alec, stop," said Tremaine. "We have two choices. We die trying, or wait to die. I prefer trying. Either way, we are dead if we fail."

"We don't even know if there is a bottom," said Kathleen.

"You're right, just like there was no top. There may not be a bottom," said Tremaine.

"It doesn't matter. Whatever is going to happen will happen on the way. It is the journey that will teach us or kill us, not the destination. I don't know what to expect, but I think you're right, we have to try." Alec walked back to the edge and looked down. He took a deep breath and asked God for guidance. "We may not need this winter gear anymore. It will only weigh us down. Let's take what we need and leave the rest."

They searched through their backpacks and removed the parkas, gloves, and boots that kept them from dying during the freezing blizzard and left them on the ground for another seeker to find. Their packs were light with a few survival essentials.

Alec smiled as he watched Tremaine coil up a rope and stuff it in his pack. *As if we have a chance of survival, we prepare ourselves*, he thought. He looked at Kathleen and knew that she was not feeling this. Alec picked up his gear and walked along the edge of the chasm. They followed him.

He searched for a path down. *There must be one*, he thought. He walked for about twenty minutes and stopped.

"What do you think?" he asked.

"What?" asked Tremaine.

"Over there." Alec pointed to a narrow ledge that descended down to the bottom and out of sight. He walked to the ledge and stopped. He looked back at Kathleen and Tremaine and smiled slightly, and then he turned back to the ledge and took a deep breath and stepped off the edge and into the unknown.

Tremaine took Kathleeen's hand, led her to the edge, and kissed her cheek. She looked down and said a prayer and stepped onto the ledge while holding on to whatever she could.

Tremaine looked back up the mountain and silently said good-bye to Issi, turned, and stepped down.

This is the place where fear lives, Tremaine thought as he made his descent into the abyss.

They walked silently one behind the other.

Alec took the lead and hoped that he was not guiding them to their deaths. He knew that whatever happened in this world would affect their life or death in the other world, the world he called home. He thought about his farm and Tilly and how much he missed her. He hoped that she was all right and that he would see her again. He thought about Gwyneth and what could have been a beautiful love if this cloud had not hung over his house, his family. He wanted so much to tell her how much he loved her and to let her know that letting her go was his greatest gift to her.

She had a real life to enjoy, he thought, *not this madness that I live in. I know she found love and managed just fine.* He smiled at the thought as he maneuvered himself downhill.

Kathleen chuckled. "I've been through some crazy things in my life, but nothing beats this wild ride," she said. "Well, I guess it was a good life, all in all."

Tremaine thought about the nightmare and wondered how much of it was a premonition to what was yet to come. Even though he knew he had to try, he really didn't want to. He didn't think his life was worth fighting for, but he knew that Alec and Kathleen's were, and he was going to do whatever it took to get them through.

He thought about his mother and the kind of life he was headed for. He missed her and wished that he could apologize to her for being such a horrible son. He wanted to tell her that he loved her and that if he had it to do all over again, it would be different. He thought about the money he stole with no regard for the people he stole from and the lies he told to protect himself. He knew he was headed for the jail cell or the wooden box, six feet under.

I guess Hell is the right place for me. It's not like I deserve any better. I'm a good person at heart, I think, but I just can't seem to pull it together. I'm sorry. I wish life had been different for me, wish I had made it different, but I guess it doesn't matter now. My soul is lost.

He remembered something that Isadora said to him. She said that he would be confronted with fear and would have to choose to surrender or fight. *Or fight,* he thought, *there's a choice. We don't have to give up. We can fight. We fight. We have each other, and together we will overcome the bad. I told my mother that if I die it would be for something that mattered. Well, it will be for something that matters: me.*

"Look, there's some level ground where we can rest." Alec pointed down a few feet to a flat area that looked like a tabletop. "It seems sturdy enough."

"Yes, I'm very tired. We've been walking for hours, and it's getting dark. We should rest there for the night," Tremaine responded.

They were all glad to be sitting down. The walking was tiresome and intense. Every step had to be meticulously placed on the small ledge, or they would find themselves falling into who knows what.

Tremaine was feeling better. He knew that he had a battle to fight; he knew he would probably lose, but he realized that defeating the horrible image that he had of himself was the first step to defeating his fear.

As the sun set they took refuge on the small plateau that protruded out from the cavernous wall. They were so tired, they didn't say much. Each of them was in deep reflection of their lives and the direction it took.

"Check your flashlights and make sure they work. We'll need them tomorrow. We won't have the sunlight for much longer," Alec said as he pulled his flashlight out of his pack and turned it on and off.

Kathleen and Tremaine did the same. Alec turned his flashlight on and scanned the area to see what they would be up against tomorrow. He moved the light down the path of the ledge to see where it may take them, and it went beyond what his eyes could see. He wondered how they would stay on the narrow ledge with only the narrow beam from the flashlight guiding their way. The flashlight hung on a rope that Alec hung around his neck.

"Don't want to lose this," he said.

Alec scanned the light down, and nothing but darkness loomed back at him. He looked at Kathleen and felt her fear.

She sat with her arms wrapped around her knees, where she laid her head. She looked up to the open sky and watched as the sky turned orange and red from the glorious sunset.

A tear rolled down her cheek as she said, "Good-bye."

Tremaine braced himself against the wall and readied himself for whatever tomorrow would bring.

Alec rose before sunrise and readied himself to begin the day's journey. He checked his backpack while Kathleen and Tremaine slept. He wanted to get an early start to use as much sunlight as possible, for soon it would be gone. As a slither of light shone through, he used his flashlight to see around him. It was rocky and dark. The rock wall descended into a darkness in which no light could survive. He heard Kathleen stirring around. He walked over to her and kneeled down.

"Kathleen, we need to get started," Alec said.

She looked up at him, happy to see a familiar face. She sat up and took a moment to ready herself.

Alec walked over to Tremaine and shook him. "Wake up, Tremaine. We need to go."

"Damn, it's morning already? Okay, I'm ready." He moved around a bit and wiped the sleep from his eyes and struggled to wake up. He stood up and grabbed his backpack and strapped it to his back and yarned uncontrollably.

He helped Kathleen stand and gave her a hug. "Well, Kathleen, I suggest we get a move on, can't dally, you know. Things to do, places to go, people to see," he said in an awful British accent that made her laugh.

Alec looked back at her and was happy to see her relax for a moment. Tremaine pulled her flashlight from her backpack, bowed and handed it to her as if it were a wand. "My lady."

"Stop, I should hit you over the head with it." She smiled and turned toward Alec with her flashlight on and ready. Little glimmers of sunlight were all that was left of the world above that guided them downward into darkness that could only exist in a nightmare.

Alec took a deep breath and looked back at them with a sad apprehension in his eyes. He turned and started his descent. Kathleen followed, and Tremaine stayed in the rear. They walked for several hours and watched as the sunlight faded into darkness, and they had to rely on their flashlights only. Walking along that ledge in virtual darkness was terrifying. They could not speak, because they couldn't lose their concentration, not even for a moment.

A flash of light caught Alec's eye. He stopped and scanned his flashlight into the darkness, but he didn't see anything.

"What is it?" asked Kathleen.

"I don't know. I thought I saw something, but now it's gone."

"Down here our minds will play tricks on us. There's no telling what we'll think we see," Tremaine said.

"Yeah, I guess you're right." But just as he said it, there it was again, an orange-colored light shining from beneath them. "Did you see that?"

"Yes, I saw it. Look, there it is again." Kathleen pointed a little farther up. "What do you think it is?"

"I don't know, but we seem to be headed straight for

it," Alec said. "Let's keep walking, and hopefully we'll find another spot to rest for the night."

They moved down the wall slowly. The farther down they went, the more of the orange light they could see. There were glimmers of light twinkling in and out, like fireflies on a summer's night. They saw the beauty of it, but at the same time it was frightening not knowing what it was, and since this journey had not produced a whole lot of happy moments, they were reasonably doubtful that anything good would come out of it.

Alec saw some level ground where they could rest. They sat and rubbed their feet and legs to try and relieve some of the discomfort from so much walking.

"I'm really not in shape for this," Kathleen said as she massaged her feet and ankles.

"I know, and it's getting really hot down here," Tremaine said. He took his backpack off and lay back.

"Well, that's what happens when you're close to Hell," Alec said as he looked back at them.

He reminded them of their greatest fears. Each of them wondered if what they feared the most would be realized in this Hell, the deepest place, where they waited for their inner fear to consume them.

All light from the sun was gone, and the darkness was unwilling to relinquish even a glimmer of light from anywhere. Except for an occasional peek of the orange color from below, the cave was completely dark. Their flashlights were their only source of light

"We don't know how long these are going to last, so we should conserve as much as possible. We should only have one on at night while we're sleeping, and we should take shifts. I'll go first, the two of you should try to rest."

"All right." Tremaine turned his flashlight off and closed his eyes. Open or closed was the same, blackness.

Kathleen laid back and tried to rest.

Alec sat against the wall and stared out into the fore-boding and ominous darkness. He tried to stay focused, but his mind kept wandering back to the fear, the "what if" situations that could cost one or all of them their lives. He didn't know whom he was most afraid for, but he couldn't shake the feeling of doom and the relentless fear of failure.

The night dragged on, and Alec was so tired. But he managed to stay awake for four hours until it was time for Tremaine to relieve him. Alec woke Tremaine and lay down to sleep. Tremaine took his position against the wall and made the light dance on the cave walls to enter-tain himself for a while. He scanned the flashlight across the walls when suddenly he saw something move. He moved the flashlight around, but he didn't see anything and then suddenly, he saw some movement along the wall but he couldn't see what it was in the dark. It was like the wall was moving.

He jumped to his feet. "What was that?"

He looked over at Alec and Kathleen as they slept soundly. He thought to wake them, but as he scanned the light around again, he didn't see anything, so he calmed himself and decided to let them sleep. He took a deep breath and sat back down. *It was nothing. My mind playing tricks on me in the dark, that's all.* He looked all around to confirm his thoughts and didn't see anything. He sat with the light shining up into his face and tried as hard as he could to stay awake, but to no avail. He lost the fight to fatigue, and his eyelids slowly closed. He fought back and tried to open them, but he couldn't fight it, and be-fore he knew it, he was sound asleep. He heard some movement around him, pebbles and stones moving about. He could feel the presence of someone or something. He remembered the shadow he saw across the wall, and he was too frightened to wake up. He didn't want to know, but he knew he had to look. He slowly opened his eyes and when he focused, he looked up into Alec's menacing face.

"Tremaine, what are you doing? You are supposed to be awake." Alec was not happy. He felt that Tremaine could have put their lives in jeopardy while they slept. "We have to be able to depend on you. You can't just decide to fall asleep at your post."

"My post." Tremaine stood. "My post? This is not the army, I am not guarding Fort Knox. I fell asleep. I'm sorry. I didn't do it on purpose, I just fell asleep." He turned and walked away from Alec.

Alec grabbed his arm. "No, no, you can't just walk away, Tremaine. This is your problem. You won't do what you are told. You don't know how to follow instructions."

"What are you saying, Alec?"

"You know what I'm talking about. You just don't know when to stop, when to leave things alone like you're asked to. You won't let it go, and now look at us." Alec was angry, but he really didn't know why.

"Leave what alone? What, Alec? Torrin's journal? That's what you're talking about? The binder? You think that if I had left it alone we wouldn't be here right now, don't you? Say it, Alec. You think this whole thing is my fault."

"I didn't say that, I only said that you need to learn to take directions and follow them. That's all I'm saying." Alec turned away from him.

"No, it's not all you're saying. You are angry at me for getting you started on this nightmare. That's what this is about, isn't it? Isn't it, Alec?"

"Damn it, yes." Alec stared at him with anger in his

eyes. "Yes, Tremaine. All you had to do was leave the trunk alone, like I asked you to."

"But, Alec, if I had, you would have ended up in that well forever, trapped like everyone else. Is that what you want?" Tremaine was puzzled by Alec's reaction to finding out and wanting to help.

Alec thought about it and calmed himself a little. He looked at Tremaine apologetically,

"I know you're right, but it would have been me. I would not be putting your life and Kathleen's life in such danger. If it were just me, I could live with that, but this—"

"Please don't let the guilt come back. I couldn't handle that," said Tremaine.

"No, no, I know that this wasn't my fault, but it hurts me that the two of you are here with me. I should have started the journey years ago, and I should have walked it alone."

"It doesn't matter now. We are here now. We are in this together and we will get out together. Let's not waste energy on what we can't fix. We have a whole day of walking ahead of us," Kathleen said. Just as she turned to pick up her backpack she saw something move against the wall. "What was that?"

"What?" Alec asked.

"Something moved. Like a shadow."

Tremaine scanned the walls with his flashlight. "I thought I saw something last night, but I blew it off as a hallucination."

They all looked all around, but couldn't see anything.

"It was like a shadow. It was moving across the wall, but now I don't see anything, but something was there. I thought for sure I saw something," Kathleen said.

"Yes, it was there and then it wasn't. Yeah, like the moment you put the light on it, it stopped moving." Tremaine kept scanning the area.

"It?" asked Alec as he looked at Tremaine.

"Well, whatever it or something is. I don't know." Tremaine shrugged.

"Oh God, now what?" Alec picked up his backpack and pointed the flashlight down the path and started walking. Tremaine and Kathleen followed.

They walked for another day. This was becoming exhausting. It seemed that they would never reach the bottom. The orange light was becoming more and more prevalent.

Alec stopped when he realized what it was. Lava. He knew that when Kathleen realized what it was, she would panic. He looked around to find a place to rest, hoping that he will be able to calm her on a flat surface, someplace safe and a little more secure. He didn't say anything. He looked forward and kept walking. He was getting unbearably hot, and Kathleen seemed more and more frightened. She trembled, and her foot slipped off the side. She caught herself, but a piece of stone fell to the bottom. She watched it as it plunged downward toward the orange light. She watched it fall and disappear into the semi-solid flow of lava.

"Lava. Oh my God, it's lava. Oh no, Alec. I can't, I can't move. Please, Alec. Please don't make me do this. I have to go back. I have to." She started to turn.

Alec looked back at her and knew that she was in trouble. He started walking back toward her.

She looked at him with tears flowing. "I can't do this. Please take me back, please," she cried.

Alec reached out to grab her arm, hoping that he could keep her stable on the small ledge.

"My deepest fear." She smiled and turned and started walking back up the ledge.

Alec held on to her arm and stopped her from moving farther. The ledge was not wide enough for her to step past Tremaine, and he didn't know if he should back up or stay or what.

"What's wrong? What's going on?" he asked.

"It's her deepest fear, falling into the lava," Alec said.

"Oh no. Don't worry, Kathleen, we won't let anything happen to you. Don't worry," Tremaine pleaded.

She felt Alec's constraint on her arm, and she yanked her arm free, but it forced her body weight too far forward and she could not stop the momentum. Just as she felt herself leaving the ledge, she said, "There are no angels in Hell."

She could hear Alec scream, and Tremaine yelled her name. It seemed surreal, as if they were yelling across time and space. She fell. She could see the lava getting closer and closer.

"Stop her," yelled Tremaine. He looked at Alec, "Stop her," he yelled.

"Stop," said Alec. "Stop, stop, stop." He took a deep breath, closed his eyes, and focused on her. He centered himself and commanded, "STOP!"

The wall shook from the thunderous sound, and Kathleen found herself face down about three feet from the lava that flowed beneath her. It was an awesome sight. She hung, realizing that Alec had stopped her just like he did Tremaine in the old mineshaft. If the lava bubbled up and touched her, she would burn to death in mid-air.

Alec lay against the wall. He was using all of his strength to hold her. He didn't know what to do next, but he didn't let her go.

"Kathleen, shield yourself; shield yourself like you did when the creature was following me. You can do it, concentrate and put the invisible wall between you and the lava. Do it, Kathleen, do it now," Tremaine pleaded at the top of his lungs.

Alec held strong. He could hear Tremaine, but he couldn't lose his concentration, so he didn't open his eyes, he didn't speak.

Kathleen closed her eyes and whispered the Lord's Prayer. As she hung suspended over the lava, she slowly waved her hands across her body. Suddenly her body felt light. She could tell that something happened because of the strange tingling feeling that she had. She used one finger and touched down. She felt what seemed like a sheet of glass between herself and the lava flow. She kept her eyes closed so as not to look at the lava and break her concentration. As the lava bubbled up to hit the shield, she allowed her body to rest upon it. Slowly, she slid her body across the glass shield to the edge of the lava flow. She inched her body over, not knowing how far she had come or how far she had to go. She was feeling her way to make sure that the shield was laid out before her. She moved slowly until she eventually touched the rock wall. When she opened her eyes, she saw solid ground. She laughed and the shield dissipated beneath her. It was gone, she dropped three feet to the ground and bruised her knee, but she didn't care. The pain felt wonderful, and she was glad to have it.

"I'm okay," she yelled. "I'm all right."

Alec let her go. His body was so limp, Tremaine had to hold him to keep him from falling off the ledge.

"Kathleen," yelled Tremaine, "are you all right?"

"Yes, I'm fine." She laughed. "I'm fine." She turned and looked back at the lava flow and felt a strange calmness about it. She came so close to it, but it didn't conquer her. She prevailed. She sat on the edge and watched the lava graciously move by her. She was in awe of it, no longer frightened. There was a beauty about it that pleased her and made her feel whole and complete.

"It may be my Hell, but it is the earth's lifeblood that flows through her body creating new land, new life, a new earth constantly. It's beautiful." She moved back away from the daunting heat and waited for Tremaine and Alec to make their way down the ledge.

Tremaine had to get Alec off that ledge. He had to find him a place to rest. Alec was exhausted and could barely walk. Holding on to him and maneuvering him down the ledge was a difficult task for Tremaine. He stayed behind him and moved him slowly, stopping every so often to let him rest. It was a steep drop from which Kathleen fell, and now Alec and Tremaine had to steadily walk down that path without losing their grip. Tremaine didn't think they could make the trip in a day. He didn't know what a day was anymore. There was nothing around him to measure time by, and he couldn't be sure that anyone's watch was right. The ledge was very steep. He couldn't see at the bottom in the dark.

"Kathleen, you still there?" he yelled to make sure she was all right.

"Yep, I'm here. How much longer?"

"I can't tell. I can't see you, so I can't tell how far it is."

"Keep talking to me, and I'll follow your voice," said Tremaine.

They followed the ledge down for what seemed like hours. It was a slow descent, but they finally made it to Kathleen. There was a flat area where Alec could lay down. He was still very drained and needed to rest.

Kathleen and Tremaine hugged. They were happy to see each other, to say the least.

"That was close." Tremaine looked into her eyes and smiled.

"Yeah, it was one of those experiences I'd rather not have," she said.

They laughed and hugged.

"How is he?" She looked down at Alec resting on the ground. She walked over to him and kneeled down to stroke his hair. "Do you think he'll be all right?'

"Yeah, I think so. It took a lot out of him to hold his concentration like that, but I think he's mostly just tired and needs some rest, and so do I." Tremaine found a spot near Alec and lay against the wall.

Kathleen did the same. "God, I hope this will be over soon. I don't know how much more of this I can take." Kathleen closed her eyes.

Tremaine took his flashlight and waved it around. He looked down the path the ledge was taking and saw no end in sight.

"There is no end to this, Kathleen. There was no top, and there is no bottom. I don't know what we're doing here. I just don't know." Tremaine took a deep breath and sadly hung his head. He wanted to cry, but knew it wouldn't help matters. He listened as Alec moaned and groaned in a deep sleep and wondered what he could be dreaming about. He knew that there was more to come, but how much more could they take before they just gave up and died? He flashed the light on Kathleen and saw her sleeping soundly.

I'm surprised she can sleep at all after what she's been through, he thought.

He held the light on Alec and watched him sleep until his eyes closed and he fell into a deep sleep that took him into a world of vivid dreams and terrifying nightmares. In his dreams he fought for his life, and his body trembled from the fear of the darkness.

He opened his eyes slightly and saw movement on the cave walls, just like before. He was still half-asleep and thought that it was part of his dream. He looked down slightly and saw the flashlight still shining on Alec, and then he looked back at the wall. It was hard to make out what it was, but he knew something was there, and it was all around them. He was frightened, but he was so tired he could barely hold his eyes open.

He closed his eyes, but forced them open again. He stared back at the wall and then back at Alec, and he stopped breathing. The light filtered out into the darkness, but he did not see Alec. He thought for a moment that he was dreaming, and that he would awake and it would be all right, but deep inside he knew something was wrong, and he needed to pull himself together and deal with it. In his exhausted, half-awake state, he closed his eyes and a single tear rolled down his cheek. He took a deep breath, opened his eyes, and stood.

"Kathleen . . . Kathleen, Alec is gone." He didn't yell. He couldn't even feel a sense of urgency about it. His mind was overwhelmed, and all he wanted to do was go home. "Kathleen, wake up."

She sat up.

"What? What is it now, damn it?"

"Alec is gone."

"Gone where?" She turned her flashlight on and walked to Tremaine. She saw his flashlight on the ground and looked out over the area, but she didn't see him. "Oh no. Please, please don't let this be happening. I can't, I can't do it, Tremaine, I can't." She started to cry. "This is too much. You hear me? Too much. What are we supposed to do now? What?" She dropped to the ground and sat on the hard rock and cried.

Tremaine sat on the ground, held his hands in his head, and tried to figure out what to do.

He walked to the ledge and moved his flashlight up the steep slope that had taken days to walk down. He stared up, hoping to see the sky. He wondered if he ever would again.

"I agree," said Kathleen.

"Agree to what?" he asked.

"You know what. What you are thinking."

"And what is that, Kathleen?"

"That we should leave. We should just start climbing right back up and get the hell out of here."

He looked back at her. He saw fear in her eyes. Her face was so battered and she was so beaten that he felt pain just watching her struggle with her own cowardice and fear. She was so scared, she was willing to leave Alec behind.

"I wasn't thinking that." Tremaine turned and looked back up the slope.

"Yes you were, I can tell. You are thinking it now. You want to get out of here just as much as I do."

Tremaine didn't flinch. "Yes, you're right, but not without Alec." He didn't raise his voice or show any signs of anger at her suggestion. He realized that she was not thinking with a clear mind, and he was too tired to get upset. He just wanted his friend back. "He's somewhere."

"He's somewhere, he's somewhere. Well, of course he's somewhere. The question is, Where? Do you think we can find out where in this darkness, in this Hell?" she yelled. She moved closer to him and forced him to look at her. She got in the light and looked into his eyes. "We won't be able to find him, Tremaine. We won't," she said calmly.

He turned away from her. "I'll never know that if I don't try. I have to try, and if I don't find him, I can say I tried. Besides, without him, this is all for nothing. He is the only one who can carry the crystal rose back to the well and free those people and carry that coin to the sun.

He is the descendant, and he has to do it. Without him, this truly was all for nothing. I can't give up."

Kathleen wiped the tears from her face and walked back to where she was sitting and sat down.

Tremaine looked at her and wanted her to be all right with this. He couldn't just abandon Alec without trying. This whole journey was about him, and more than that, Alec was his friend.

"Kathleen, each of us must face our deepest fear. You dealt with yours, and I'll have to confront mine. Wherever Alec's is, he's dealing with it now. We have to help him just like he helped you. Do you understand?" He knelt down and brushed the hair from her face and wiped away her tears.

"Ok, you're right. I'll try," she whispered.

He hugged her and kissed her forehead. He stood and walked to the edge and looked all around.

"Do you know what his fear is?" Tremaine asked.

"Yes, yes, I know." Kathleen stood and walked to the edge. "He was afraid of ending up in the wall of the well."

They looked at each other and simultaneously realized that Alec was in the cave wall. He was there somewhere, but finding him would be all but impossible. He could be as deep as deep can go or somewhere above them. They didn't even know if he was conscious and would respond if they called out to him, but they had to try.

"Alec," yelled Tremaine. He moved around as best he could in the dark, hoping to hear something. "Alec," he yelled again and again.

Kathleen moved around slowly and called out his name.

"Alec, can you hear us? Alec, please answer, please." Her cries went unanswered. She looked back at Tremaine. "What do we do? This is impossible."

* * *

Alec lay on the ground semi-conscious. He knew something had happened to him, but he wasn't awake enough to figure out what. He could faintly hear Tremaine calling him, but it seemed so distant, he thought it was a dream. He struggled to sit up.

"Where am I? What happened?" he whispered.

He was exhausted and faint. He realized that neither Tremaine nor Kathleen were nearby. His flashlight still hung around his neck, and he finally got it turned on. When he scanned the wall around him, he was panic-stricken when he realized that he was trapped inside the cave wall. He started to breathe rapidly. He stood up and walked along the wall, and as far as he could see, there was wall on each side of him. The distance from front to back was about twelve inches. There was barely enough room to turn around. It was as though he was in a coffin that stretched for miles. He wasn't sure what direction he should be walking in, so he stopped. They could be above him or below. He was stumped. He sat on a rock and wondered how anyone could ever find him. He knew they would try, but how, in a cave that goes on forever, how?

This is my fate, he thought. *This is where I was going to end up anyway. My deepest fear. I guess I had to see the nightmare that Torrin caused for so many people. I had to see the hell they experience and the hopelessness that destroys your soul and dooms you to an eternal Hell. The thing is, if I die here, my soul will end up there anyway. So what was the purpose of all this? I can't believe we went through all this for it to end this way. It can't be over, it just can't be.*

"ALEC!" yelled Tremaine.

He heard his name. Tremaine was calling him. It was faint and he couldn't tell what direction it came from. He was very still and listened intently. For a moment he had a ray of hope that he may be found.

"TREMAINE," yelled Alec. "Tremaine, I'm here," he yelled.

"Did you hear that? He's here, did you hear that?" Tremaine was so excited to hear his voice. "He's alive, Kathleen, he's alive." He smiled and started moving his flashlight in the direction of the sound, but he saw nothing.

"Alec, Alec, keep talking until we find you," he yelled.

"I hear you. I'm here, inside the wall," he yelled.

The sound bounced off the walls all over the place. It echoed throughout the cave, which made it very difficult to get the direction of the sound.

"Alec," he yelled, and Alec's name rushed back to him over and over again.

"I'm here, Tremaine, I'm here," Alec yelled.

Tremaine looked all around, trying to pinpoint the direction of his voice.

"I think it's coming from there," he said as he pointed down toward the abyss.

"No, it sounded like it was up there to me." Kathleen pointed to the opposite side of the cave way above them.

"I don't know." Tremaine looked up and then down. He was so confused he stepped back from the edge and leaned against the wall. "I don't know, Kathleen, you may be right. I can't tell."

She lowered her flashlight and turned back toward Tremaine and then she saw a glimmer of light from the wall just beneath her.

"What was that?" She walked toward it and looked around. "Look, there it is again. I think it's him."

Tremaine looked down and waited and suddenly he saw the light. It was faint, but something was there. "I see it. What do you think it is?"

Kathleen looked behind her and waved her flashlight around.

"It's not here," she said.

"What?" Tremaine was puzzled.

"Alec, wave your flashlight around," she yelled. They both looked on as the faint light moved up and down and across the cave wall. The cracks in the wall allowed a glimmer of light to filter through, just enough to show them where to find him.

"Oh my God, Alec, we see you, we see you," Tremaine cried as he started climbing down to the source of the light. "Talk to me, Alec. Keep talking."

"Tremaine, I hear you. I'm here, behind the wall. Do you hear me?"

"We hear you, Alec, we hear you. We're coming."

Tremaine and Kathleen climbed down as fast as they could.

"Keep talking, Alec. Keep talking."

"The wall is all around me. I can't see anything. It's dark, very dark. I don't know if I can take this. The wall is closing in around me. I can't breathe. I-I-I don't know if I can take this. Help me, help me."

Tremaine could hear the fear in Alec's voice. He felt helpless and knew that even if they reached Alec, they still didn't know how to get him from behind the wall.

Alec fell against the wall. The darkness was unbearable. It was hot, and the air was dense. He struggled to breathe and stay conscious. Fear gripped him as he thought about dying in that wall just like Torrin, Michael, and David. He started to shake from the fear. The darkness overwhelmed him as he began to hallucinate about the horrible deaths of his forefathers. He could see the life force being sucked out of him, leaving the horrible, leather-like skin behind on a disfigured, horrid skeleton. He saw himself struggling to get out of the wall of the well. He could see the people of the village pushing against the wall in agony and despair to escape the Devil's clutches. He was there with them, living the horror, enduring eternity in a living Hell.

"Alec," yelled Tremaine, "Alec, talk to me."

Alec dropped the flashlight as he slumped between the walls and crouched on the ground in fear. The light faded out, leaving him in total darkness.

"Where's the light? We lost the light. Do you see it? Oh God, please, where is he?" Kathleen looked all around but she didn't see it anymore. "Maybe it went out. We have to find him." Tears rolled down her face from the hopelessness of it.

"Don't worry, Kathleen, we'll find him. We will." Tremaine stepped off at a landing and started moving along the wall. "It was here. The light came from here. Alec," he yelled. "Alec, speak to me. Where are you?"

He slowly moved his hands along the rock wall, hoping to find the crack that the light came through, but there were too many cracks. As he moved along the wall he felt some loose rock that seemed easy to move. He picked at it until a tiny hole appeared that he could get his finger through. He looked up and down the long stretch of wall and wondered where Alec could be and if this was the place to start, but it didn't matter. The stone was hard and unforgiving. It was the only way in.

"Alec, Alec, please talk to us, please. Do you think he's dead? What could have happened to him?"

Alec opened his eyes for a moment when he heard Kathleen's voice, but couldn't find the strength to call out to her. There wasn't much air, and he was losing his ability to focus. He knew there was no way to get behind the wall.

"Alec," a soft voice came from all around him. He forced his eyes open and there was a soft white light shining around him and a figure stood before him. He tried very hard to focus, but he couldn't.

"Alec," the voice whispered.

"Who, who is it?" He tried to stand, but he stumbled and fell against the rock.

"Alec, it's me." The voice was soft and comforting.

He managed to open his eyes and look into the light and saw the sweet lovely face of Gwyneth smiling back at him. Her beautiful auburn hair flowed about her as her brown eyes danced in the light. His fear was calmed as he stared into her brown eyes.

"Oh my, oh my, Gwyneth, is that you?"

He stumbled as he tried to move toward her. He reached for her, and she extended her hand to him. She held his hand and moved closer to him. She lay against the wall and held him in her arms.

"Gwyneth." Tears rolled down his face. "How are you here? How can this be? I'm dead, and if I am, that would mean that you are—"

"Don't talk. Save your strength. You have lots to do." She stroked his hair.

"I-I'm dead?"

"No, no, you won't die. You can't, because you are not the last of your family, and you have to save your child and grandchildren."

"A child, what are you saying? I have a child?"

"Yes, my dear. We have a son. His name is Edward, Edward Hamilton. He's in Arizona with his wife and three children. I know now why you didn't want us to be together, but it was too late. When I left you I was carrying your child. I married, and Edward was raised not knowing, until recently. He found some of my letters that told him who you are. He is confused and he needs your help to understand. Find him."

"But you, where are you now?"

"I am no longer in the physical world, but I can see when the people that I love suffer. I had to come; I had to tell you. You see, you can't give up, Alec. You can't. Your grandchildren need you. They know nothing of this, and won't understand why this is happening to them or what to do. Please try, please." She stood and kissed him on the lips and started backing into the light. He watched her fade into the light and out of sight."

"Gwyneth!" he cried. "Gwyneth, please don't leave me, please. I'm sorry, I'm so sorry." He reached for her and fell back onto the rock. "Oh God, I have a son. I can't let him die like this. I can't let it go on."

"Alec," Tremaine yelled and yelled.

Tremaine was so frustrated. He moved up and down the wall of rock, trying to find a weak point, but couldn't. He didn't see any way of getting behind that wall. All he could think about was Alec dying inside that impenetrable stone. He became so angry that he hit the wall with all his strength and the stone gave way. He stepped back when he saw the stone move.

"Did you see that?"

"Yes, yes, I saw it. Try again," said Kathleen.

"Maybe I—" He looked at his fist. He took a deep breath and pounded the stone again, and again, it gave way just a little more.

"Oh God, Tremaine, you have the strength to do it. You can do it." She held her breath in anticipation of the wall caving in.

Tremaine struck the wall again and again. It took all his strength, but he didn't stop until he saw the stone give way to the dark, empty space behind it.

When Kathleen saw the hole in the wall she fell to her knees. She couldn't believe what she had just seen, but she understood that in this world they all could do great things.

"Give me a flashlight."

Kathleen grabbed the flashlight from her backpack and handed it to him.

He pointed the light up and down, but he needed more room to see with the light. He put the light down and used his fist to pound away at the hard granite stone.

Alec saw a momentary flash of light and knew they were looking for him. The hole created by Tremaine allowed some air into his space and he felt better.

"Air is good, always a good thing." Alec smiled. He was still very weak. It seemed like he had been encased in the wall for hours. He had to let them know where he was. He had to scream. He had to let them know that he was alive and he needed to get back to save the life of his son and grandchildren. He had to be successful. He had to survive. In a single moment there was something in his life that was greater than himself. He finally realized why he had to take the journey—Gwyneth and the tie that will forever bind them, Edward.

He screamed as loud as he could, "I'M HERE," and then he fell across the rocks and passed out.

When they heard the sound of his voice they were hopeful. They pounded away at the stone until Tremaine finally got the hole open wide enough to see inside with the flashlight. He scanned up and down the stone wall.

"We have to get inside. Alec," he yelled as he moved the light up and down the long dark space between the inner and outer walls. The space was so narrow, it didn't seem that anyone could stand in between the two walls. He kept looking up and down, but he saw nothing.

"What was that?" Kathleen asked.

"What?" asked Tremaine as he turned and looked at her. "What did you see?"

"It seemed that the wall was moving. I've had that feeling before. I'm so tired of this place, tired of being here. My mind is going, I'm sure," she said.

"No, no, I've had that same feeling. Like every now and then the wall seems to have a wave of motion. I thought I was imagining things, but if you see it too, I don't know." He looked around and saw nothing. "Well, we have to focus on Alec for now." He turned back to the hole in the wall. "You should go in and look for him."

"What? Me? You think I should do it?"

"I can't get through this hole, but you can. I can be here still chipping away at it while you look for him, so he will be able to climb out after you find him."

"Why can't we wait for you to get the hole big enough now and we go together?"

"He may not have that much time left. It could take hours to open this wall and hours to find him. We could be doing both at the same time. We need to find him now."

"Okay, you're right. I'll try," she said. She tested her flashlight to make sure it was working and peered into the hole. She looked back at Tremaine, took a deep breath, and climbed up and over. "It's like being in a coffin." She looked up and down. "Which way should I go?"

"Call out to him. Hopefully he'll answer," said Tremaine.

"Alec, Alec," she yelled over and over again. "Can you hear me, Alec? Answer, please answer." She waited, but heard nothing. "What should I do?"

"Wait a minute," Tremaine said as they both listened intently.

Alec lay upon the rock near death. He heard the sound of Gwyneth's voice softly caressing him.

"You have to try, Alec. Wake up, you must try."

The voice was faint and weak, but Alec knew that he had to respond to let them know where he was.

"I'm here," he said faintly. "I'm here."

"Alec," yelled Tremaine. "Alec!"

"Tremaine," he yelled with all the strength he had. "Tremaine!"

"Did you hear it?" He smiled at Kathleen. "He's alive. It came from that way." He pointed to her left, and she started walking. He watched her walk into the darkness and out of sight. "Kathleen," he yelled, "keep talking to me. Make sure I can hear you."

"I will," she said as she moved slowly down the narrow path following the thin stream of light. She was unusually calm for someone walking between two daunting walls of rock, but for some reason, it seemed safe and neutral, away from all the madness on the other side. "Alec," she yelled.

Tremaine could hear her calling for Alec, so he knew she was all right so far. He continued to pound away at the rock so that Alec could climb through. It was the only way out.

"Alec," she called out again and again. She turned the flashlight toward herself and she tore a piece of white fabric from her blouse. She laid it on the rock to help her find her way back. She kept walking and yelling. She stopped and yelled back to Tremaine, but she got no response. "Tremaine," she yelled again, but there was dark silence, not a sound.

Suddenly, she heard the faint sound of Alec's voice. "Tremaine," he whispered. "Tremaine."

"Alec, Alec, I'm here. I hear you." Kathleen moved as fast as she could toward the sound of his voice. She waved the flashlight around until she saw him lying across the rock barely moving. She checked his body to make sure he wasn't hurt. She found his flashlight on the ground and she grabbed it and hung it around his neck, and then she tried to lift him. Alec was almost twice her size, so it was a difficult thing to move him along such a small space. She laid him on her back and dragged him inch by inch down the narrow path. "Alec, Alec, try to walk. Please, Alec, try.

"Kathleen, it's you. I'm going to be all right. I'm going to live. I have to, Kathleen, I have to," he whispered.

As she moved him closer and closer to fresh air, he became stronger.

"Yes, Alec, you will be fine. We'll get you out of here." She stopped for a moment to catch her breath. She moved the flashlight around and saw the white fabric flash back at her and smiled. She was on the right track. "Tremaine," she yelled. "Tremaine, can you hear me?" She heard nothing. "Maybe I'm still too far away. Alec, can you walk?"

"Yes, I'm fine," he said as he forced himself to stand. He took a deep breath and held onto the wall as he maneuvered himself down the path.

"Tremaine," she yelled again and again. "Why doesn't he answer? I hope everything is all right." She started to get concerned and wondered if she should have left him.

"Oh no." Alec stopped. He was terrified. "Oh no."

"What is it?"

"His deepest fear. Oh God, Kathleen. Don't you see? Each of us had to live through our deepest fear. Remember when Isadora said that we had to face them? You faced yours at the lava flow, and now this is mine, but Tremaine's was beyond horrible. If his comes true, I'm not sure how we can help him."

"You're right. He was there for each of us, and now he's alone. We have to hurry."

Kathleen began to walk as fast as she could. She looked back at Alec and watched him try to keep up. He was getting stronger and stronger with every step. Finally they made it to the opening and climbed out. Tremaine wasn't there. They looked all around and saw nothing that would give them any clue where he was, and suddenly his voice rang out in terror.

"HELP ME, THEY GOT ME! HELP!"

Alec looked up to see Tremaine being attacked by small demonic creatures coming from the wall. They were like a swarm of bees coming from everywhere. The walls seemed alive as the creatures moved slowly toward their victim. They were pulling him up the path.

Tremaine screamed for help. He was so frightened, and he didn't know if Alec was safe or not, so he didn't think there was anyone to help. He fought with all his might. He kicked and flung the creatures into the abyss, but they kept coming. There were so many of them. They were like little demons, the demons from his nightmare. They were there the whole time lying against the rock wall and waiting.

Alec's heart sank, he had no idea how he was going to save his friend and the fear of losing him in this horrible way was gripping his heart.

Kathleen screamed when she saw Tremaine being pulled up the path by these horrible creatures.

Alec ran toward him and threw as many of the creatures off of him as he could.

Tremaine struggled to free himself. The creatures pulled him close to the edge and he started to go over when Alec reached in and caught his arm.

"Hold on, Tremaine. Hold on." Alec did all that he could, but the creatures were too many.

Alec tried to calm himself so that he could stop Tremaine's fall, but he couldn't focus. The creatures were all over him. They pulled at his arm, forcing him to lose his grip on Tremaine. He couldn't stay focused on stopping his fall and holding on at the same time. He also knew that Kathleen was behind him and helpless. He heard her scream as the creatures moved toward her like a swarm of ants on the desert floor. He looked back to see if she was all right when he was overpowered and forced back.

Kathleen moved back as far as she could and watched in horror as the creatures attacked them and watched as Alec lost his grip on Tremaine. It seemed to move in slow motion.

"Stop," yelled Alec, but he couldn't focus. The creatures were all over him. He was throwing them off one by one, but they kept coming. He couldn't think of Tremaine with the creatures fighting him and moving toward Kathleen.

Kathleen was so frightened that she too would be pulled down into the lava that she lost her grip and screamed in horror. When she realized what just happened, she fell to the ground and cried.

Tremaine reached up to the heavens as he fell, carrying dozens of the demonic creatures with him. He knew the outcome and prayed that his death would be swift. He thought of his mother and great-grandfather, the Black man with the bright blue eyes, the day he met Alec, and the day he found Torrin's journal. He saw his great-grandfather sitting in the chair in his basement chanting. He was so real to him, so alive, that, for a moment, he knew that he was home and that everything would be all right.

"Hello, Great-grandfather." His body went limp as his soul was released and his body was gone.

Just as Tremaine's body vanished into nothing, the creatures scurried back to the rock wall and out of sight. They melted into the wall as if they were never there. Alec lay on the ground in shock. He moved to the edge and looked down, hoping that what had just happened was only imagined and that Tremaine was standing on a rock down below, but he wasn't. He lay as still as the rock around him, not knowing what to do or why. Kathleen cried until she passed out.

The hours passed slowly. They slept from sheer exhaustion. The ordeal had been more than anyone could bear, and now the worst possible outcome lay heavily on their hearts.

Kathleen opened her eyes and sat up. She looked at the dark cave walls and tried to focus her eyes. She remembered. She rested her head on her knees and a tear rolled down her cheek as she felt the empty space in her heart where Tremaine once was. She looked around and saw Alec lying a few feet from her. She wiped the tears from her eyes and she forced herself to stand. She walked slowly to him and kneeled down.

"Alec." She touched him gently. "Alec."

He began to groan and stir around. He opened his eyes, looked up at her, and screamed in agony.

She held him in her arms and rocked him like a child as she let him grieve over the loss of his friend.

"He was just a child. Kathleen, how could I let this happen? How could I? Oh God, please bring him back, please."

She held him tightly until he calmed down. He lay in her arms helpless.

"This isn't your fault, Alec. You couldn't stop it," she said.

"It is my fault. This whole thing is my fault. He wouldn't be here if it were not for me and all of my family's curses and deals with the Devil. It is because of me that Tremaine is dead. It is my fault," he cried.

"Now look, we have been through enough. I will not let you compound this by bringing back all of your issues with guilt. I will not endure it anymore. It's done. What's done is done. Whatever we were supposed to do, we can't do it." She stood up. "I'm leaving." She looked up the path as if she were looking to Heaven. She found her backpack and her flashlight and started walking up the path.

Alec watched her as she ascended. He didn't know how to feel about it. He looked back at the lava flow where Tremaine fell in and felt excruciating pain. He struggled to stand up and wondered if he would ever get over this. He found his backpack and strapped it on, picked up his flashlight, and started walking behind Kathleen. He stopped for a moment and looked back at the lava flow and around the cave wall.

"Good-bye, my friend." The thought that Tremaine died in vain was devastating to Alec. To return home with nothing to show for the death of Alaya's son was unthinkable. Alaya knew that this would take his life, she warned him of it, but he knew he could not have stopped Tremaine from coming.

This will kill her, he thought, *Her only child. John will never forgive me for this, I'm sure. I guess my punishment will be to live for eternity in the wall of the well.*

Kathleen walked with earnest resolve. She didn't flinch as she marched right by as if shielded from any aggressor, internal or external. She carried her shield of faith, strength, and resolve as if it were a banner that wrapped around her, keeping her safe from all the crippling blows that life could dish out.

Alec watched her move forward and wondered how she carried on. He wasn't sure if he had the strength to take the next step. As he ascended the path, he realized that it took them what seemed like three or four days to descend into the abyss, and now it seems to only take hours to walk out.

"Something is different," he said.

"Yes, I can already see some light. I don't understand," she said.

"We were never that far from the surface physically. The whole thing took place in our minds."

"In the mind's eye." She smiled. "I think you're right."

"Then, is Tremaine really dead?" he asked.

"I don't know." She looked back at him. "I guess that if he believed he was dying, then he probably did," she said.

"I wonder if the same laws apply here as back there." He stopped and looked back down into the abyss and wondered if Tremaine was really there.

Chapter Six

From Here to There

The small hint of light entering the chasm was starting to dim as night fell above them. They were so tired and wanted to stop, but decided that being out of that hole in the ground was more important than sleep. They kept walking until Kathleen peered up through the crack and saw the moon.

"Ah, oh my," she gasped. "Do you see it, do you see it, Alec?"

"Yes, I see it." He smiled as he looked up and marveled at the glowing round white ball that hung in the night sky. "It's perfect."

They were close, too close to stop. Seeing the moon gave them a renewed sense of urgency, a burst of energy that carried them onward. They both felt a weight lift from them, even though they did not find the crystal rose. They were leaving with nothing but the clothes they came with and each other. They were leaving with the memory of a friend and a long journey that took them to the inner depths of their souls.

They were both different people than they were when

they started this journey, and even though they lost Tremaine, both were thankful for the enlightenment that they now embraced. They were free from the burdens that come with life and living. Realizing who they were and what they wanted from their lives, regardless of how long or short it was, gave them a courage that they didn't have before, and now they were ready to face whatever life had to offer. They carried Tremaine with them, and his life became theirs.

A cool breeze blew down upon them, and Kathleen stopped and took a deep breath of the cool, fresh air. She began to walk faster, knowing that the top was just a few feet away. The moonlight shined brightly in the night sky, and they could see all around them.

Finally Kathleen placed her hand on solid ground and she began to cry. All of the anguish melted away as she pulled herself up and out of the crack in the earth. Alec followed her, and they both lay on the ground laughing and crying that the ordeal was over.

"No more. I'm done. You can stick a fork in me," she said.

Alec laughed. He hadn't laughed in such a long time that it felt strange. For some reason, it made it think of Tilly. He remembered the joy she brought him and wondered if she was all right.

A soft voice came from nowhere. "She's fine."

"What, what, did you hear that?" He came to his feet.

"Hear what?" Kathleen stood. "Please, Alec, please don't start hearing things. This has to be over, it has to be."

"Did you know that here and there are one and the same, and where you're going will always become where you've been? The present can only last a moment before the future overtakes it, and it becomes the past and what's done is done, or is it? Where are you now? Who are you now? Who are we?" The voice emerged from the darkness and Isadora stood before them. She was smiling warmly, as if she had been waiting for them to come up from the darkness.

"Isadora, why did you leave us? Where did you go?" Kathleen walked toward her and hugged her.

Isadora looked at her and smiled. "I didn't leave you; you left me. It was your journey."

"We lost Tremaine," Alec said sadly.

"You can never lose him, Alec, and you know why." She looked into his eyes as if she expected him to answer a question, but Alec didn't understand. The whole thing just made him angry.

"What are you talking about? He's dead. He died in the cave down there."

"Down where?" Isadora asked.

"Down . . ." Alec looked behind him and the chasm was gone. The earth was whole and there was no sign that the past three or four days happened. "We were down there. We were there for several days."

"What is this, Isadora? What is this? We were there. Tremaine was attacked and fell. I fell and Alec was trapped in the wall. It did happen, it did.

"If it didn't happen, then where is Tremaine?" she asked.

"I didn't say it didn't happen."

Isadora smiled.

Alec didn't understand. He knew that Isadora wanted something from him, but what? He stared up at the moon and wanted so much to change everything. He realized that this curse was not his fault, but he did carry the burden of redemption and salvation for all of those people in the wall of the well. He wanted to save them and himself, but to what avail? He felt that he had lost everything—his farm, Tremaine, and his will. The battle left him hopeless and without Tremaine.

"How can we leave this place?"

"Leave what place?" she asked.

"Don't play with me. I'm in no mood for riddles. I am tired. I've heard it all before, and all I want to do is go home. If I end up in the well, then so be it. I've had enough. This was Tremaine's journey as much as mine, and now he's gone. Whatever the outcome, I don't care."

"Tremaine is still on his journey," she said.

"Look, just point me to the exit sign."

"Exit from where?"

"Issi!" he yelled.

"Look, I don't mean to be difficult, but I don't know what you want. It seems to me that you can get the answer yourself."

"You said that I could never lose Tremaine, and I knew why. What does that mean?" Alec pondered the thought. He tried to figure out what it was that she thought he knew. He didn't know, but somehow it had something to do with Tremaine.

"You know the answer, Alec. Who are we?" she asked.

"Who are we? I don't know. I'm Alec, and she's Kathleen, and you're you, I guess. I don't know what you're asking."

"Yes, you do," she said just as she phased back out of existence.

"Noooo, Issi, please come back. Please don't leave us here like this. What are we supposed to do? God, please, I need—I can't, please let it be over." Kathleen fell to her knees and cried. "If I ever get back, I'm going to find another line of work. I don't even want to know about the hereafter or afterlife or spiritual anything. What happened to the white light and happy reunions? Everything I thought was wrong, everything."

"Who are we? Who are we? What is it? What is it? What does that mean? I don't know. I don't know, damn it." Alec angrily kicked a rock and paced around, trying to figure it out.

Kathleen looked at him and felt his pain. She knew that he was carrying the weight of Tremaine's death on his shoulders, and now he was trying desperately to get her home. He had given up on saving himself and now his only focus was her. She wiped her eyes and walked over to him, took his hands, and held them.

"Alec, calm down. Calm down. This must be something you can figure out, or else she would not have left you with it. But you can't think when you're all wound up like this. Come over here and sit." They sat by a large stone. She pulled a bottle of water from her backpack and gave it to him. "Take a drink."

He took the bottle and drank the water. He was still tense and a little scared. "Tell me about your farm. I've never been on a farm. Kind of a city girl, you know," she said.

He looked at her and smiled a little. "It was the home built by Torrin. My family has been there four generations, and I guess I'll be the last. The town has grown up around it, and I know they are just waiting for me to die before they sell it off bit by bit. I had corn and a small patch of soybeans. I had horses and chickens. The cabin has grown over the years. My father added a few rooms, and so did my grandfather before him. I think it started with two rooms: a kitchen and a bedroom."

"Where are your animals now?"

"I gave the chickens away, and a neighbor is watching Tilly for me."

"Tilly?"

"Yeah, she was my best friend. We were both two old farm hands that figured we'd see each other through to the end. We took care of each other, you know. It was like everything was connected. Everything was dependent on everything else, and we thrived with each other. We belonged to each other."

"Who are we?" Kathleen softly asked.

"We are one."

The light that started to glow in front of them was alarming but soothing. It was frightening, but they didn't want to run. They knew that whatever came out of the light was going to be wonderful. The light slowly took a shape. It condensed into a narrow band of light that was so bright, you could barely look at it. As it narrowed, it formed itself in to a rose. There it was; it was suspended in front of them like the glory of God. It was luminescent and created a peace that neither of them had ever felt before.

Alec walked around it to see if it was coming from somewhere, if it was connected to something, but it wasn't, it was just there.

"We are one," he whispered.

"Yes, yes, we are one in the eyes of the Creator. We are all one life force that is connected to each other and the universe. When we harm someone, we harm ourselves, and when we help someone, we help ourselves, for we are of the same consciousness. All that is, is God. He is the one true self." She laughed. "It seems so simple, but we were so far removed from it that we couldn't see it."

Alec smiled and took her hand. They were so overwhelmed by it, they weren't sure what to do. Alec reached for the crystal rose and grabbed it, and suddenly, they found themselves back in the white space where life and death pass each other as time moves on. It was where they met Issi and now must leave Tremaine behind.

They looked around and watched as people moved in and out of existence. They hoped they would see Issi or

Tremaine as he moved into his next existence, but neither of them appeared. Alec held on to Kathleen's hand. He didn't want to lose her too, so he never let her out of his sight.

"Where to now?" she asked as she looked around for an exit.

"I'm not sure. How did we get here before?" asked Alec.

"We were meditating. Yes, we need to focus our minds on our world. Close your eyes and concentrate, focus."

They stood very still with their eyes closed and thought about sitting in Kathleen's sunroom, where this journey had begun. Alec had a hard time concentrating on the sunroom. His mind wandered to Tremaine and his great-grandfather's house. Their bodies relaxed, and they could feel their spirits lift away. Alec was nervous, but he wanted this to be over. He could feel the rose radiating with pulsating light. The light was so intense that it overshadowed everything else around it. He held on to it and allowed it to carry him and Kathleen through the vortex between life and death and back to the world that he knows as home.

Alec could hear John chanting in the distance. He didn't understand, because the meditation that John had tried to use didn't work; that's why they'd sought Kathleen's help in the first place. He didn't understand why John would still be chanting, but he followed the sound. It was alluring and pulling on him to come. He held onto the crystal rose with one hand and Kathleen with the other. He seemed to be floating like a feather when suddenly he was being pulled down. He was spiraling out of control. He looked up and saw Kathleen floating above him. He didn't realize that he had let her go; he couldn't hold on. He lost her and he screamed for her. He cried out her name over and over again until he seemed to hit bottom.

* * *

John and Alaya watched as the light formed in Alec's hand as he lay upon the cot. The light got brighter and brighter and formed itself into a luminous crystal rose.

Alec unknowingly held on to it as he gasped for air and opened his eyes. He looked around and found himself in the basement of John's home, lying on the cot where he and Tremaine tried to perform the meditation. He realized that the meditation did work and that he had never left this room. He wondered about Kathleen. Alec looked to his right at the cot next to his and saw that Tremaine was not there and he screamed.

"Nooooo," he cried, "No, God, I hoped that you, but I guess not, I guess you didn't save him."

Alaya put her hand on John's shoulder and he stopped chanting and collapsed in her arms.

Alec sat up and tried to get his bearings. He didn't understand what had happened, but he was starting to wonder if he never left John's house. Did he really meet Kathleen? The whole journey was made in the spirit in a few hours.

Alaya helped John to his room so he could lie down. Even though it was just a few hours, it was exhausting for him. It took total control of his mind to maintain a link between the two worlds, and at his age the experience drained his life force tremendously.

"Alaya, I am so sorry about Tremaine. I can't tell you how much I regret what happened. I . . ."

"Wait now, don't be writing my eulogy just yet." Tremaine walked into the room carrying a glass of water. "Here, I know you'll need this."

"Tremaine." Alec jumped to his feet and stumbled as he tried to gather himself.

"Wait, wait. It's all right. Just sit and rest a minute, you can't just jump in and out of worlds and not expect some effect on you. You sit still. Here, drink this. I know you're thirsty, I know I was. I must've drank a gallon of water since I've been back."

Alec was dying of thirst, so he drank the water and placed the glass on a nearby table. He grabbed on to Tremaine's arm and held on to it and stared into his face and smiled. He tried not to be too happy, just in case it was yet another illusion, but he wanted it so much, it was hard not to believe.

Tremaine forced him to lie back down, and he slowly loosened his grip on Tremaine's arm.

"How?" asked Alec.

Tremaine raised his right hand to mimic the traditional native greeting.

"How?" He looked so silly, they both laughed.

"You're here, but I saw you perish." Alec became more serious as he stared into Tremaine's eyes, wondering if it was really him.

"Not really, you really didn't see me perish," he replied.

"I saw you fall into the lava. I saw you burn."

"No, you didn't."

"I did, I did see it. I'm sure, but I guess I can't be sure of anything, can I?"

"You see, the Navajo people believe that the physical and spiritual world blend together. So from the physical world, Great-grandfather has been with us throughout the journey, and when he realized that I was in trouble, he pulled my spirit out of the body before I hit the lava and the body that you thought perished only existed because the spirit was in it. The moment the spirit left, the body vanished. I never really hit the lava flow. If Great-grandfather had not pulled me out, the connection between my spirit and my body would have been lost. I would have died on this cot, but instead, I awakened here just as you did. The world that we were in is for the spirit; the physical was just an illusion."

"Thank God." Alec took a deep breath and sat back up.

"Where is Kathleen?" asked Tremaine.

"I lost her in the vortex. I couldn't hold on to her, and we got separated."

"She was in the vortex, so she must be back here somewhere. Maybe she went home."

"Yes, maybe, if she existed at all." Alec tried to stand and remembered that he had the crystal rose in his hand. He was so elated about seeing Tremaine, that he'd forgotten he had it.

Tremaine looked upon it. "Is that it?"

"Yes."

"How did you find it?

"Isadora came back and . . ."

"Issi . . . Issi came back." His face saddened at the thought of her. He missed her and wished for something more.

"Well, only for a moment. Just long enough to give us the answer."

"It's magnificent."

Tremaine reached out slowly to touch it, and just as his fingers touched the rose a cold, foul wind blew through the house. The walls shook as things fell from the shelves, windows flew open and shattered, and lights flickered on and off. A dark shadow moved swiftly through the room and the foul smell moved with it. Tremaine pulled back.

Alec stood and watched as the shadow moved up the wall and through the ceiling.

"*Nimitz,*" John screamed from his bed.

They ran upstairs to find him sitting up in his bed, terrified. Sweat was pouring from his face, and his hands shook from fear. He was cold, and his heart was pounding. He yelled again, "*Nimitz.*"

Tremaine threw a blanket over his shoulders and held him until he calmed down.

"It's all right, Great-grandfather, it's all right," Tremaine repeated over and over.

Alec walked to the window and looked out at the darkness melting into the evening sky. He looked back at Tremaine,

"What was that?" asked Alec.

"I've seen it before," said Tremaine as he rubbed his great-grandfather's shoulders to try and calm him.

Alaya came in with a pill and a glass of water and gave it to John.

John swallowed the pill and drank the warm water and started to relax.

"Where?" asked Alec.

"In your barn."

Alec looked confused.

"The day I found Torrin's binder, a dark shadow moved through the barn and the smell was the same. I blew it off as my imagination, but now, I don't know."

"You should have told me about that," said Alec.

"What would you have done at that time? You wouldn't have believed me anyway." Tremaine allowed Alaya to take over calming John.

Alec realized that Tremaine was right and turned back toward the window. He was frightened. The ordeal had been overwhelming, but to think that there was more to come was devastating.

"What did he say? What did John call it?" asked Alec.

"*Nimitz*, it is the lord of the demons. It is not native to Navajo, but it translates as *the most evil*," said Alaya.

Alec looked at the rose that he held in his hand and wondered what the most evil would do to get it.

"You must hurry. Now that you have the rose, it will not stop until it is destroyed. Now that it has been moved from the spiritual to the physical, it can be destroyed, and you must not let that happen. It must be returned. If it is not, God help us all. He will do everything he can to stop you. He never thought you would figure it out, so he rested until the power of the rose pulled him out of his serenity. With the rose removed from its rightful place, he can perform unimaginable acts of evil. You must protect it, and you must hurry."

Tears rolled down John's face as he lay back in the bed. He took Tremaine's hand and held it.

"Oh my God, we have awakened the Devil," said Tremaine.

"No, my son, he has always been awake. But now, he has an even greater sense of purpose, and his destruction will be without measure." John dropped his hand and closed his eyes to sleep.

Tremaine looked at Alaya and saw the terror in her eyes.

"I guess you were right. I'm not ready for this," he said.

"No, maybe I was wrong and you are the only one who is." She looked at the crystal rose and up at Alec. "I don't know why my child was chosen to free you, but I now believe that only he can do it. Maybe the outcome is as much for him as it is for you, I don't know. But I feel that what you have just come through was to prepare you for this fight. You have the shield now, and your hearts are pure and strong, and you have to know that you can win. You can be successful, because if you aren't and he senses fear, he will kill you. I can only believe that if God tasked you with this, He will give you the strength to endure it. I know that you are tired, but the time to rest is later. Take what you need and go, go now." She walked over to Tremaine and kissed his cheek. "You are Navajo, it is your gift."

"I know that now." He hugged her and kissed her cheek.

"I hope this is one of those things that we'll look back on someday and laugh about." Alec looked at Tremaine, took a big sigh, and walked out of the room. He found his jacket and the keys to the truck.

Tremaine and Alaya followed him into the living room. Tremaine pulled his things together and kissed her again and said good-bye. Alec walked to the fireplace mantel and picked up the Bible and the crucifix. He looked back at Alaya.

"Yes, Alec, take them," she said. She pulled the crucifix from around her neck and placed it around Tremaine's. "Good-bye." She turned and walked back into John's room and closed the door.

They walked out, got into the truck, and headed down the driveway. There was nothing to say. They both thought about what Alaya said and realized that fear was their worst enemy. They replaced fear with determination. Tremaine wanted to save the life of his friend and free the people from the well. Alec wanted to free the people from the well and keep the world from falling into chaos. They both wanted to get the rose back to its rightful place, but they knew that one of them would have to die to do it.

Chapter Seven

If You Feed It, It Will Grow

"Where are you going?" Tremaine watched Alec turn the car in the opposite direction of the highway back to Arizona.

"I need to know about Kathleen," he said.

"You mean, if she was real?"

"Yeah, I have to find out." Alec drove the truck down the street past the university where she worked, and down the road about thirty minutes, until he reached the street where her beautiful cottage was. He turned and looked for the narrow driveway that they turned onto to get to her house. He didn't see it. He parked the truck, stepped out and looked all around, but he didn't see it.

Tremaine stepped out, and they both stood where the driveway should be, but it wasn't there. The small row homes beside the cottage still lined the street. There was a small grocery and a music store at the corner and a busy intersection at the other corner. Everything was the same, but where the house once stood was now a vacant lot full of tall grass and weeds. The house was gone.

"Are you sure this is where it was?" asked Tremaine.

"Yes, I'm certain. I made sure I followed her every turn, and as I recall, it was only one turn from the street the university is on to her street. I'm sure it was here." Alec was heartbroken. He wanted to see her again. He wanted to know that she was all right.

"May I help you?" a small voice came from the house next door. The small, frail woman walked out to the fence to see what was going on. "Are you lost?" she asked.

"Was there ever a house there?" Alec asked as he pointed to the vacant lot.

"Oh my, yes, years and years ago." She remembered a time long past and smiled. "About forty maybe fifty years ago there was a young Asian woman who lived here. She was very beautiful. The story goes that her husband thought that she was having an affair, and while she slept he took the children and left, but before he drove off, he set the house on fire. It burned to the ground and she died inside. It was a horrible story, and to this day, people say she comes back here looking for her children. But it's just a ghost story, you know."

"What was her name?" Alec asked.

"I think it was Kate or Karen or something like that," the lady said.

"Kathleen? Kathleen Cho," said Tremaine as he looked at the lady to see her reaction.

"Yes, that was it. In fact she worked at the university up the street. My goodness, how could you know that?" She giggled.

"No one ever built on the land?" asked Alec.

"No, rumor has it that Mr. Cho paid the taxes on the land and it remains his to this day. I don't know if he will ever sell it. They say he loved her so much that he couldn't bear the thought of her with another man."

"Thank you." Alec turned and got back into the truck.

Tremaine ran to the other side and climbed in. He pulled from the curb and drove down the street.

"Wait, stop." Alec pulled over and Tremaine got out and walked into the music store. Alec had no idea what he was up to, so he just waited. Tremaine came out carrying an instrument case for a clarinet that he placed the rose inside. It was perfect for carrying it and concealing it.

Alec went around the corner and drove to the university. He parked the truck and got out.

"Wait here." He walked to the administration building and inquired about Kathleen Cho. "I am looking for Professor Cho, does anyone by that name work here?"

The young clerk checked her computer for the name of the professors on crystal rose and could not find it. "No, I'm sorry, but that name does not come up. Are you sure it was this university?"

"Yes, I'm sure. There's no one by that name working here, and you're sure."

"Yes, sir, I'm sure."

She could see the stress in his face. "Is everything all right?" she asked.

"Yes, yes, I'm fine."

He turned and slowly walked out. He looked around and remembered the scene when he and Tremaine were there. He walked back outside and looked down to the bottom of the steps, where she had been waiting for them. How could it have been so real? *Who was she*? he thought.

He walked to the truck, climbed inside, and drove toward the highway. He didn't say anything, and Tremaine realized that he wasn't able to find her or any connection to her.

They rode in silence for a while.

"So, you didn't believe that whole ghost story. Actually, it made sense to me. She was in the other world waiting for us, and when we got here, she became our guide. She was the link from this world to the next," Tremaine said.

"Yeah, maybe you're right. That whole scene in her house was strange. We were already in the spirit when we met her. But she seemed so scared and frightened. She was so real and she had to confront her fears just liked we did. Why would she, if she wasn't real?"

"She was real. She was just as much real in her world as we are in ours. Maybe there are trials and tribulations in every existence that we have to deal with. I don't know. I'm just talking without a clue."

"I'll admit, I am a little angry," said Alec.

"At what?"

"At the way she made us think that she was in danger and that she didn't know what to do, that whole helpless routine. If I hadn't been worried about her, I could have saved you."

"Maybe, I don't know. In that world the danger could have been as real for her as it was for us. But I know what you mean. I guess I'm a little angry too." Tremaine stared out the window.

"Isadora." Alec glanced over at him and could see his sadness.

"Yeah, the way she left was crazy. Maybe she was the guide. I don't know. I'm tired. I'll sleep a little and you wake me in a few hours and I'll take over, okay?" Tremaine laid the seat back as far as it would go and closed his eyes.

"All right," replied Alec as he focused on the road and wondered about what lay ahead.

Alec drove for a few hours. He could feel his eyes closing and sleep trying to overtake him. He pulled over to the side of the road and tried to shake it off. He looked at Tremaine sleeping soundly and didn't want to wake him.

It was late at night, and the moonlight was bright in the night sky. The stars twinkled in the darkness but were overshadowed every time a car passed by with headlights shining brightly. Everything seemed calm, and Alec leaned against the window and closed his eyes for a moment. He opened them quickly when another car passed by.

Something was different. He sat up and looked around. It was so dark he could barely see anything. He looked up at the sky, and it was pitch black. There was no moon, stars, streetlights, nothing. He pulled the flashlight from the glove compartment and turned it on, and suddenly it stood before him. It was foul and evil. It was a man, or something like a man, with horrible dark eyes that peered through him. He couldn't speak as he looked into the darkest soul he had ever seen. Suddenly, he felt hands around his neck choking him. He tried to free himself, but he couldn't. He couldn't feel the hands, but yet he was choking. There was nothing to grab on to. He struggled to breathe. As he gasped for air, he reached over and jostled Tremaine.

When Tremaine saw Alec struggling he tried to help him, but didn't know how. He looked out the window and saw the dark man and yelled at him to stop, but he didn't let Alec go. Alec was beginning to turn blue.

"Alec, he can't hurt you unless you let him in. Don't let him into your mind. Alec, close your eyes and think of something pleasant. Think of Tilly, yes, and the farm. Calm down and relax and know that it isn't real. Say The Lord's Prayer."

"Our Father who art in Heaven." Alec struggled, but he whispered the prayer as best he could.

Tremaine got out of the truck, the crucifix in his hand.

"Hallowed be thy name."

He held the crucifix up and forced the man to look upon it.

The evil creature pulled back. "You will not succeed," the evil voice said.

"Thy kingdom come, Thy will be done."

He lost his grip on Alec and he stopped choking.

Alec tried to relax as he took deep breaths. He saw Tremaine standing outside of the truck and feared for his life. He rolled the window down.

"Tremaine, get in the truck. Get in the truck now," Alec yelled.

Tremaine backed up and climbed back into the truck.

Alec started the motor and pulled off. He could see the man in his rearview mirror standing in the darkness as he turned the corner and out of sight.

"Are you all right?" Tremaine asked.

"Yeah, I think so. How did you stop him?" asked Alec.

"It was the cross. I don't think he can look at it."

"Ok, then we won't lose these." Alec pulled the cross that he got from Alaya from his pocket and hung it around his neck. He took the Bible and placed it on the dashboard and patted it a few times. "We need all the help we can get."

Tremaine took over the driving for a while, and Alec took a break.

"I need to make a pit stop," said Alec as he pulled the seat back up.

"All right, we'll pull over at the next exit."

Tremaine drove twenty more minutes and then saw a small diner on the side of the road. The gas station across the street had a line of cars waiting to gas up. It was a long stretch between this little oasis in the desert and the next town. They pulled over, went inside the diner, and took a seat.

Alec looked at the menu. "I gotta go. Order me a turkey sandwich." He got up and went to the restroom.

"What'll it be?" the tall, dark-haired waitress asked.

"I'll have a burger, and he'll have the turkey."

"What do you want to drink?" she asked.

"Ah, make it two Cokes."

"All right." She pushed the pencil back into her hair, put the pad back in her pocket and went back to the counter.

Alec came back and Tremaine took his turn. It didn't take long for the food to arrive, and they both enjoyed a good meal for the first time in what seemed like weeks. They knew now that the whole ordeal took only hours, but their body clocks were telling them that they had lost days.

"It's very strange, isn't it?" asked Tremaine.

"What?"

"The way this seems all surreal kinda, you know?" Tremaine said.

"Yeah, it's like looking at a moving picture and I'm in the picture looking at myself," said Alec.

"Sometimes I feel that I'm still not in my body. It's like I'm looking down on myself. I wonder if that will ever change, if things will ever be the same again." Tremaine smiled a bit, hoping to get a yes answer, even if Alec wasn't sure. He wanted to be reassured about something, even if it was a lie. He looked out the window and saw the dark, evil man standing across the street at the gas station. "Oh my God, look."

Alec looked up just in time to see the dark man wave his hand and the pumps at the gas station burst into flames. A line of cars blew up one by one. The force was so great, it shattered the window at the diner.

The people who could get out of their cars ran across the street, and those that couldn't burned to death while screaming for mercy. The flames bellowed up into the sky, showering debris everywhere. The people in the diner looked on in horror.

"My wife, oh God, my wife." One man ran out into the street, only to find that his car was enveloped by the flames and his loving wife was gone. He fell to the ground in agony.

Another lady screamed, "My baby, my baby," as she ran toward the flame and got too close. She burned to death before the people around her were able to put the flames out.

The dark man walked out of the flames and stood beside the people and watched them try to save her life. "It's just as well. She would have committed suicide at the death of her children anyway." He walked to the diner and stared inside at Alec and Tremaine. "You will not succeed," he said as he moved slowly away. He never looked back at the horror that he'd caused.

The sound of fire and rescue trucks resounded in everyone's ears, and the sight of the devastation was mind-boggling. Alec and Tremaine were devastated. They knew that the removal of the rose put him on this rampage. He would do anything to stop them from getting to that well. They never imagined anything like this and realized that it will only get worse.

They ran from the diner to the truck and got back on the road. They were both scared out of their minds, but they kept driving. At this point they didn't know what else to do. Alec drove for a while and then Tremaine. They tried to rest, but couldn't.

"Why doesn't he just take it? Just take the rose?" asked Tremaine.

"I don't think he can. If he could, he would have, back there, but he can't, he can't touch it. He can break our spirit or even kill us; either way he will win unless we succeed. Somehow, I don't think this is just about me. I can't help but wonder how many other unsuspecting souls are trapped around the world. If we do this, it may be greater than anything we can imagine. This seems larger than just me and my family. Someone wants him stopped," Alec said.

"Well, I guess we'll have to take the beating and survive at all costs. Especially you. Without you this is meaningless."

"Not completely," said Alec.

"What do you mean?" asked Tremaine.

Alec took a deep breath and wondered if he should say anything about this at all. He felt that Tremaine wouldn't believe him because he wasn't sure he believed it.

"What is it, Alec?"

"I think I have a son."

Tremaine looked over at him, puzzled by the statement. "Isn't that the kind of thing you would know?"

"Not necessarily. When I was trapped behind the wall, Gwyneth came to me and she told me that I had a son named Edward in Arizona and that he has children."

Tremaine thought about it for a moment. "You were unconscious some of the time. Do you think it could have been a hallucination or a dream?"

"I think that it could have been, but I don't think so. I saw her. She held me. I just don't think it was a dream," said Alec.

"I don't know, Alec. Some crazy things happened in that world, and then we find out that it was all in our heads. Could it be that this was in your head too? That it was only real because you wanted it to be?"

"But I don't want it to be. In fact, it's the last thing I want. I gave Gwyneth up just so this wouldn't happen."

"I guess you didn't give her up soon enough." Tremaine smiled.

"Yeah, I guess. It was thirty years ago, and my desires were stronger than my brain. God, I hope I only dreamt it, but I don't think so."

"If you're right, that's serious. That means that you are not the last of your line and that if you don't stop this now, your son, his children, and their children will all end up there. Oh God, Alec, what're you going to do?"

"I don't know."

"He doesn't know about you?" asked Tremaine.

"I'm not sure. I think she said that he recently found some letters that told him about me, but I can't be sure."

"If we don't succeed, we might need his help," said Tremaine.

"Yes, I was thinking the same thing, even if I could find him, I don't know if I can make him understand, If he will—Oh no."

Alec and Tremaine heard the engine sputter and choke. The truck started slowing down as Tremaine pulled off the road. The truck rolled into a dead stop. Tremaine turned the key, but nothing.

"You know what we forgot to do before the gas station blew up back there? Get some gas." Tremaine opened the door and got out.

"Now what?" asked Alec.

"I guess we walk." With the rose tucked safely in the case under his arm, Tremaine pulled his belongings from the truck and started walking.

They'd had very little sleep and dawn was coming over the horizon. They stayed on the highway and walked along the side of the road for miles until they came to a small town.

A bright red truck zoomed by fast, almost running them off the road.

"Damn, did you see that?' Tremaine watched the truck barrel down the road.

"I guess she's in a hurry. She looked familiar," said Alec.

They walked into the small town to get some gas and hopefully convince someone going west to drop them off back at the truck. The town was small and quaint. There were a few modern-looking buildings, like the post office and the local community center, where the local theater club and the high school basketball team both performed. Shops and houses lined the main street, which had one hotel and four or five restaurants. It was a dying town that wouldn't last another fifty years.

The young people who graduated from the one-room school left the day after graduation and only visited on holidays and funerals. A tall church rested at the end of the street and towered over the rest of the town. The town had the feel of Mayberry, where Andy, Barney, and Floyd would sit in front of the barbershop for hours on end. You could almost smell Aunt Bee's peach pie and expect to see Opie riding his new bike any minute. Nothing much ever happened here, until today.

Just as Alec and Tremaine entered the main street, the dark shadow that they had come to recognize crossed in front of them. They stopped and looked all around. They knew he was there, somewhere. Everything seemed very still, even though there were people moving about from shop to shop. For them, it was like watching a movie in slow motion, taking in every frame of the picture bit by bit. A snapshot here, a snapshot there, and there he was, standing in front of the church.

The people paid him little attention. He was still and quiet, and with little fanfare, he raised his hand and waited.

Alec saw the bright red truck that flew past them move from the gas station to a local diner across the street. The young Black girl who stepped out of the truck seemed out of place in this uni-cultural town. Alec focused on her and wondered if she would survive what was about to happen.

The buildings started to shake and rumble. The street-lights burst and windows broke into the street. People ran out into the street to see what was going on. Build-ings cracked and fell. Some seemed to sink into the ground. People were screaming and running for loved ones and home.

Alec and Tremaine looked behind them and saw the huge crack in the earth coming straight down the main street.

"It's an earthquake," someone yelled.

Tremaine jumped to the other side just before a gaping hole would have separated the two of them. They ran to-ward the church, along with many people, while the dark man just stood there.

Just as they reached the diner, a man fell into the crack and Alec stopped to grab him.

"Hold on," yelled Alec.

He held the man's arm as he dangled in midair. He tried to grab hold of something, but the earth shook so hard, it was difficult to steady himself. Alec held on. He remembered when he couldn't hold onto Tremaine in the cave, and he was afraid that the same thing would hap-pen here.

"Help me, Tremaine, help me."

Tremaine reached down and grabbed the man's other arm and pulled him up while another man running from the store was hit by falling debris and fell into the crack and into the abyss. Brick and glass fell everywhere, caus-ing death and injury.

The lovely young lady ran from the diner just before it collapsed and was struck by stone falling from the col-lapsing building. Alec saw her and pulled her away be-fore blocks of stone caved in onto the street. He carried her down a side street into an open area and laid her down on the ground. He held her in his arms and looked upon her face, the soft beautiful face of Isadora. He didn't want to leave her there, but he had to find Tremaine.

Tremaine tried with all his might to lift a wood beam that had a man trapped.

"I'll be right back," he said as he went to find something he could use for leverage.

The young man thought he was being abandoned and he screamed for mercy.

"Please don't leave me here. Please, I don't want to die like this. Please," he cried.

The small quaint town was transformed into utter chaos. People were running everywhere trying to find someone, save themselves, or save someone else. It seemed like hours, but the earth finally stopped shaking, and the crack stopped just at the steps of the towering church. The church was spared, and it became the place of refuge.

Evil walked down Main Street and surveyed the damage as Tremaine worked his way through the debris and found a two-by-four that might work. Just as he grabbed it, he was struck from behind and knocked unconscious.

"Hello," said Alec as he watched the young lady open her eyes and try to focus.

"Oh my God, what happened?" She tried to sit up.

"There was an earthquake," he said.

"In New Mexico? An earthquake? What the hell is going on?" She held her head where it hurt the most and forced herself to stand up.

"Listen, will you be all right? I have to check on a friend."

"Yeah, sure, I just need to get back to my truck, and I'm out of here," she said as she started walking toward the main street.

Alec walked with her. When they reached the street

she looked around for her truck and didn't see it, but she did see a young man lying on the ground down the street. "Is that your friend?" She pointed.

"Oh God, Tremaine, no, please God, no."

Alec ran. He kneeled down, picked him up and carried him back behind the fallen debris.

The young lady followed him. "Will he be all right?" she asked.

"I don't know." Alec gently slapped Tremaine's face, hoping that it would wake him. "Tremaine, Tremaine," he called out to him. "Wake up, Tremaine." Alec took a deep breath of relief when he saw Tremaine's eyes open.

He tried to sit up, but couldn't. He grabbed his head and cringed from the pain.

"Damn, what happened? I—" He saw her. He couldn't say anything. He stared into her face and wondered if he was hallucinating. "Issi."

She wasn't sure how to react to him. His stare was daunting, and she hesitated to respond to him. She stepped back and nervously extended her hand.

"Hello, I'm Randi Lake."

Tremaine couldn't stop staring at her. He took her hand and said hello. She helped him stand up, and they began to walk.

"I'm Tremaine Fleming. Randi, your name is Randi."

"Yeah."

Tremaine realized that she was different. He remembered when she came through the space where life and death met and how she became Issi in her new existence. To him she was still Issi with a different name, and he was delighted to see her again.

"You really remind me of someone. A lot."

He stopped and stared into her eyes. He couldn't believe it was her. He knew it was her, the same person. The name was different, but it was her. He wanted to grab her and kiss her and tell her how he felt, but he couldn't. Randi didn't know him, so he would have to take things slow.

Just as they made it back to the main street, Tremaine remembered the man trapped under the wood beam.

"Oh no, I-I have to take care of something." He walked very fast down the street until he reached the man, who was still lying there. "I'm here. I didn't forget about you."

Alec and Randi followed and tried to help pull the wood beam away from him, but couldn't. The man lay still and quiet. Alec kneeled down to check the man's pulse. Tremaine looked all around for something that he could use to move the beam.

"No, Tremaine, it's over," said Alec.

He looked back at Randi, and she understood what he meant.

"I've got to help him. I told him that I would help him." Tremaine kept looking for whatever he could find.

"He's dead, Tremaine. The weight of the wood was too much. He's gone," said Alec.

Tremaine was devastated. He couldn't talk.

"You couldn't help. You couldn't help yourself. You did the best you could."

Tremaine couldn't speak. He started walking away from it, just walking away.

"Tremaine, where is the rose?" Alec's heart started pounding, knowing that panic would be the next level if Tremaine lost it.

Tremaine lifted his arm, where he had tucked the case and realized it was gone. He couldn't speak, he couldn't move. His mind and body was numb. He didn't know what happened to it, and he didn't know where to start looking. He hung his head. He couldn't think. His mind was jumbled and wandering in nine different directions. He couldn't focus.

Randi didn't understand, but it was easy to see that he was in a great deal of stress. She looked at Alec and saw horror on his face and Tremaine looked like he wanted to scream. She wanted to help, but had no idea how.

"What is it? Where is the last place you were when you remember having it?" Randi asked.

Alec walked back to the place where he'd found Tremaine unconscious and looked around, but it wasn't there. He walked back.

"It's not there."

Alec sat on a pile of rocks and stared out at the street and watched the chaos going on around him. People were hurrying about trying to find their way. Children were crying, and men and women were digging through rock and rubble to find those trapped beneath.

Tremaine stood in place, still and numb. He knew the town was a disaster zone, but he couldn't see it. He tuned everything out. All he could hear was the pounding of his own heart. Emergency and Rescue moved into the town in droves, and they were all stunned at the horrible sight. Tremaine could not believe the horror that was caused by removing the crystal rose and wondered if he'd made the right choice to try. *I wanted this so much. I wanted to help. I had no idea that this could happen. I never thought that something like this could happen. I've killed so many. They are all dead because of me and my quest for righteousness*, he thought.

"Damn," he whispered. He looked back at Randi, not knowing how to answer her.

As she looked into his sad eyes, she saw the face of Evil walk by, leaving a cold, foul stench in the air.

Evil looked into Alec's face and said, "You will not succeed." He held a slight grin on his sinister face. He turned and walked down Main Street and out of town. He never looked back at the horror he'd caused.

Randi felt fear. "My God, what was that?" She knew there was something horrid about the man, but she had no idea that he was the cause of the destruction around her.

Alec looked out over the town and for the first time really saw what happened. The devastation and chaos was massive. The small town was struggling to grasp what had happened and scattered around trying to find something that would explain it.

Rescue workers from neighboring counties tried to save as many lives as they could. People were trapped and lost as loved ones ran throughout the area, yelling out their names and looking through the debris. Fire erupted throughout, and pieces of buildings gave way from the weight of collapsed structures.

Alec watched as a woman searched for her child. He watched her wander around and felt a sorrow that he had never known. She frantically called out Robby's name and he wanted to help. He walked toward her when he heard the sound of someone crying behind some fallen rock. He started to dig through the rock and got the attention of Tremaine and a few rescue workers. They dug for a while until they came to a wall and there he was, trapped behind a large slap of stone that protected him from the fallen rocks.

"Robby, Robby."

Alec reached in and pulled the child out.

The woman cried as she wrapped her arms around her child. The rescue workers got him to a safe place to check him out and bandage his wounds. Alec was so pleased to see something good happen, he broke down. He was so mixed up that he couldn't think.

"What do we do now?" Tremaine asked.

"We find it." Alec looked at him with a determination that Tremaine hadn't seen in a while. "This will not happen. We know that he doesn't have it, because he can't hold it, but he can control someone that's weak in faith and faint of heart. Someone has it nearby. I can feel it. I know it. We'll split up and cover the town. Tremaine, you check over there." Alec pointed in a easterly direction. "Randi, you look down there."

"Wait. I'm not in this. I don't even know what I'm looking for. I appreciate your saving my life and everything, but I don't want anything to do with that crazed man that just walked by, which means I don't want anything to do with whatever the two of you are doing." She slowly backed away from them and walked toward her truck.

"No, no, please don't go." Tremaine was talking to Randi with his mouth, but to Issi with his heart. "Please, we could use your help."

"Look, I know I remind you of someone, but—"

"No, no, that's not it. If you leave, we are stuck here. Our truck ran out of gas a few miles down the road, and we may need you to help us get back to it. Besides, I don't think you can drive out of here right now anyway."

"That's okay, I'll walk." She smiled and kept walking.

Alec caught up with her and grabbed her arm.

"Okay, Randi, can you take us to our truck now and we'll come back to look for the rose?"

She looked at the desperation in Alex's eyes and couldn't say no. "All right, I'll give you a lift. Come on."

They climbed over rock and debris and finally got to what was once a beautiful bright red truck. The truck had been spattered with rocks, glass, and falling pieces of buildings. She got inside and found the key in her bag. She could barely see through the window, and when she turned the key, the engine struggled to turn over. She tried again and again until it started to roar. It was a beautiful sound. They were happy that something went right.

They tossed the rocks and stones that lay on the truck

onto the broken road and found some old towels in the bed to clean the windows. As Tremaine was wiping the windows he felt a cool breeze. It startled him and he had a confused feeling of anxiety and calm at the same time. He stopped and looked around and saw his great-grandfather standing across the street. He wondered if he was really there or if it was a hallucination. He walked to the end of the truck and watched as his great-grandfather waved to him. Tremaine couldn't tell if he was waving hello or good-bye.

"Are you all right?" asked Alec.

"Yeah, yeah, I'm ok." Tremaine could feel that something was wrong. His great-grandfather was in trouble, and he felt helpless to do anything about it.

Alec didn't buy it. It was obvious that Tremaine was very disturbed, but at what? Alec wondered if it was from losing the crystal rose, but he didn't think so. "Tremaine, what is it?" he demanded.

"Great-grandfather . . . there's something wrong. He's fading away. I have to go to him."

"What . . . how do you know? What's going on?" Alec moved to Tremaine's side. "What is it?"

"He's there. I can see him. He's across the street." Tremaine stared across the broken street into John's fading eyes.

Alec looked around but saw nothing. After what they'd been through together, he couldn't dismiss Tremaine's claim, but he also knew that he couldn't lose sight of the present mess they were in. Tremaine stepped off the curb to go to him when Alec grabbed his arm.

"Ok, look, there's a lot going on right now. We have to focus on the need at hand. Let's find that rose and get the hell out of here."

Tremaine turned to look at Alec, and when he turned back, John was gone. Tremaine wanted to leave right then, but he knew that he couldn't. He had to finish the job. He had to find that crystal rose.

"You're right. I'll start over here," he said as he climbed over mounds of rubble and eased around narrow ledges to peer through broken glass windows and down impassable alleys.

"Wow, he's got issues." Randi watched Tremaine maneuver around the torn-up town.

"You don't know the half of it," said Alec as he looked on. He turned to her and tried his best to explain what she was looking for. "Randi, we are looking for a rose." He waited for her response.

She looked at him oddly. "Like a flower?"

"No, not a regular rose. I mean a holy rose made from crystal."

"Holy? Like as in God and angels?"

"You may want to stay with that thought." Alec wanted her to get it.

She giggled and started backing up toward her truck.

"Wait, Randi. I can explain . . . or maybe I can't, but you have to believe me when I say that I understand that you don't understand."

"Oh, I understand, all right. I understand that you and Spock over there are two beer bottles short of a six-pack. I don't think I even want to know. Crazed dark men gliding by, he sees visions, and now you are looking for a holy crystal rose. We are still on planet earth? Because the next thing I expect to hear is that we've been transported to Vulcan and we're at war with the Romulans or the Klingons or some other crazy-ass thing." She turned to open the truck.

Alec grabbed her hand. "Wait, Randi . . . please wait. I promise you I can explain this, but even if I did, the only way for you to believe it is to see it."

"See what?" Her curiosity was mounting. As crazy as

it was, it was intriguing and captivating as well as obviously dangerous. The combination was an adrenaline rush like she'd never had before. The journalist side of her wanted to know more, but the scared side of her wanted to run like hell. Randi was studying journalism at Oklahoma State University. The death of her mother took her back home to Phoenix, and on her return trip she'd made the mistake of stopping in this small town in the middle of nowhere to get some gas and found herself mixed up with Alec and Tremaine and their quest for justice. She worked part-time for the school newspaper and, for a moment, thought that this may be the story that could land her that prestigious job after graduation. If she survived, and they aren't crazy, and the rose is real and—She popped herself on the forehead for even considering staying in the madness. She turned and opened the door to the truck and climbed inside.

"There's a well," said Alec.

"Ok, there're lots of wells across America," she said.

"Not like this one."

"Ok, I'll bite. What's different?"

"There are people trapped in it." Alec knew he needed her and could not let her get away. He held onto the truck door and stared into her eyes, hoping that she would try to understand.

"People trapped. Did you call the police?" she asked.

"Logical question, but this is not a logical situation. You see, it's their souls that are trapped."

"Okay, well, I'm gonna see if I can maneuver myself out of here." She started the truck and backed up. She worked the truck in the small space until she was free. She had to drive over rock and debris, but she finally made it to the end of the street and she headed out toward the highway.

Alec watched as the bright red truck got smaller and

smaller in the distance. He turned his attention back to finding the rose. They had to find it. He saw Tremaine venture down an alley and made his way to him.

Tremaine was desperate. He tried to concentrate and focus so that he wouldn't miss even the smallest clue, but his mind wandered, and everything seemed so shattered that he couldn't think straight. He nervously walked around, praying that God would give him some help, some guidance.

"No luck," said Alec as he followed Tremaine into the alley.

"Not so far," Tremaine said sadly. "She left, didn't she?"

"Yeah, couldn't convince her." Alec sighed.

Tremaine didn't react to the news. He didn't look up; he kept walking around looking in every possible spot, and then he stopped, looked at Alec, and smiled.

"What?" asked Alec.

"We don't have to look. It will find us." Tremaine smiled.

"What do you mean?"

"As soon as the cover is removed, the light will be so bright that it will show itself. All we have to do is wait."

They walked back to the church and sat on the steps. They watched as the townspeople moved in and out of the church with their injured and sometimes dead. The people who had to leave their damaged homes walked in with the few items they could carry. Some had only the clothes on their backs. For them, everything was lost. Many had nowhere to go and no idea what to do, so they migrated to the church, hoping for guidance or just solace from the madness.

The pastor of the church, Pastor Simmons, stood in the doorway helping people enter God's house. A few of the members were inside setting up tables for food and lay-ing blankets on the floor and benches for people to stay the night. Anyone whose house wasn't destroyed gave refuge to those who had nowhere to go. Many donated food, water, clothing, and blankets. It was heartwarming to see the kindness of people in desperate times, but the horror of the event overshadowed the moment with death and destruction everywhere.

Tremaine noticed a young man walking toward the church carrying a long black leather case that could carry an instrument. It was strapped across his shoulder. "Look." Tremaine pointed to the young man.

Alec noticed the case and stood up. "It looks like it," he said.

Tremaine stood and they melded into the crowd of people walking into the church. They tried to keep their eyes on the young man, but there were so many people, it was difficult. The church was huge. It was a new church with a huge dome and balcony seating. The church was the center of living for the townspeople, and they spent much of their lives there. People from all around would attend and Pastor Simmons was well-liked and respected amongst his parishioners. The townspeople saved for years to build the new church and were shocked when it was still standing after the earthquake. They knew it was a miracle from God, and so it was the most likely place to find refuge and hope.

Tremaine and Alec entered the beautiful church with its stained glass windows and the huge gold cross that dressed the wall behind the pulpit. Two huge stained glass windows from floor to ceiling flanked the cross that allowed streams of light from the setting sun to seep through and cast a yellow glow over the room. Even in its chaos, it was beautiful.

They started moving toward the young man. They didn't want to scare him or cause a scene, so they approached him slowly and cautiously. The young man took a seat on the floor and leaned against the wall. He seemed content and completely unaware of what he had strapped around his shoulder.

Tremaine took a seat beside him, and Alec stood on the other side and stared out the window.

The young man looked up at Alec and wondered why he stood so close to him. He scooted over a bit and bumped into Tremaine.

"Sorry, man, sorry," he said as he scooted back the other way a bit.

"That's okay, no problem," Tremaine replied as he studied the case. "What's that? Is it an instrument?"

"Yeah."

"What sort of instrument?" Tremaine asked.

The young man looked at him curiously. "Just an instrument, that's all," he replied. The young man started to feel a little crowded and tried to stand up.

Alec stepped in front of him, and Tremaine grabbed his arm and pulled him back down. He bounced back to the floor and looked up at Alec.

"Look, I don't have anything that you could want. If you want to steal the instrument, I'll tell you, man, it's worthless. It's used and won't get you a penny," he said. The young man didn't look trustworthy. He seemed rebellious and a little rough around the edges. It was obvious that he was troubled and probably accustomed to taking things that didn't belong to him. He tried to get up again, and again Tremaine stopped him.

"I need to see your instrument," Tremaine said.

"What for?" he demanded.

"Just open the case and let me see it." Tremaine was adamant.

Alec never looked down. He stood in front of the young man and looked all around.

The young man hesitated, but he pulled the case from his shoulder and flipped the lock and opened it. Tremaine waited for the blinding light, but there wasn't any. He stared down into the case at an old silver clarinet.

The young man was startled. He couldn't understand why anyone would want to steal an old clarinet. He waited and watched them stare at it.

Tremaine stood up and looked around frantically.

"It's in here, I know it is." His eye caught the pastor standing at the front door.

The pastor was talking to a young man who was carrying a black case. "What is that?" the pastor examined the case.

"I don't know, sir, but I think you should have it." The young man hesitated, but handed the long black case to the pastor.

Pastor Simmons wasn't sure if he should take it or not. He reached for it and then pulled back. "Well, what is it?"

"I don't know, but I don't think just anybody should have it."

"Have what?"

"Please, sir, please. I just don't think I should have it. I don't think it's of this world." The young man handed it to the pastor and backed away. He turned and walked away from the church.

Tremaine knew it was the rose. He started moving in between people as fast as he could to get there before the pastor opened it. Alec followed him. They watched as the Pastor flipped opened the lock and lift the top just as Tremaine grabbed his arm.

"Noooo," yelled Tremaine.

Everything seemed to move in slow motion as if time was slowing down. It reminded them of the white space where life and death met and where they met Issi. He saw the astonished look on the pastor's face as the crystal rose glowed so brightly that it filled all space around them. People stopped and marveled over it. Pastor Simmons lifted it from the case and tried to hold onto it, but it gently slipped from his grasp and hung in mid-air, shining a blinding light. The light became so bright that they couldn't look upon it. A few peered out to see the streets miraculously buckle back in place. Stones and pieces of iron seemed to float back to their rightful place and wedge themselves back into buildings and walls. Fires went out, and cars and trucks reformed themselves as if by wizardry or sorcery. It was unexplainable when people who were thought to be dead began to stir around. Wounds healed and bones mended themselves, and those who once lay breathless along the street and inside the church gazed into the light that gave them life.

When Randi's bright red truck that was badly damaged by falling rocks started to buckle and repair itself, she stopped on the side of the road and got out. She stood back as the truck took on the look of the beautiful red truck she'd bought just a year ago. Her breathing was irregular as she tried to come to terms with what was happening and why. She took deep breaths, hoping that it would help calm her. She thought about the town where the earthquake happened and the story that Alec told her. She walked back to the truck, and all around it, and there wasn't a scratch, not a dent. There was no sign that the truck was ever damaged. She ran her hand along the side and walked up and down, wondering if she should get in.

"Objects just don't fix themselves; they just don't. What the hell is going on here?" She was afraid, but she was even more curious. She jumped back into her shiny new truck and turned around.

* * *

Alec reached out and grabbed the rose and forced it back into the case. He took it from Pastor Simmons's arms and fled down the steps and into the street. Everyone was so shocked over the events that had just taken place that they didn't think to run after them.

By the time they gathered themselves and realized what happened, Alec and Tremaine were at the end of the street. A few people ran after them. They wanted that rose. They wanted to grab what they knew to be a piece of God, and they were going to do anything to get it.

The helicopters that carried the television crews who were covering the small town's earthquake hovered overhead. The helicopter crews followed them and watched their every move. They thought they had the miraculous transformation on film, but when they played it back, all they could see was a white light and then the town was whole again. How it happened was a mystery, and Alec and Tremaine were at the heart of the story.

They ran as fast as they could, but they were losing ground and knew it would be only minutes before the crowd overtook them when Alec saw the red truck.

"Randi," Alec whispered.

Tremaine was glad to see her. They ran toward the truck. Randi could see that they were about to become part of a modern-day lynching. She sped up, turned the truck around, and opened the doors.

"Jump in," she yelled.

They grabbed the doors and held on. She hit the gas pedal before they were inside and fled the scene as fast as she could. She got some good distance between the town and them before she pulled over and stopped.

"What the hell happened? The town, it was intact. I saw it, it was like nothing happened, but I know something did. My truck, look at my truck, what is this? You"— She looked at Alec—"what you were saying about souls in a well and the holy crystal rose, all of that was true. How, what...what happened back there?" She stumbled over her words for a few minutes.

"We need to keep driving. We can explain, but you will have to be open-minded about it," Alec said.

"Open-minded. I just saw my truck and a whole town repair itself and he wants me to be open-minded." She laughed a little. She pulled the truck back onto the road and headed toward Oklahoma City.

"You know, you could call this story in before anyone else gets it to a major newspaper. That will look pretty good on a resume." Tremaine smiled and nodded his head.

"Do you see those guys in the helicopters that are everywhere? They already have the story, and now we are the story. So I think we need a how-to-survive strategy, because once this is out, we will be wanted by everyone, everywhere. How did I get mixed up in this? We'll keep driving, and hopefully we can get by, since no crime has been committed." She looked at each of them. "No crime has been committed, right?" she asked just as she saw a tall dark man standing in the roadway directly in front of her. She slowed the truck down and prepared to stop.

Alec looked up. "No, no, don't stop," he yelled.

"What? I have to stop. I'll run over him if I don't." She was scared and confused. She didn't know what to do, but she knew she couldn't run over someone with her truck. She could intentionally kill him.

Alec saw her hesitation and placed his foot over hers and pressed down on the gas pedal. The truck sped up faster and faster until it was upon him. As the truck barreled into him, Randi screamed in horror. She pulled the truck over as Alec lifted his foot from the gas pedal. She stopped the truck, jumped out, and ran back to where the accident took place, but there was no one there. There was no body lying in the street.

Tremaine knew she was about to lose it. He walked toward her and pulled her into his arms and held her while she cried.

"What was that?" she cried.

"Let's get back in the truck."

They walked back.

"Why don't I drive?" Tremaine opened up the back door, and she jumped in without a word. She couldn't talk. She was trying to rationalize everything that was happening around her, but she couldn't.

"Tell me . . . tell me everything," she said.

Alec didn't miss anything. He started with Tremaine showing up at his farm without cause and how he found Torrin's binder in the barn. He told her about the well and the souls that were trapped down there and how they came to be there, about Tremaine's great-grandfather John and the journey into the realm of death where they met Isadora, who they believed was Randi incarnated, and who the dark man really was."

"So I am a reincarnation of someone you met when you were dead and the man I just ran over is the Devil?" She thought for a moment. "You know, when I say it out loud, it doesn't sound so bad. I don't want to believe you, but after everything that's happened, I don't know what else to believe." A flash of light caught her eye. "What's that, those lights up ahead?" She looked out the window.

"Oh no, it's a roadblock." Alec looked at Tremaine. He slowed the truck down. There was enough traffic on the street to mask their presence for a little while.

"We could ram it," said Tremaine.

"What? I just got my truck back," said Randi. "I don't think that would be wise. I mean, as of right now, we haven't committed a crime. Neither of us broke any laws, so even if they arrested us, they can't hold us."

"So you're suggesting that we turn ourselves in," replied Tremaine.

"No, I suggest we stop and see what they want."

"They want the rose," said Alec, "and if they get it, we may never get it back."

"Let's not have it. Can we hide it somewhere in this desert and after the madness dies down, come back and get it?" said Tremaine.

"Stop," said Alec. "Let's think about this."

Tremaine pulled onto the shoulder of the road. "If we do that, where would we hide it? What if we never make it back here? How will we find it?"

"We can mark it somehow. Like you said, they are going to take it, so you may never get it back anyway," Randi said.

"She's right; we'll be in litigation for years trying to recover it. They'll call it a national security threat, and we'll never see it again," Tremaine said. He looked into the rearview mirror and watched as a black car pulled up behind them and stopped. "Look."

Alec and Randi turned to look out the rear window and saw Pastor Simmons exiting the car. Alec got out of the truck and walked around to meet him.

"What do you want?"

"I know what it is. I held it in my hand and I know what it is. How did you get it? It shouldn't be here. You have to take it back. Do you hear me? You have to take it back before chaos consumes us. Do you hear me?" The pastor was overwhelmed and still shaking from the events that happened in his small town. He started walking toward the front of the truck when Alec stepped in front of him.

"No, no . . . what do you want?" Alec asked again.

"I want to see it. I want to know what could do, what I

just saw. I need to feel it again." The look on Pastor Simmons's face was daunting. He struggled with his words, and he knew that his experience was miraculous, but he could feel that devastation came with it.

Alec looked down the road and saw cars and helicopters encroaching upon them.

"Pastor, I need your help." He walked back to the truck and grabbed the case. He looked at Tremaine. "I will meet you at the well."

Tremaine understood.

Alec grabbed Pastor Simmons's arm and guided him back to his car. They got inside. "Turn around and go back toward the town."

"I don't understand." Pastor Simmons started the car and began to turn. "Where are we going? We can't go back to the town; they will kill you for this."

"I know, but we have to evade the news crew and the roadblock. You just keep driving until I tell you to stop." The pastor drove toward the onslaught of news reporters and townspeople until Alec said, "Make this left."

He turned off the highway onto a rural road and sped away unnoticed. They watched as the news reporters sped by in mass pursuit of the bright red truck.

Randi climbed into the front seat and the two of them looked like a young couple out for an evening drive. Tremaine came upon the roadblock, where he was stopped and asked to exit the truck. They both got out and stood on the side of the road while the truck was searched inside and out, top to bottom.

"There were three of them," Officer Thompson said.

"Yeah, are you sure this is the truck? Maybe this isn't them," said Officer Green.

"It's gotta be," replied Officer Thompson.

"It's them." A gruff-looking man came from behind a van. He was a tall, medium-built man with dark skin. His bald head glistened in the sunlight, and his brown eyes danced around to capture everything in his field of view. He walked toward Tremaine and Randi. "Where is it?" he asked.

"Where is what?" Tremaine appeared confused by the question.

"So, the third man must have gotten out along the way and took it with him." He looked around. "You can tell me where it is, or we will have to take matters into our own hands and when we do that, things don't always end well. Do you understand?" Lieutenant Dryer tried to be as persuasive as possible.

"No, no, I don't understand. What are you talking about? What have I done? Do I need a lawyer?" Tremaine played it off well.

But Randi was genuinely frightened. She didn't have any loyalty to him or Alec, but she also knew she couldn't tell. Whatever was happening to them involved her, and she knew that telling would create another set of issues that may be worse.

Tremaine looked at her and, with his eyes, asked her to be strong as they walked them to separate cars and forced them inside. An officer followed them in her truck.

"Who are you, where are you taking us?" Tremaine pleaded with the men in dark suits with no identification or association with anyone or anything.

"Are you the police? FBI? What! What's going on here?"

They sped off, leaving a few men behind to look for Alec and the rose, who by then was moving south toward the New Mexico desert.

"What happens now?" asked Pastor Simmons.

"Just keep driving," replied Alec.

"I will be missed. They will look for me."

"No one is kidnapping you. Remember, you followed

us. No one can link you to us, and as soon as I'm in Oklahoma, you can go back home."

"What's in Oklahoma?" Pastor Simmons's curiosity was getting the better of him. There was obvious risk involved in this, but he couldn't help himself, he wanted to know.

"My home," answered Alec. He looked up at him and smiled, knowing that he wanted more. Alec had no idea where he was going.

Pastor Simmons kept driving down a long stretch of highway and wondered if he would ever see his small town again. He was regretting his choice to follow them.

"What is the name of the town back there again?"

"Mitchellville," said Pastor Simmons. He nervously looked at Alec. "What if I give you the car? I can catch a bus back home and then you can be on your way."

Alec smiled. "How do I know you won't tell them that I have your car and where we are headed? The moment you step out of the car, you can call the police."

"But I won't. I promise." The pastor was ready for this to be over. "If you force me to stay, it really will be kidnapping. That's a crime, you know."

"Yeah, I know. But if it is your plan to hightail it back home, why did you follow us in the first place? You said you wanted to know. You wanted to feel it again, and now you want to jump and run. What did you think would happen when you started out looking for us? What was going through your mind?"

"I just need to know that I wasn't dreaming. That it really does exist," he said softly.

"Oh, I see, and now that it has gotten a little hard, you don't want to know anymore. Is that it? You want to know, but not bad enough to do anything about it. Sounds cowardly." Alec turned and looked out the window at the flat land and the blanket of bright stars that canvassed the dark sky.

"I'm not a coward, but I'm also not crazy. I never expected to be pulled into a manhunt. I never expected to be kidnapped. I mean, it's not the kind of thing that you plan for, you know." Pastor Simmons smiled at the thought of planning for such an event. "I don't know what I expected. I just had to come."

Alec was silent for a while. He stared out the window seemingly mesmerized by the landscape. "Do you believe in fate?" he asked.

Pastor Simmons wasn't sure how to answer that. He hesitated. "Yes, yes, I do. I do believe that life draws you to certain things and people that sometimes test your faith and your beliefs. It is our choice to act upon it or not, but I do believe that we are put in certain places at certain times to do a particular thing." As he was talking, he realized what Alec was thinking. "You believe this is fate . . . that I am here for a reason."

"It allowed you to hold it."

"What do you mean?"

"The rose. The reason the man brought it to you was because he could not touch it. He knew it. He felt strongly that to touch it would be sudden death. I had to go through purification before I could touch it," Alec said.

"What kind of purification?" the pastor asked

"That's a story for another day. It's safe to say that you must be a man of great kindness and free from worldly burdens. Somehow you have managed to live a pure life, and I believe it found you."

"Nonsense." Pastor Simmons was stunned by what Alec said. His heart was racing, and he couldn't calm himself. "I admit that I live a austere and celibate life, but whether that makes me pure or not, I don't know. I try not to let the trappings of the world become my need, but I admit there are times when I wish for things and, well, you know, but I made a vow and I intend to keep it, God be willing."

Alec looked at him and smiled.

"We have to find somewhere to stay for the night. Let's stop at the next motel we see, and if you are still here in the morning, I'll tell you the story of how we got the rose and what we have to do. If you are not here in the morning, then I ask you to give me a day head start before you tell the authorities where I am. Can you promise me that? If you do, I will believe you."

"I promise." Pastor Simmons was all mixed up. He didn't want to believe Alec, but he had to believe what he'd seen in his small town. He had to believe the possibility that the crystal rose could have chosen him, and if so, what should he do?

He drove for another thirty minutes before he saw a motel on the side of the road. It was a run-down, unassuming place with few customers and fewer amenities, but all they wanted was a quick shower and a place to sleep. Alec thought that it was isolated enough that a manhunt may overlook it. He pulled into the parking lot and they both walked into the small lobby. The motel was old and musty and smelled of mold. The carpet should have been replaced ten years ago, and the walls needed a fresh coat of paint.

"It will do," said Alec.

Just as Alec walked into the lobby he could hear the news broadcast from the television that was mounted on the wall near the counter. They were talking about the miraculous event that occurred in Mitchellville and showed sketches of him and Tremaine.

"The two sketches that you see are composite drawings of the two men that are being pursued for questioning. Eyewitnesses say that the earthquake occurred not long after these two men, whose names are unknown, entered the town. The police are looking for a red Ford truck being driven by a young Black woman. Apparently she helped them flee the area after the appearance of the bright light, and the town miraculously repaired itself and the people presumed injured or dead regained life and wounds were healed. It is by far the most fantastic story I have ever had to broadcast, and if I had not seen the pictures of the devastation after the earthquake, I would not believe it." Anchorwoman Jennifer Post was visibly shaken by the story and wasn't sure if she was telling the story as fact or fiction.

Alec looked at the sketches and noticed the resemblance to himself and started to back out of the lobby before anyone saw him. Luckily, there were only a handful of people there, but all it took was one person to recognize him.

Pastor Simmons looked back at Alec and followed him outside.

"Ok, you have a choice to make. You can go in there and get the room and allow me to finish my job, or you can report me to the clerk and it will be over by morning. Either way, it's up to you."

"You wait in the car. I'll be right back." Pastor Simmons looked Alec straight in the eyes, as if reassuring him that he would support his cause. He walked back inside and got one room with two beds in the name of James White.

"Thank you," said the clerk as he passed over the key. "Room 106," he said. He was so enthralled with the story, he didn't look to see whose name was on the register.

Pastor Simmons took the key and walked out. He got in the car and drove around back. They walked into Room 106, closed the curtains, turned on the television, and watched the broadcast news tell the most fantastic story they had ever heard.

They both slept soundly while Tremaine and Randi sat in a holding room at the police station. A man and woman from the Federal Bureau of Investigation, National Security Administration and the local police department moved in and out of the room, asking the same questions over and over again.

"Who are you? Who are you working with? What caused the bright light? Did the light repair the town?"

They both held their ground and professed nothing. Since they didn't have the rose, they claimed ignorance.

"God, how many times do I have to say it? We were driving back to Oklahoma. We are on our way back from her mother's funeral. I don't know anything about what you're talking about." Tremaine was tired and frustrated and felt that if he had to say that again he would explode.

Captain Hicks knocked on the door and opened it slightly. He poked his head inside the room. "Blake, can I speak with you?"

Lieutenant Blake gave Tremaine a daunting stare and walked out. "What is it?" Lieutenant Blake looked frustrated.

"Are you getting anywhere?" asked Captain Hicks.

"No, no, but I know somehow they are involved."

"I don't know. Their story about her mother's funeral is true, and there were eyewitnesses to her presence at the funeral, so they could be telling the truth that they were on their way back to Oklahoma," said Captain Hicks.

"What about him? Did anyone see him there?" asked the lieutenant.

"No, but he may have come along just to help her drive, but didn't go to the funeral with her. The point is, they could be telling the truth." Captain Hicks wanted it to be over. "Either find a reason to keep them, or let them go."

"Ok, I hear you. But I'm putting a tail on them. I can

feel that he's lying, and if I'm right, he will lead us to it."
Lieutenant Blake walked back inside the holding room.
"All right you win for now, but I will be watching you. I
will not let you get away with this."

"Get away with what!" Tremaine stood, anger in his
eyes. "What did I do that you should be holding me and
harassing me like this? What did I do?" He stared at
Lieutenant Blake and waited for his response.

"You know how all this happened."

"Let's say I do. So what? What crime was committed?"
Tremaine stepped back and headed for the door. He
looked back at the Lieutenant and walked out.

Randi was waiting in the hallway. She was so glad to
see him, she threw her arms around him. It shocked him
a little, but he liked it.

As they walked toward the door, Tremaine heard the
news broadcast proclaiming a rise in crime, death, and
injury all across the country and internationally since the
event occurred in Mitchellville. Political leaders around
the world were encased in bitter disputes, and each of
them was ready to destroy each other for irrational, insane reasons. Rational thinking had ceased, and emotional
fervor claimed the planet.

"We have to hurry," said Tremaine.

"What do you have to hurry to do? Does all of this
have something to do with the light?" Lieutenant Blake
had followed them to the front entrance.

Tremaine turned and looked at him.

"We need to hurry home," he said and grabbed
Randi's hand and walked out.

It was eleven o'clock at night, and driving would be
impossible. They found a motel to rest for the night. Tremaine had no money, and Randi had little, so they had to
share one room and even though they asked for two
beds, they were astounded to open the door and see the

one large king-sized bed. Randi's heart skipped a beat while Tremaine smiled.

"We need to get this changed. We asked for two beds, didn't we?" She started to walk back to the lobby.

He grabbed her arm. "Look, we can do this. That bed is big enough for four people. I'm sure we can both sleep without touching each other."

She looked at him suspiciously and wondered if she should.

"Well, I guess you're right. I mean we are both adults, so it should be all right. But, if you roll over, so help me, you'll be talking like a munchkin."

"All right, all right, I get it. Besides, I'm so tired, I'll be asleep before you lay down."

They walked inside, threw off their shoes and fell across the bed. He forced himself into the bathroom and re-entered the room in his boxer shorts minutes later.

She stared at his beautiful physique. Under the over-sized clothes he wore was a young man with firm, chiseled muscles and flat abs. His arms were tight, and she just wanted to reach out and touch his biceps. At that moment, she wanted to be Issi and wanted to remember everything.

He knew he caught her off guard and he held back the smile. He slid into bed and wrapped the covers close around him.

She regained her composure, grabbed her purse, and walked into the bathroom. A little later she peeked out into the room to see if he was asleep. He seemed to be sleeping soundly, so she felt it was safe to sneak by in her bra and panties. On her tiptoes, she slowly walked into the room, placed her clothes on the chair, and when she turned around his big brown eyes were staring straight at her. She was so embarrassed that she tried to cover herself with her hands. But to get any coverage, she needed four more hands. She ran for the bed, pulled the covers back, and slipped inside.

She snarled at him. "You see, you see, that's what I'm talking about."

He chuckled. "You're cute." He smiled and turned over.

The night passed quickly. They were both so tired that they slept soundly. When he awoke they were wrapped in each other's arms. He held her and studied her pretty face as she slept nestled in his arms. He gently kissed her forehead and softly caressed her hair.

She stirred around a little and eventually woke up looking into his eyes. It took her a moment to realize where she was. She looked around and at his chest, but she didn't move. She felt comfortable and secure in his arms.

She didn't want to invest in a new relationship, because she hadn't had much luck with men before, and she didn't want to replay that same old script with someone else. She wasn't ready. But she wasn't threatened by him. She had to admit, he was growing on her.

When he looks at me, does he see Issi or Randi? she thought. *Who am I to him?*

He kissed her gently as she let her doubts melt into lust and desire. She held him as he caressed her body and gently moved her under him. Their bodies melted into one as she called his name when he thrust his body into her. She knew this was a moment in time that may never become the love of her dreams, but the moment was exhilarating, and she enjoyed the passion of a man for the first time in a while. She felt like a woman. She felt feminine and free. She allowed herself to submit to the moment and not think about tomorrow.

When Alec awoke and saw Pastor Simmons still there, he took a deep breath of relief. All night he waited for the knock on the door, but as he hoped, Pastor Simmons kept his word and did not tell the authorities where they were. He crawled out of bed and headed for the bathroom. He looked at the pastor and smiled. The pastor acknowledged him with a nod and went about packing for the long journey ahead.

The two men pulled themselves together and headed outside, and within moments, they could hear the helicopter blades roaring in the morning sky.

"It wasn't me. I promise." The pastor was adamant that he did not contact the authorities. He looked into the sky. "They're just wandering. They don't know we're here."

"Maybe you're right." Alec hesitated as he watched the sky. He couldn't see the helicopter, but he could hear it. "Let's get out of here before they show up."

They started the car and headed out onto the highway. Alec knew that they would not have much time before the authorities discovered them. He wondered about Tremaine and Randi and hoped that they made it back to the well. After everything he'd been through, he was scared. He remembered Kathleen and wished she were here. He remembered how he felt when he thought he'd lost Tremaine and the pain caused by hate and guilt. He listened to the news and knew that all of the chaos going on in the world was because of him. So many people dying and killing.

"How can I not feel guilt?" he whispered.

"What did you say?" asked Pastor Simmons.

Alec nervously glanced at him. He didn't realize that he spoke out loud.

"I was listening to the news. It's scary."

"What does all of this have to do with the rose and you?"

"Yeah, I did promise to tell you everything. The reason

all of this madness is going on is because we removed the crystal rose from its heavenly place, and if we don't get it back, the world will destroy itself."

"Take it back to where? Where did it come from?" Pastor Simmons was so curious, he could hardly wait to hear the story.

Alec took a deep breath and tried his best to explain.

Pastor Simmons sat in awe of his tale. Part of him found it so unbelievable that he immediately discarded the thought, but then he had to admit, everything he'd seen so far had been outside of real life, so he couldn't dismiss it so easily.

"What happened to the souls? How does Tremaine fit into all of this . . . and Randi? How did you—"

"Wait, wait. I'll get to all of it." Alec smiled a little. He knew he was taking a chance telling this to anyone, but then who would believe him? "Tremaine was staying with me on my farm and discovered a ledger left by Torrin telling the whole story. It also told that the souls were trapped in the wall of the well where Torrin threw in the coin. Tremaine climbed into the well and discovered that the ledger was true and the souls are trapped."

"Wait a minute, wait just one damn minute. Are you telling me that there are souls stuck in a well? Is that what I'm hearing?"

"Yes."

"Wow! Go on." The pastor couldn't wait to get to the end of this story.

"Yes, well, once I discovered the truth, Tremaine and I started out on a journey to find the rose to release the souls."

"How did you know where to look?"

"There was a riddle in the ledger left by Torrin that gave us a clue. You see, Torrin, Michael, and my father

David all tried to find the rose, but couldn't. Through the help of Tremaine's great-grandfather, we were able to cross over into the realm of death and purge ourselves of our greatest fears."

"The realm of death." Pastor Simmons smiled at the thought. "So you died and came back?"

"Well, yeah, I guess you could say that." Alec knew how crazy he sounded, but for him, it was all real.

"So now what?"

"One of the verses in the riddle is that if we remove the rose from its rightful place, chaos will plague the earth and we will have to return it. But it is the only means of freeing the souls."

"One of which you will become, if you don't break the curse."

"Yes." Alec glanced over at him and wondered what he thought of him.

"Do you think this is selfish? I mean, with everything that's going on. Maybe I should have taken my lumps and joined my family in the well for an eternity. I mean, they caused this mess, and others shouldn't have to pay for it."

"Do you have children?" asked Pastor Simmons.

Alec started to say no, but then he remembered what Gwyneth told him when he was lost behind the cave wall.

"Yes, I do," he answered hesitantly.

"Then you can never know when or if this will ever end. Your children and the children of the townspeople could be trapped for a millennium. I can understand why you would try, but what I don't understand is why I'm here."

"I'm not sure either, but it allowed you to touch it, so there is a reason, and I'm sure we will find out."

"I don't think I want to—What was that!" Pastor Simmons felt cold as a dark shadow moved through the car. It was bone-chilling cold and foreboding. He looked around to see the dark figure of a man sitting in the back-seat. He jumped around in his seat as Alec pulled the rose close to him.

"You will not win. I have already destroyed your friends. They are dead, and you will be soon." The dark shadow moved across the backseat and out the rear window and out of sight.

"Oh, and I forgot to tell you that we are being chased by the Devil," Alec said calmly.

Pastor Simmons was still in shock. He turned slowly and stared at Alec for several minutes and wondered how he could be taking this so calmly. He sat in the seat and watched his hands shake from fright.

"That's good to know . . . I think." He took a deep breath and tried to calm himself. "Why didn't he take it?"

"He can't touch it." Alec laid the rose on the backseat and kept driving toward Oklahoma.

"Do you think they are dead, like he said?" the pastor asked.

"I don't know. You can't believe him. All I can do is pray for God's help and hope," said Alec.

"Yes, pray."

CHAPTER EIGHT

Full Circle

Tremaine and Randi stayed close to each other as they watched the people around them move from being normal human beings to hard-core criminals and murderers. There were riots going on everywhere. People had lost their souls, their humanity. Even those who would never say an unkind word found themselves feeling hate and envy. They all wanted something, but they couldn't figure out what, and they had to do anything to get it.

Randi gasped at the man who was chasing a neighbor up the road with a knife to kill him. He screamed in anger that he was tired of being polite and that he always hated him. The lady across the street with her husband and two children looked at them and said she couldn't do it anymore and walked away.

"Jewel," he screamed, but she didn't look back. She walked as if she was under a spell, as if she were being pulled into the arms of a jealous lover.

An explosion rattled the buildings around them and fires and smoke bellowed into the sky.

"Please hurry," Randi whispered to Tremaine. He

filled the gas tank and moved the truck out onto the road just before the gas station owner came out of the store with a double-barrel shotgun and fired off a round that ignited the tanks. The explosion was enormous and Tremaine sped up to escape the encroaching blaze. He got back onto the highway and moved east as fast as he could. They were both shaking.

"What's going on, Tremaine? What's happened to everyone?" Randi couldn't remember ever being that scared.

"It's the rose. We have to get it back. Until we do, we will be inside this horror." Tremaine kissed her gently and put his arm around her. He drove as fast as he could and prayed as hard as he could.

When he saw the wonderful sign WELCOME TO OKLAHOMA, he almost cried. "A few more miles, a few more miles," he whispered. He drove for a few more minutes when the truck got really cold. He knew what it was. "He's here."

"Who's here? Why is it so cold?" Randi was even more scared.

"You are already dead. Make a wish, and I will save your life." The dark man sat in the back seat of the truck. His evil tone was daunting as he smiled and slithered out the back window.

Randi screamed in horror. "Stop, stop, let me out."

She grabbed the door handle to open it, but Tremaine reached over and stopped her.

"No, Randi, no, you don't want to get out. It's all right, he can't really hurt us unless we let him. Calm down, calm down."

She sat back in the seat. She couldn't think, her breath was short, and her hands were shaking.

"Oh no." Tremaine hit his brakes when he saw the traffic jam a few yards ahead. He hit the brakes, but the truck didn't slow down. He kept pumping the brake pedal, but the truck kept plowing down the road.

"Oh God, what's happening?" she cried.

"Put your seat belt on and hold on," Tremaine said.

Randi clamped the seat belt across her and held on as her beautiful red truck hit the edge of a car that propelled the truck into the air and off the road into an embankment.

Just before hitting the trees, the dark man's face flashed in front of them with an ominous smile on his face. "You are already dead." He smiled and grinned.

What took only moments seemed to be an eternity. Everything seemed to be in slow motion, as if they were watching the show from outside the truck. They looked at each other and felt the warmth and love between them.

Tremaine whispered, "Randi," and the truck hit the ground and plowed into the trees below.

They lay there unconscious, just as John felt Tremaine's agonizing pain throughout his body. He sat up in his bed and screamed in agony.

Alaya ran to his side and tried to calm him. "What is it, Grandfather? What's happened?" She held him and tried to comfort him, but he began to pull himself out of his bed.

This was the bed that John had planned to die in, but now he knew that his fate was not his to own.

"I must go. My child called out to me. He is in trouble," John said as he forced himself to the edge of the bed.

"It's Tremaine, isn't it?" Alaya asked.

"Yes."

"Where is he? How will you find him?" she asked.

"I will follow his voice. Help me," he said as he stood and walked to the wardrobe to pull out the clothes to wear.

She helped him dress and helped him to the truck. She grabbed a few essentials and locked the door behind her. She guided the truck down the long driveway and out onto the road.

"Which way?" she asked

"Follow his voice," he said, pointing east.

"You will have to guide me, Grandfather. I cannot hear him."

"I will guide you."

As Alec and Pastor Simmons crossed into the state of Oklahoma they could feel the presence of the dark man. People were moving about everywhere, committing one heinous act after the other. News reports from all over the world spoke of atrocities being committed everywhere. People were destroying great works of art, defacing monuments, burning homes and schools, killing and maiming each other.

"I hope you can stop this. It seems—"

"Stop . . . I hear, I hear him," said Alec.

"Hear who?"

"John, I can hear him. Something's wrong. I can feel it. It's around here. Something happened here." Alec stopped the car and pulled onto the shoulder. He could see the traffic jam a mile ahead and knew that he should not go that far.

"Now wait a minute. Wait a minute. We can't stop. We both know that the authorities are on our heels. Are you crazy?" Pastor Simmons didn't understand.

"Remember I told you that we entered the realm of death with the help of Tremaine's great-great-grandfather? He is Navajo."

"Yes, so?"

"Somehow because of that connection, because he had to connect with our spirit, he is still linked with us. It's like he's part of me now. It's hard to explain, but I know I have to stop."

"Okay, okay, stop and do what?"

"I'm not sure, but . . ." He waited and listened. "It's

over there. He walked to the edge of the road and looked down the embankment and saw pieces of the red truck strewn all over the place. "Oh God, Tremaine." He looked back at Pastor Simmons. "Grab the crystal rose and come on."

"Who me?" The Pastor didn't want to touch it again. He nervously reached into the car and pulled it out just as he heard the helicopter blades whirling in the evening sky. He grabbed the case and ran down the hill behind Alec. By the time they reached the battered broken truck, the helicopter was setting down on the highway.

"Let's get them out of there." Alec forced the door opened and pulled Tremaine and Randi from the truck. They were both in bad shape. "I'll carry Tremaine, and you take her." Alec picked up Tremaine's broken body and tried his best to carry him. Alec was not a young man, so Tremaine's dead weight seemed more than he could bear.

"Here, I'll take him. You take her," said Pastor Simmons. He took Tremaine into his arms, and Alec lifted a much lighter Randi, and they walked into the woods hoping to find some shelter. They knew it would only be moments before the authorities figured it out and began the hunt.

They walked for an hour, and eventually came across an old abandoned farm. The house was barely standing, but Alec knew they couldn't go on carrying them. They forced the old door open and made it inside. Alec laid Tremaine down on an old sofa and Pastor Simmons put Randi's small body in a large chair.

"Let me take a look at him." Pastor Simmons sat beside Tremaine and started to check his body for broken bones.

"Do you know what you're doing?" asked Alec.

"Kinda. I have a medical degree from Johns Hopkins."

"You're a doctor?"

"Yes, it was my first love, until I decided to answer the call."

"Really?" Alec looked surprised. He looked around as he heard Randi stirring about. He went to her. "It's okay, just sit still."

She screamed and reached for her head.

Alec quickly placed his hand over her mouth to keep the authorities from hearing her. "It's all right. Please be calm."

She looked into his eyes, and when she realized who he was, she hugged him desperately and cried.

"Tremaine, how is he? Is he all right? What happened? There was this man, an awful man and he made the car crash and . . . I . . ."

"It's all right, Randi. We're here now, and Tremaine is going to be fine. Just please be quiet; we are being followed."

She looked over and saw Tremaine on the sofa and tried to stand to go to him, but she couldn't. The moment she tried to move, excruciating pain grabbed her ribs and head and she fell back into the chair.

"He'll be all right. You just sit here. I'll see what I can find around here that we can use."

Alec looked around in the old house. The farmhouse was made of logs. It reminded him of his cabin and farm with the big fireplace and the huge kitchen. He searched around and found sheets and blankets, a bottle of liquor, an old rifle, a box of bullets and a box of matches. He immediately filled the gun barrel with the bullets and took a long swallow of the liquor.

"I needed that," he said. He walked back into the living room, where Tremaine was still unconscious and Randi was struggling with the pain.

Pastor Simmons took the sheets and began to tear them into strips. He wrapped Randi's rib cage and poured some of the liquor on a cloth and wiped the cut on her head. He wrapped a bandage around her head and gave her the bottle.

"Here, take a drink."

She took the bottle and turned it up. She took in as much as she could before gagging.

"Now, lay back and try to rest."

He walked over to Tremaine and used the wet cloth to clean his wounds. "He may have a concussion. He hit his head pretty hard." Pastor Simmons dabbed the cloth around the wound gently to clean it. "Did you check the medicine cabinets?" he asked Alec.

"No, no, I didn't," answered Alec.

Pastor Simmons stood and walked to the bathroom. He looked around and found some bandages and a sewing kit. He threaded the needle and soaked the needle and thread in the liquor. He wiped the wound again and began to sew the wound closed on Tremaine's head. He covered the stitches with bandages, and then he wrapped his head with a stripping from the sheets.

"We are going to have a problem real soon, because we shouldn't move him. If they find us, what'll we do?" the pastor asked.

Alec showed him the gun.

"Are you sure it will fire? It looks older than you."

"Well, every now and then, I still fire up, so maybe this old girl will too." Alec smiled. "I think I'll take a look around."

He walked outside and looked around. He went into the barn and found nothing but old horse stalls, hay, a few tools hanging from the walls, and an old rusted tractor. As he was walking back he noticed a storm cellar. He opened it and went inside. It was large enough for the four of them to stay for a while. He needed a way to mask it. He pulled some old dried bushes and twigs from the ground and placed a pile of debris near the storm door.

He walked back inside the house. "I may have found us a place to hide. I'll get Randi, you grab Tremaine." Alec helped each of them inside, and then he got out and pulled the bushes, twigs, and broken pieces of wood over the door. He made sure it could not be seen. He opened the door and slipped inside with one arm still outside to reposition the wood on top. He didn't know if he covered the door completely, but he tried. They were not down there long before the sound of voices came from outside.

"This place looks abandoned," said Sergeant Long.

"The perfect place to hide," Lieutenant Dryer replied.

Four or five men walked inside to find the place empty. They looked all around, but nothing.

"They were here. I know it. They are still here somewhere. They have to be," Lieutenant Dryer said.

He went into the living room and sat in the chair and looked at the sofa and noticed a spot of blood. He got up and walked over to examine it. "It's still wet."

He walked outside. "They are here somewhere. I don't care if it takes all night, find them.

The policemen searched the area for hours. When they couldn't find anything around the farm, they started searching the surrounding woods, but they couldn't find them. Lieutenant Dryer was furious. He could feel them, and he wanted so much to know what was going on. He was more curious about the crystal rose than he was about finding them.

"I know you're here," he yelled. "If you come out, nothing will happen to you, I promise. All I want is to talk to you about what happened. That seems simple enough." He was just about to give up when he stumbled on a pile of wood and bushes that moved away when he pushed them. He started to lift the pieces of wood away and discovered the storm cellar door.

Alec knew that they were in trouble. He positioned his rifle to shoot the moment the door opened. He never thought he would be positioning himself to kill a man. He always thought that a man who would commit murder was the lowest of the low, but there he was holding a gun preparing to commit the most heinous of all acts, taking another man's life.

"Look at this," said Lieutenant Dryer as he reached down to open the door.

"What are you doing?" a voice came from across the yard.

Lieutenant Dryer stopped and looked up to see an old man and a woman staring at him.

"What do you want, old man?"

"What are you doing here?"

"Look, this is police business. This has nothing to do with you."

"You are on my land. What happens on my land has everything to do with me." John stood proud and strong. He felt energized for the first time in years. He remained calm and waited for their response.

"This isn't your land," said Sergeant Long.

Everyone stood around watching the exchange. Lieutenant Dryer walked toward John and stood directly in front of him.

"Look, I will throw you off your land if you don't leave and let us take care of our business here."

"Do you have a warrant?" John asked calmly.

"No one lives here." Lieutenant Dryer was frustrated. He forgot all about the storm cellar.

"I did not say I lived here. I said it is my land. My ancestors are buried here. My people consider this sacred land. Why do you think it has been left this way for so many years? If you do not have a warrant you can not search here."

Lieutenant Dryer did not have a search warrant. He didn't really believe John, but he couldn't disprove him, so he had to go. He gathered his detail and walked back toward the highway.

"That old ancestral burial ground thing gets them every time." Alaya smiled at his wit and helped him move around the farm. "Yes, Tremaine, I hear you. Where are you?"

He turned and walked to the storm cellar and opened it. Alec was so afraid that he would have to shoot someone. He didn't know what was going on, but he couldn't hear the policemen anymore, so he knew something stopped them from opening the door. He stood ready to defend the lives of everyone in the cellar with his own knowing that without him, all was lost. For a moment he thought he heard John's voice.

"No, it is me."

He wasn't sure, but he relaxed his stance, so when the door opened he hesitated.

"Thank God." He took a deep breath and calmed himself when he looked into John's face. "Are they gone?"

"Yes, I think so," said John.

Alec climbed out of the cellar and helped Pastor Simmons lift Randi and Tremaine out. John was startled when he saw Pastor Simmons. He looked into his eyes as if his soul was clear to him.

The pastor smiled at him and took his hand. "I did not expect to see you this soon," Pastor Simmons whispered.

"I am ready," said John.

"Help me get Tremaine inside," said Alec as he tried to carry him.

Pastor Simmons took Tremaine from Alec's weak arms and carried him inside. He laid him back on the sofa and checked his bandages to make sure everything was still intact.

Alec helped Randi to a chair. "How are you holding up?" he asked.

"I'm fine, I'll be fine, but what about him? Do we need to get him to a doctor?" she asked.

"No, he is here with us. We just have to allow his spirit to heal his body. We have to wait a little longer for him to come back to us, but he will." John sat beside Tremaine.

"We can't stay here. I guarantee that Lieutenant Dryer is standing in the woods watching us right now," said Alec.

"If that's true, we can't make it back to the car either," said Randi.

"You're right. We have to find another way." Alec walked to the window and studied the forest that surrounded them. He knew they were out there just waiting for them to try to make it back to the road.

"They don't know who I am. They won't connect me with you, so I can move about freely. I think I'll see what's going on. I'll walk out the back and try to get behind them." Pastor Simmons headed for the back door.

"Do you think you'll need this?" Alec held up the rifle.

"No, you keep it. You may need it if I don't return. Besides, I have to appear to be lost if I am discovered wandering around out here."

"Good luck." Alec closed the door behind him and locked it. The old house was so fragile that he had to smile at locking a door that one push could knock down easily. But, nevertheless, he felt safer with it locked.

Pastor Simmons followed a path through the woods that led him toward the road. He moved through trees and bushes and climbed on fallen trunks.

After about thirty minutes, he heard voices chatting about the people hiding at the farm. Pastor Simmons kneeled down to listen. He searched the area to see where they were. He felt an ominous cold around him and knew that he was not alone. He finally saw the policemen standing amongst the trees just below the road. What was most chilling was the dark figure that passed amongst them without notice. Pastor Simmons knew who he was. He stayed low and tried to get as close as he could. He listened as they plotted on how to flush Alec and the others out of the farmhouse.

"It's only a few of them. What are we waiting for? Let's just kill them and take the light," one of the policemen said.

"And then what? Who is going to face the murder charge?" asked Lieutenant Dryer.

"What murder charge? Have you seen what's happening to us? Everybody's lost their minds. No one will care about these few people, with all the carnage going on out there." The policeman pointed to the road.

Pastor Simmons realized that he was right. They wouldn't care, and not only that, even if he got to the car, he couldn't get through the massive traffic jam and hoards of crazy people that seemed to be everywhere. He looked around and saw an old dirt road that must have been used by the farm owners to get back and forth to the main road. If he could get to the car without incident, he may be able to bring it down through the woods without being seen. He knew it was unlikely, but when you're down to one option, you use the one you got. He watched as the dark man waved his hand across Sergeant Long's face and moved along as on air.

"I'm done waiting." Sergeant Long took his gun from his holster and started walking. "I got better things to do. We can have the light. I want it and I want it now."

A few of the other policemen followed him. Just as Lieutenant Dryer stumped out his cigarette and started to follow them, Pastor Simmons stood up and startled Sergeant Long. He pointed his weapon and fired.

Pastor Simmons waved his hand and stopped them. All things stopped around him. The bullet hung in mid-air, and Lieutenant Dryer was staring at Pastor Simmons as if surprised to see anyone in these woods.

Sergeant Long held his gun, and the others looked along the path of the bullet. They were frozen in time. Birds hung in mid-air, and bees seemed trapped by the flowers that encased them. No one could move, not a word or sound was heard, not even the breaking twigs that cracked under his feet as he walked toward the dark man.

"So you have been helping them all along." The dark man walked toward Pastor Simmons through the policemen standing frozen in time.

"It is time for this to end," Pastor Simmons replied.

"Look around. I'm just beginning."

"You cannot keep them. Among them are chosen ones. You knew this when you gave them the riddle. You knew that someday it had to end."

"He made a wish. I granted it. It should stand firm throughout the ages." The dark man was adamant.

"I didn't make a wish, I owe you nothing, and I will do everything in my power to get them to the well."

"Your powers are weak, they will die, and I will have his soul and all of those that are his."

"I have him, and you know what that means." Pastor Simmons waved his hand all around as if to indicate the oneness of God that surrounded them.

"I will always win. If it's not Torrin Wilhelm, it will be someone else. Selfish desire will always corrupt what you try so hard to hold on to."

"And what is that?"

"Hope." The dark man smiled. "You always hope that they will be someone other than who they are, but you see, I know them. They are more like me than they are like you."

"You are wrong."

The dark man moved closer to intimidate him.

Pastor Simmons closed his eyes, and a beautiful white glow shone around him. He was radiating in a soft white light that kept him from harm.

The dark man reached out to touch him and the light burned his hand. He backed up.

"Mmmmm, well, I guess we shall see. Only time will tell," he said as he faded into the trees.

Pastor Simmons walked to the street and got the car. He brought it back to the farmhouse. Just as he got out of the car he waved his hand, and everything went back to that moment in time.

Sergeant Long found himself shooting at a tree.

"What, I thought I saw somebody. I—what was it?" Sergeant Long stuttered.

"Yeah, there was someone. I saw him too," said Lieutenant Dryer. He looked all around but no one was there. He knew it had something to do with Tremaine and Randi and those folks hiding out at that farm.

It took them a few minutes to get their bearings and remember what they were getting ready to do. "We were going back to the farm, right?"

"Yeah, yeah." Sergeant Long started walking. Just as they reached the farm they heard what sounded like an automobile roaring by through the woods behind the farm. When they stopped and looked they were shocked to see a car passing them on an old dirt road headed to the main highway and they were caught out in the middle of the woods close to an hour's walk back to the road.

Lieutenant Dryer was furious. He was beside himself and couldn't figure out how they got a car. There wasn't one there when they were searching around. He wanted to know how all of them could have missed seeing the car. He ran back toward the highway and they all followed him. He yelled the all the way back at each of them for missing the car. "How could we miss it?" he kept asking.

Alec made it back to the road with everyone piled into the car. He stopped at John's truck. John decided to stay with Tremaine, so Pastor Simmons and Alaya drove the truck. They drove away from the crowd and turned off the highway onto side streets.

They were in Oklahoma, so Alec had a good idea how to get back home. He couldn't wait to see his farm, and he hoped that Tilly was all right. They were just a few hours away, and his heart was pounding with excitement at being this close. He also knew that the dark man wasn't done with them yet. He knew that Lieutenant Dryer would soon be on his tail and he was afraid for Tremaine, but most importantly, he was afraid for himself. He was the key, and he knew that if anything happened to him, all was lost.

"John." Alec looked in his rearview mirror at him.

John looked up.

"I need for you to tell him something. If you do, do you think he will understand?"

"Yes, he can hear me."

"If I don't make it, he has to contact a man in Arizona, in Phoenix. His name is Edward Hamilton. He has to make him understand and give him the crystal rose. He can finish the job."

"Who is this man?" John asked.

"My son."

Alec focused on the road. He looked in the mirror to make sure Alaya and Pastor Simmons was behind him. He drove through small towns and communities on the outskirts of Oklahoma City. He took back streets and alleys, and everywhere they went, the streets were filled with people running about, doing all sorts of horrible things. They were fighting each other like it was the end of the world. As if they'd all just gotten news that all life would end tomorrow and today was their last day to live, and for many it was true. It all seemed so primal.

Less than an hour away, I'll be home, Alec thought.

Randi sat in the front seat and watched as the madness went on around her. She was startled when a bottle hit the front window and cracked it. She screamed and covered her face.

Alec weaved between the crowds and debris in the street as best he could, and John held onto Tremaine tightly in the back seat.

People were breaking windows, setting buildings on fire, stealing, and looting. It was nothing to see someone shoot an unarmed person without provocation.

Someone jumped into the back of Alaya's truck and broke the back window and tried to get in. Pastor Simmons moved to the backseat and fought with him. He eventually took a piece of broken glass and slit the man's throat.

"Oh God, what is happening to us? What's going on?" Alaya cried.

Pastor Simmons sat in the back and held his head in his hands. For him this was the ultimate sin, and Alaya could see his grief over it.

"Don't do that. He was going to kill us. It was him or us. You did the only thing you could. We have to survive, or this is the way it will be forever. You did what you had to do."

"I know. I just wish there could have been another way," he said.

"That's it," Alec screamed as he turned down a small street. "That's my home over there." He pointed down the street. He couldn't have been happier. He was going to stop inside and then head straight for the well with the rose.

The farm was looking a little worn. The grass needed cutting, and weeds had overtaken the farm, but it was a beautiful sight to Alec. He couldn't wait to get inside and settle down. He parked the truck and helped Randi get out. Pastor Simmons carried Tremaine inside, and Alaya helped John.

Alec walked Pastor Simmons to a bedroom, where he laid Tremaine down, and walked Alaya and John to another bedroom, where she helped John settle down to rest.

Randi stretched out on the living room sofa, and Pastor Simmons and Alaya followed Alec into the kitchen.

"Let me see what I can find to eat. I know I didn't leave much, but I think I had some cans of soup around here somewhere."

He checked the shelves and under the sink and found several cans of soup, a jar of olives, and cans of fruit. He pulled open the drawer and got the can opener and found a pot, rinsed it out, and put it on the stove.

The soup smelled good.

Alaya found several bowls and washed them out and sat them on the table. Alec filled each bowl and poured another can in the pot to boil. Alaya took a bowl to Randi. She placed it on the coffee table and helped her sit up. She was so hungry, she practically drank the soup.

Alaya took another bowl into John's room. She helped him sit up and spoon-fed him as much as he could eat, which wasn't very much.

He was exhausted. The trip was tiring for everyone, but for a one hundred-year-old man, it drained what little strength he had away. He lay back down and fell into a deep sleep.

Alaya walked back into the kitchen and sat at the table.

She didn't speak much; she ate some soup and listened as Alec and Pastor Simmons planned out the next move.

"So, this is where it all began." Pastor Simmons looked all around.

"Yeah, I guess you could say that. The place looked a lot different then, when Torrin was here," Alec replied.

"What are you going to do now?" asked Pastor Simmons.

"I guess I'll have to take the rose to the well."

"And then what?"

"I don't know." Alec looked surprised that he really didn't know what he was supposed to do with the crystal rose.

"You don't know? Then how will you know if you succeed?"

"I don't know that either. I only know that this rose is supposed to free them. How? I don't know."

"Well, I guess we'll play it by ear and see what happens." Pastor Simmons took a sip of his soup. "Good soup."

Alec finished his soup and a can of peaches and walked back to check on Tremaine. He could hear him talking. He walked into the room. Tremaine was sitting up in the bed, but his eyes were closed. He was talking to someone, but no one was in the room.

"Alaya, come here."

She walked in. Pastor Simmons followed her.

"Kathleen, we lost you. Where have you been?" said Tremaine.

"Who is he talking to?" Alaya asked. She looked all around and saw no one. "Who is Kathleen?"

"She was with us on our death journey. She was our guide," said Alec. He walked to Tremaine and sat on the bed and looked at his face. Tremaine was still unconscious, but Kathleen had somehow tapped into his subconscious.

"Tell me, Kathleen, what do you want me to know?" Tremaine said. "He is here. The shadow hovers over this house. He will stop us. He is evil."

"What is it?" asked Alaya.

"Great-grandfather, I am here. Yes, Great-grandfather, I will do as you say." Tremaine lay back down on the bed as if nothing happened and slept.

Pastor Simmons checked his eyes and his breathing.

"He's sleeping. I think he's just sleeping. He should wake on his own in a few hours," said Pastor Simmons.

Alec opened the curtains and looked out the window and noticed how dark it was outside. He went into the living room and opened the front door and it was pitch-black outside. Pastor Simmons looked out over his shoulders.

Randi opened the curtains. "What's wrong?" she asked.

"What time is it?" asked Alec.

"Around nine, I guess," said Pastor Simmons. "What's wrong? It's night time."

"Where is the moon, street lights, stars, any light?" asked Alec. He stepped back inside and closed the door. "It's him. We have to get to that well."

"In this darkness? Can you tell where it is?" asked Alaya.

"I'll have to try," he said.

"What's going on? Where are we?" Tremaine stood in the hallway looking confused and bewildered.

"Oh my God, you're awake." Alaya ran to him and hugged him.

Alec threw his arms around him too.

Tremaine didn't understand the excitement, but he let them hug him and figured he would ask later. He looked over at Randi and smiled. He walked over to her and hugged her.

"I thought I had lost you," she said.

"Never," he replied. He kissed her cheek and turned to Alec. "How did we get here? Are we back at your house? What happened?" He had a thousand questions.

"What is the last thing you remember?" asked Alec.

Tremaine thought for a moment and cringed when he thought about the accident.

"Oh, oh we hit the car. We hit the car. I couldn't stop, the brakes didn't work. We were in the air and then, the truck . . . the red truck. I remember the accident. Randi, how are you? Are you all right?" He reached for her.

"I'm fine. It's you we are worried about. You have been unconscious since the accident."

"Wow, you're kidding. But I remember things. Great-grandfather, I spoke to him, I remember. And Kathleen, I remember. Mother, why are you here, and where is Great-grandfather?" Tremaine was so confused. He felt that he was fluid and communicating all along, so now to hear that he wasn't conscious made him wonder what was real.

"Your great-grandfather is here," said Alec.

"Here where?"

"He's sleeping."

"I know I spoke with him. I don't understand."

"You did. Somehow while in your subconscious state you were able to communicate with your grandfather. He knew you were in trouble after the accident and he had to come," said Alaya.

"You spoke to Kathleen. What did she say? Do you re-member?" asked Alec.

"Yeah, Kathleen, she told me to be careful. She said that the dark man was near and that he would stop us. She said that your life was in danger and that we had to hurry."

"You need to look outside," said Alec.

Tremaine opened the front door and stared out at the darkness.

"Do you have a flashlight?" asked Tremaine.

"Yeah." Alec went into the kitchen and came back with a large flashlight.

Tremaine turned it on and moved the light around in the darkness. When he flashed the light directly ahead, the face of evil flashed back at him. He was so startled he dropped the flashlight and it rolled outside. When he started to reach for it, something grabbed his hand and started to pull him outside into the darkness.

"Help me!" he yelled and held onto the doorframe.

Alec and Pastor Simmons grabbed him and jerked him back inside.

He sat on the floor and tried to calm down. "Oh my God, what are we going to do?"

They stayed inside the house until morning. They tried to sleep, but couldn't. The first thing on their minds was finishing this. John walked to the door and opened it, and even though it was eight o'clock in the morning it was pitch-black outside.

"It's the same. We can't go out there." Alec was so frustrated. He didn't know what to do. He ran out of ideas and options and plans and he couldn't think about it anymore. "I'm tired. I've had enough."

"Edward," John replied.

"What did you say?" Alec looked at him.

"I said *Edward*. That's why you can't stop. Edward and your grandchildren. So now, what is next?" John took a seat and closed his eyes to think.

They all gathered in the kitchen and tried to replenish their fatigued bodies. They ate cans of fruit and drank old coffee. Alec showed them the binder left by Torrin, and Tremaine told them how he found it in the barn and how angry Alec was at him for snooping around. Tremaine talked about working in the field and feeding the chickens and the horses.

Alaya noticed the joy in his eyes when he spoke of his time here. She was happy to know that he found some peace. He was so troubled when she left him that she worried that he would never find his way. But she admired the man that he had become. She was proud of him and she knew that John was too.

He gave a piece of himself to someone else and looked for nothing in return, that takes courage, she thought. She was still afraid for him, but it was all right. Whatever happened, it would be all right because she was sure he had found his way, and if he left this life today, he would stand in the company of great men that came before him. She smiled, took a sip of coffee, and frowned at the bitter taste.

"This is awful," she said and put the cup down.

They laughed at her expression.

"Wow, I haven't laughed in so long, I forgot what that felt like." Alec hung his head. There was a sadness about him that ran deep within.

"Remember, Alec, the guilt is not yours to bear. We are close, and we will figure this out too. Don't worry." Tremaine tried to comfort him.

They talked for hours.

Alec noticed John standing in the kitchen doorway.

"The rose will give us light and keep us safe," he said.

"What?" asked Alec.

"We will use the rose to find the well," he said.

"But we can't open the case, we have no idea what will happen," said Tremaine.

"If it is anything like what happened in Mitchellville, then it could be a good thing. I mean, it restored the town. I think he's right," said Pastor Simmons.

"Well, I guess it's worth a try, because we can't stay in here forever," said Tremaine.

"Should we all go?" asked Alec.

"No, I don't want my grandfather out there. We will stay," said Alaya.

"I agree. Randi, I want you to stay here too," said Tremaine.

"No, I'm going. After all of this, there's no way I'm not going. I have to see this. I have to." Randi was adamant. She got herself involved in this to see it to the end. This was the story of a lifetime.

"Randi, you can barely stand. I can't allow it," said Tremaine.

She laughed. "Can't allow, mmmm, I think that's funny. Can't allow—So one night gives you the right to tell me what I can and cannot do?" The pin was dropping and everyone heard it.

Alaya looked at Tremaine, Pastor Simmons looked at Randi, Alec smiled at Tremaine, and John turned and walked out.

"We will all go," said John.

"No, Grandfather. You can't go. You're not strong enough," Alaya cried.

They walked out of the kitchen and into the living room, where John was staring out the window. He turned and looked into Alaya's loving eyes and smiled and then he looked at Pastor Simmons. They stared at each other as if communicating on a level that only they could understand.

Pastor Simmons reached out and took his hand. "Yes, I agree, we all should go," said Pastor Simmons.

"No, I can't let you, Grandfather." Alaya knew his health was failing and this could kill him. It was too much; she couldn't allow it.

"Child, I know it seems that this journey was for Alec and Tremaine, but no, it is for all of us. We were brought together for a reason, and each of us must climb this mountain to see what is at the top for us. If it is the time of my death, then it is already ordained. I will pass to the next place whether I'm here or there. When it is my time, it is my time. The Creator has given me more years than I ever deserved to have, and maybe it was to see this through." He turned and looked back outside. "All of us will go."

Lieutenant Dryer decided to break the rules and follow them into Oklahoma. He found out who Alec was and where he lived, and he was heading straight for the farm.

Sergeant Long felt that he had already gone too far outside of their jurisdiction and was not going to risk his job over this manhunt. He contacted Captain Hicks, who turned the matter over to the Oklahoma authorities.

By the time Lieutenant Dryer arrived at the farm, it was surrounded by police cars and television vans. People hovered around the farm and tried to push their way through the crowds. He knew he could not be involved in an official capacity, so he stayed back near the television crews. Tensions were high.

The police officers called out to Alec and Tremaine, demanding that they come out. They were prepared to storm the farm if they had to. Lieutenant Dryer stood back and watched the Oklahoma police chief try to maintain some order out of the chaos.

They could see the farm clearly. The sky was blue, and the surrounding town was bustling with people. The police chief pleaded with them to come out, but he heard nothing. The farm was silent. He didn't know that they couldn't hear him. He didn't know that they were being deceived.

Alec placed the rose on the coffee table and waited for the moment when it was time to open it. He was nervous about the outcome. As soon as he reached for it, the door and windows flung open. The wind whipped through the cabin blowing anything that wasn't nailed down all over the place and the temperature dropped to freezing.

The dark man stood at the door staring at the holy crystal rose. "You know it can't help you. You are not even in the world." He moved forward toward Alec. "I will win, and you will live for eternity in the wall of the well. Your soul is my soul."

Pastor Simmons stepped between them just as the dark man reached out for Alec. Pastor Simmons closed his eyes, and the soft white light that surrounded him in the forest glowed around him. He did not stop time, so everyone saw him transform into pure light. Alec moved back against the wall, and Tremaine dropped the glass he was carrying. Randi and Alaya looked on in amazement, and John closed his eyes from the blinding light.

The dark man pulled his hand back when it touched the light and began to burn. He glided back to the door and faded into the darkness.

Pastor Simmons turned and looked at everyone. He said nothing, just waited for their reaction.

"Who are you? What are you?" Alec asked. He wasn't scared or frightened. He knew it was a heavenly thing that just happened, but it seemed that Pastor Simmons was not who he proclaimed to be. "That's why you could touch the rose, you are . . ."

"It doesn't matter. We have to get this done," said Pastor Simmons.

"Oh, it matters. It matters a lot," said Tremaine.

"The darkness is in us," said John. He sat with his eyes closed.

"What does that mean?" asked Randi.

"It means that the darkness that surrounds this house is coming from us. He is using our fear and guilt to keep us away from the light. He is deceiving us. We have to do this now," said Pastor Simmons.

Lieutenant Dryer stood by a van and waited for the eventual outcome of the elusive manhunt.

A voice came from behind him. "I can show you what this is all about." He turned around to see a tall man in a dark suit. He was pleasant-looking with dark hair and eyes, and a strange, slanted grin.

"What do you mean? Who are you?"

"I'm just somebody who knows."

"Knows what?"

"What this is all about. It's about a wish. A wish someone made years ago."

"What are you talking about?" Lieutenant Dryer was becoming a little frustrated with the man. "Either tell me or don't, but stop the double-talk."

"I can do better than that. I can show you."

"Where?"

The dark man pointed to the well. Lieutenant Dryer was curious. He looked toward the well and wondered if he should allow himself to take the risk. The dark man walked toward the well and even though Lieutenant Dryer hesitated, he followed.

"You know that old saying, be careful what you wish for, you just might get it?" The dark man looked back at him and smiled.

"Yeah, I've heard it, but what does that have to do with this?"

"Well, years ago a wish was granted at that well. It was a wonderful thing. Lives were saved and for a time all was good."

"What does this have to do with what's happening down there?"

"Everything." He smiled.

* * *

Alec, Tremaine, John, Alaya, Randi, and Pastor Simmons joined hand in hand and opened the door. Alec opened the case and removed the rose. The moment it was removed from the case, the light filled all that surrounded it. The light was so bright and intense that they could barely look at it. But to them, it was only a point of light in the darkness. They were walking blind and allowing the rose to guide their way. They were linked together, hand in hand, as they walked through the darkness.

The people outside were overwhelmed by it and tried to look at it, but couldn't. They could barely make out the six figures moving along slowly with the light shining all around them.

The dark man and Lieutenant Dryer was consumed by the light. Lieutenant Dryer pulled his sunglasses out and put them on, and even though it helped some, the light was still blinding. The dark man pulled a coin from his pocket and handed it to Lieutenant Dryer.

He looked at it but hesitated to take it. "What is it?" he asked.

"Take it and throw it in the well."

He hesitated. He looked at the brightest light he'd ever seen moving closer and closer to him and wondered what the light had to do with the well and this man.

"Take it and you can have all you have ever wanted."

Lieutenant Dryer looked at the man and without thinking, he took the coin.

"All that I ever wanted," he said.

"Whatever you desire, it will be yours if you throw the coin into the well." The dark man knew that if he could get him to throw that coin into the well, Alec would die and the journey would be over, at least for a time.

Lieutenant Dryer knew that it wasn't the right thing to do, but his lust for things and envy of others made him want all of the things he knew he would never have working a job day to day. The light moved closer and closer.

Alec could see Lieutenant Dryer. He saw the dark man, and fear gripped him when he saw the coin.

"Oh my God," Alec cried.

Tremaine looked up and saw Lieutenant Dryer toss the coin high into the air. His heart stopped. At the moment the coin was tossed, the veil of darkness that surrounded them faded and they knew the journey was over.

Alec ran toward the well. He ran like a man in his twenties and never took his eyes off the coin. He leaped forward and caught the coin just as it started to fall into the well. He grabbed it out of the air as he hung seemingly suspended in space and time. He held the coin close to his heart as he plunged down into the well.

"Help him," yelled Tremaine. He looked at Pastor Simmons and cried, "Help him."

"It may be too late," he replied.

"No, no, it can't be. It can't." Tremaine ran to the well and started to climb down. He could hear the dark man laughing and wanted to kill him.

Lieutenant Dryer looked into the evil eyes of this man and knew he had been deceived by the Devil himself. He was in shock. He backed away slowly not knowing what to do or say.

"For what is the value of a man who loses his soul?" The dark man laughed.

Lieutenant Dryer looked at John and Alaya, Randi, and Pastor Simmons and knew that he had to do something. He slowly walked to the well and looked inside. He ran to Pastor Simmons. "Come with me. We have to find a way for them to get out."

He started running toward the farm. Pastor Simmons followed. They went into the barn and searched for anything that would help them get them out of that well.

Lieutenant Dryer was frantic. He searched everywhere, but couldn't find anything that would work.

"What about this?" Pastor Simmons stood behind the old tractor where suddenly a coil of rope appeared.

"Yeah, yeah, that will work just find. That's funny, I looked there, but I didn't see anything." Lieutenant Dryer looked a bit confused.

"We are all so frantic it's no telling what we could overlook."

Pastor Simmons guided him to the barn door and back outside. They ran back to the well and tied the rope to a nearby tree.

"Come on," said Lieutenant Dryer as he began to climb down the rope.

Pastor Simmons looked at the dark man standing nearby and decided that it would be best if he stayed above. "No, you go ahead. I think I should stay here."

Lieutenant Dryer moved slowly down the rope. He swung himself down until he hit the bottom. He couldn't believe it. He couldn't move. He saw the wall move around him, faces screaming, hands pushing, the agony and the pain. He saw it, but it was so unreal that he thought he was hallucinating.

"This can't be real," he whispered.

"Oh, it's real all right, and if we don't keep that coin of yours from hitting the bottom, Alec will end up in that wall with them," said Tremaine.

"How did this happen?"

"Now is not the time. If we survive, I will explain everything." Tremaine was tending to Alec.

Alec hit the bottom and landed on top of all the coins that had been thrown in over the past one hundred years. He was hurt. He lay still and held onto the coin with one hand and the crystal rose with the other.

Lieutenant Dryer reached for the rose.

"I'll hold this," he said.

"Noooo, no, you can't touch it. You would not survive. Trust me." Tremaine took the coin from Alec's hand and placed it in his pocket and then he took the rose. "Help me move him over there." He pointed to an open space.

"Why can you touch it?" Lieutenant Dryer asked.

"It's a long story, but I have been through purification and you haven't. It would kill you. Trust me." Tremaine hoped he would understand and not try to touch it.

"Now what?" he asked.

"We have to find the original coin. The first coin that was thrown in," said Tremaine.

Lieutenant Dryer looked at the pile of coins and gasped.

"You have got to be kidding. That's not possible. It would take years, and how could you tell which one was the first one, even if you saw it?"

"It has a weeping angel on one side and a joyous angel on the other side," said Tremaine.

"It doesn't matter, it can't be done. We don't have that many years left in our lives to find that coin."

"Use the rose, Tremaine." Alec whispered. "Hold it out and let it guide you."

Tremaine held the rose over the pile of coins and watched as each individual coin rose from the pile and hung in mid-air. The light of the crystal rose shone brighter and brighter.

Pastor Simmons smiled. "He isn't dead. He held onto the coin and it never hit the bottom."

The dark man was furious. He started to leap down into the well when Pastor Simmons grabbed him and pulled him back. He pushed him away from the well and stood still. He allowed his inner light to shine, knowing that the dark man would not be able to come close to it. He stood between him and the well.

"Again, you lose," said Pastor Simmons.

"He'll never find the coin," said the dark man.

"He won't have to," said Pastor Simmons as he blocked the dark man's every attempt to enter the well.

As the coins floated to the top, the whole well was filled from top to bottom of coins suspended in mid-air. Lieutenant Dryer was overwhelmed. He couldn't speak; he didn't know what to think. It was beautiful to watch the light shining from each coin as if they encased the spirit of each person trapped in the wall.

Tremaine searched the coins intently trying to find the first one, the coin thrown in by Torrin so many years ago. There were so many, and it seemed so daunting, until a blue light caught his eye. It was different from the others. It seemed to have a song emanating from it. He walked through the coins that hung around him toward it until he could see the face of the joyous angel. He found it.

"Alec, it's here. I found it."

Alec tried to stand but couldn't.

"Help him. He has to be the one to touch it. It's his coin."

Lieutenant Dryer helped Alec to his feet and walked him to the coin. "Can you do this, Alec?"

"I will do it." He reached for the coin and grabbed it. He held it in his hand tightly and close to his heart. "I've got to get it outside before sunset."

They didn't know how they were going to get Alec up that rope, but they had to come up with something.

"Dryer, you go up. I'll tie the rope around Alec and you pull him up." Tremaine held the rope.

"Okay, I got ya." Lieutenant Dryer started to climb. It was difficult to climb over forms of bodies moving in and out of the wall. He was shocked when he reached the landing to find Pastor Simmons in a heavenly light and the dark man pacing around nervously at the edge of some trees.

"I'm ready," he yelled to Tremaine.

Tremaine tied the rope around Alec, who was still suffering from the effects of the fall and could barely speak because he was in so much pain.

"You have the coin?" Tremaine asked gently.

"Yes, I have it." Alec opened his hand and looked at the face of the angel that cried when Torrin threw the coin in the well. He closed it and held on to it.

"We're ready down here. Pull," yelled Tremaine.

Lieutenant Dryer pulled on that rope with all his strength. Alaya and Randi joined in to help him.

"It is almost sunset, you must hurry," said John.

The dark man snarled at the Pastor Simmons for blocking his path, but couldn't figure out how to move him. He noticed the rope tied around the tree and made his way to it. He quickly untied it, which forced more of the weight forward.

Lieutenant Dryer, Alaya and Randi faltered a bit, but held their ground. When Randi fell, it caught Pastor Simmons off guard and he lost his concentration. He turned and focused on the rope and didn't notice when the dark man was suddenly upon him. Before he could turn back around he felt the sting of his hand across his face.

The dark man struck him hard enough that he fell to the ground. Without any interference, he could force Alec back into the well. He knew the sun would be setting in moments, and every day gave him another chance at Alec's death before the souls were released.

Lieutenant Dryer and Randi and Alaya never stopped pulling, grabbing the rope hand over hand.

The dark man walked to the edge to force Alec back into the well when Alec's small frail hand pushed the coin onto the surface just before the last ray of sunlight faded away.

As the sunlight touched the coin, it started to disintegrate into dust. The souls of both angels were released from the coin. The angel of light rose to the heavens in a shining light, and the angel of darkness flew to the dark man and entered his soul.

"I know you think you've won, but you haven't. There will be another Torrin and yet another. The well is full of selfish wishes that man will pay for with his soul." He agonized over the loss, turned to smoke, and faded away.

They pulled Alec to the surface and he lay on the ground. Alaya tended to him and tried to comfort him. Lieutenant Dryer tied the rope back around the tree and threw it back into the well for Tremaine.

"Tremaine, are you all right," Randi yelled.

"Yeah, I'm fine."

He stood in the well and watched each coin disappear as a soul was freed from the wall. Points of light fled from the wall and floated up into the evening sky. The lights filled the well. It was a glorious sight. Tremaine was so amazed by it.

This moment made all of the work worthwhile. It gave purpose to their journey and peace to his heart. He was a different man now, and he knew his life would be different. He had the courage to take control of the direction his life would take and knew to hold on to the love in his life at all costs.

Everyone above watched as the freed souls moved from their earthbound hell to the heavens above.

"Pure consciousness," said Randi.

"Pure love," said Pastor Simmons.

They watched in awe at the spectacle of lights.

Tremaine grabbed the rope and pulled himself to the surface. The lights were moving all around him, as if to show their love and gratitude for being there for them.

He climbed onto the surface and took Randi into his arms. He kissed her gently and they held each other tightly.

Tremaine stood at the edge and watched as the last coin disappeared and the last point of light left the well.

But, before it lifted away, it took the form of Torrin. He looked into Alec's face and smiled. "Thank you," he whispered and floated up and out of sight.

They stood at the well, still trying to absorb all of what just happened. Alec hugged Tremaine and thanked him. He didn't have the words to express his feelings, so he just held him. Tears formed in his eyes, and Alec couldn't contain himself. He turned and walked away and cried.

"Oh no, man tears. We can't have that. Not after this. We should be beating ourselves in the chest and swinging from trees like the king of the jungle," said Lieutenant Dryer.

They all laughed.

"We have to take it back, you know," said Pastor Simmons.

Tremaine and Alec stared at each other.

"Oh no, you're right. I forgot," said Tremaine.

"We always knew we had to make the journey twice. The question is how?" asked Alec.

Pastor Simmons turned and looked at John.

John walked over and hugged Alaya. He took Tremaine's hand and shook it.

"You are a man now. You take care of your mother and this young lady. You made me proud and reminded me of what it was like to live. It was the best present an old man could have gotten." He shook Alec's hand. "Are you sure you're not Navajo?"

Alec laughed.

John turned to Pastor Simmons. "I am ready."

"Ready for what?" asked Tremaine.

"It is my time, Tremaine. I will take the rose and return it," he said.

"How're you gonna do that? How are you gonna get back?" Tremaine asked.

"He's not coming back," said Alaya. "Grandfather, you don't have to do this."

"It is my time, and I am tired. I've been ready to go for twenty years. My job is done now, and I want to see my wife and children. It is your time now. Live it with lust and joy because it is wonderful." He held Alaya in his arms. "Don't worry, child, I will be fine. You just remember, all of you remember, that the only thing that matters in this world are the things that you can carry in your heart to the next world." He took the rose from Tremaine and stood by Pastor Simmons.

"Who are you?" Alec looked at Pastor Simmons and watched as he transformed from the man known as Pastor Simmons to Kathleen Cho. She laughed a happy laugh and said hello.

"Kathleen, how? What . . . It was you all the time. You were helping us all the time." Alec was shocked and couldn't believe his eyes.

"No," Kathleen said and transformed again into the Black man with the bright blue eyes.

"Oh my God. I don't believe it. You have been with us all the time. This is the guy, remember? This is the guy who brought me to you in the first place. He kept following me until I was at your farm. You knew what would happen. You put us together." Tremaine was so surprised. He couldn't stop smiling.

"So, when we were in the cave and Kathleen fell, she was never in any danger?" said Alec.

"No, and neither were you. You had each other, and John was always there. He never let go."

He laughed as he took John's hand, and two points of light faded into the night sky. John's lifeless body fell to the ground.

Tremaine picked him up and carried him back to the cabin and called 911. It saddened Alaya and Tremaine to lose John, but they were thankful that they had the chance to say good-bye.

By morning the world was back to normal. All over the news there were stories about miraculous healings, dead people coming back, and burned buildings, broken windows, exploded gas stations, and dented cars repairing themselves back to their original form. The whole world was in a church, mosque, synagogue, or temple. Surely this was the work of God.

Lieutenant Dryer stayed the night. He couldn't imagine trying to focus on driving after everything that happened. "Well, what do you think?" he asked Alec as they sat at the kitchen table sipping on stale coffee.

"I don't know. I just hope no one comes along and creates a whole new religion out of it. I hope after a while it will become like UFO sightings—you don't know whether to believe it or not."

"This will be talked about two, three hundred years from now. It will be unexplainable, so it will always be on the minds of seekers who will be trying to find out what really happened," said Lieutenant Dryer. "And you know they will haunt you and Tremaine for the rest of your lives trying to get the answer."

"I suppose you're right. I hadn't thought about that."

"Well, I guess I should be getting home." Lieutenant Dryer headed for the door. He stopped and looked at Tremaine, Randi, and Alaya sitting in the living room and smiled. "This was one wild ride. Just think I almost put you in the wall. It makes you think about what you will do for what you think you need."

"Why did you throw the coin in?" Tremaine asked.

"I don't know. I guess for a moment I saw myself being more than I ever thought I could be. That's silly, but I ached for it. I thought I needed it." Lieutenant Dryer's face saddened at the thought of what could have happened.

"It's like my grandfather said, 'You only need what your heart can carry,'" said Alaya.

"Yeah, yeah, you're right." He smiled at everyone, opened the door, and walked out.

"Now what?" Tremaine asked.

"I don't know," Alec replied.

"What about the binder? What do you plan to do with it? You can't leave it, because someone will try to take that same journey if they read it without truly understanding. It could turn out to be a disaster," said Randi.

"She's right," said Tremaine.

Alec thought about it for a moment. He walked to the table where Torrin's journal was and picked it up.

"There's someone in Arizona that I need to meet," Alec said. "What about you?"

Tremaine looked at Alaya. "Well, if it's okay with you, I would like to stay on Great-grandfather's farm with you."

"I think I would like that," she replied.

"Randi, you finish school and come to visit whenever you can. I'll come see you too, and when you finish we'll get married and see where life takes us from there. How about that?"

"It's the best idea you've had all day." She hugged him and kissed him.

Alec took a sip of coffee.

"God, this is the worst coffee. I can't drink this anymore." He grabbed the keys to the truck, grabbed his jacket and tucked the binder under his arm. He looked around the cabin and smiled. "This place is nothing like it was when Torrin first built it." He took a deep breath. "I'm buying breakfast." He opened the door.

"I'm in." Tremaine stood and walked outside. Randi was behind him.

"Me too," said Alaya as she grabbed her purse and pulled out her keys.

Alec took one last look. He knew he would never come back to the farm. He thought of Gwyneth and Tilly and the first day he met Tremaine. He smiled and closed the door.

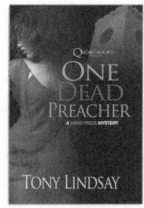

DEMON HUNTER SERIES

DEMON HUNTER SERIES BOOK ONE

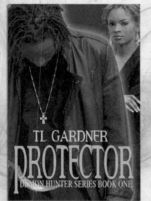

PROTECTOR

ISBN-13: 978-1933967134

DEMON HUNTER SERIES BOOK TWO

SACRIFICE

ISBN-13: 978-1933967387

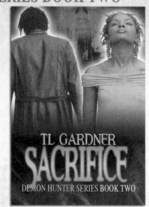

TL GARDNER

MORE TITLES FROM

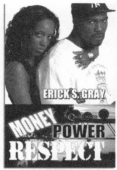
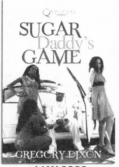